The Hobby Horse Murder

Banbury Cross Murder Mystery Series Book Three

Ben Westerham

I0556304

Memory of Murder
Lesson for a Thief
Collector of Crimes (anthology)
Shattered Dreams (anthology)

50FOR30 SERIES OF MICRO SHORT STORIES
50for30 Series One
50for30 Series Two

MULTI-AUTHOR ANTHOLOGIES
Breakneck

Published by Close9 Publishing
ISBN 978-1-911085-81-2

It can seem frightening sometimes how quickly life can swing from sweet joy to deep despair. To all of you who are in a tough and challenging place right now, know that you are never alone, no matter how dark the world might seem. May this book bring a little joy and happiness to your life.

It's all English to me

A word on the language that's used in this book, so you know what to expect. The version of English that is used here is British. This ought not to present much in the way of a problem for non-British readers. If you do find the occasional word or phrase a little odd, then I hope you still understand the essence of what is being said.

Ride a cock-horse to Banbury Cross

Ride a cock-horse to Banbury Cross,
To see a fine lady upon a white horse;
With rings on her fingers and bells on her toes,
She shall have music wherever she goes.

This is a typical modern version of the popular nursery rhyme. There are numerous earlier recorded versions that start with the same opening line.

Chapter One

James Puncheon couldn't settle. The coffee no doubt hadn't helped. Perhaps he would have been better advised to have stuck to a glass of water. He placed his half-empty cup on the sideboard and pushed himself up and out of the leather armchair he'd occupied for the previous five minutes. His copy of *The Daily Telegraph* already lay discarded on the floor of the hotel room he had checked into the previous day.

The coffee might not have helped his mood, but that wasn't the cause of his irritation. Irritation? He scratched the back of his neck as he began to walk slowly towards the door. Was it irritation or something else? Damn it, the room was too warm. And the bloody coffee had been too hot. Worse, it had arrived with cold milk. Idiots. He shook his head. Perhaps he ought to open the curtains and maybe one of the windows. Yes, but not yet. There were things on his mind.

A woman's voice, shrill and young, passed along the corridor, tailing off towards the stairs. He didn't recognise it. As he reached the door, he turned, tapped his fingers on the sides of his legs, then retraced his steps across the heavy, dark carpet, the pristine condition of which made clear it was new. A shame it was such a hideous pattern, he mused.

This wouldn't do, it really wouldn't. They were all there now. The usual crowd, plus some awful woman Sally Dingle had brought with them, quite clearly with the intention of foisting her on him in yet another effort to find him a new lady friend. No doubt Sally meant well enough, but she really should know better than to engage in matchmaking. Anyway, he wasn't in the market for a romantic relationship; although Sally wouldn't know it. He was already seeing someone. At least, he hoped to high heaven Sally didn't know.

And that was it, wasn't it? That was the cause of his... frustration. That was it. He wasn't so much irritated as frustrated. They were so close to each other and yet they might as well have been a hundred miles apart. Who wouldn't be feeling frustrated?

He picked up his teaspoon and gave the coffee a slow, thoughtful stir, then dropped the spoon on the tray and drew the fingers of one hand across his chin. Bloody hell, a man at his age ought to be able to show some patience. He was nearly fifty now, not some hopeless teenager desperate to jump into bed with a girl for the first time.

Laughter came from the street outside. Happy people in a happy world. He lingered, looking down at the dark swirling liquid in his cup. He knew where his happiness lay, but that was the problem. Right now his happiness was out of reach and, despite what they told each other, there was no certainty things would ever change. Damn it.

But it was Laura's comments that had set him so on edge. Did she really know all about his clandestine relationship or had she just been fishing, hoping he'd take the bait? As his ex-wife, she was more likely than anyone to spot what was happening under their noses. She used to be able to read him like the proverbial book and, even if they'd been divorced for a few years now, things weren't very likely to have changed as far as that sort of thing was concerned. She seemed pretty clear in her own mind what she thought was happening, but did she really know? Christ, he hoped not. Had he said too much to her? He began to reply their conversation in his mind, but promptly found himself interrupted by a solid rapping at the heavy wooden door. He walked back across the room and opened it, wondering who it was disturbing him at this hour.

"Yes?"

THE WEATHER HAD BEEN fabulous all morning. Bright sunshine and warm with it. In fact, it was so good, Inspector Leslie Dykeman had gone out on a limb and decided to leave his coat at home, settling for his well-worn brown woollen jacket. No doubt it would rain at some point, but what the hell, he was up for taking a chance, for living life in the fast lane. Anyway, there were always plenty of shops to duck into if things did get a bit on the wet side.

Banbury's annual Hobby Horse Festival did not always enjoy such accommodating weather. In fact, mused Dykeman over his breakfast toast and tea, they'd not had a dry day for the Festival in any of the previous three years. Last year was an almost total wash out. Bad for business, was that, or so the

Chief Inspector had kept telling him. Meant the public stayed at home, where it was warm and dry, and didn't show up to spend their hard-earned money. What the hell he was supposed to do about it, God only knew.

As it happened, there was another reason he was particularly looking forward to this year's Festival. He smiled to himself as he wondered at the possibilities. Sometimes, things were simply and helpfully served up on a plate for you; all you had to do was tuck in and gorge yourself. And he was going to gorge himself on this one. His shoulders jiggled up and down as he laughed. For once, he wished he owned a camera, just so he could take a few pictures for posterity. Hilarious. But all was not lost there. He was certain the photographers from the newspapers would be thick on the ground and a quiet word or two from him would ensure he got his wish.

Nine-fourteen. He was due to meet his sergeant, Shapes, in half an hour at the top end of the market place, outside the old cinema. Half an hour after that, the procession was supposed to set off on a meandering loop around the town centre. Nearly two hours of humiliation and embarrassment for the less enthusiastic members of the group who would be taking part, prime amongst whom was Shapes. Dykeman began to laugh so much he had to put his cup and saucer down before he spilt the contents all over his lap.

DYKEMAN MADE HIS WAY along the High Street, heading for the Market Place. The number of people out on the streets was already highly impressive for such a small market town. On two or three occasions he found himself struggling to squeeze through the heaving masses in places where temporary stalls and entertainers narrowed the space available.

Even the snotty-nosed, squealing kids seemed to be well-behaved, distracted by all the fun on offer. That was a rarity. In his experience, kids, especially the youngest ones, were best avoided. Too bloody demanding and prone to thinking the whole wide world revolved around them. He might well be keen on having a little more romance in his life, but kids were definitely not part of what he had in mind.

He was tempted to stop at one or two of the stalls; to have a go at hurling balls at coconuts perched on top of metal posts or firing off air-guns at plastic ducks wobbling past on a ferocious torrent of water that ran along a metal trough. Any other time he would have given in to the temptation, but he was too keen to catch up with Shapes before it was too late. He quickened his pace.

A narrow alleyway brought Dykeman out into the top end of Market Place. The place was packed, busy even by the standards of a normal market day, when it would heave and throb with eager shoppers. He marvelled at where so many people could have come from. It was amazing what a bit of decent weather could do. He stopped for a moment and took it all in. Amongst the general frenzy, he could pick out several groups of Morris dancers, wearing their ridiculous outfits and those annoying bells that rang every time one of them so much as sneezed. And the sticks they used when they were dancing, well they were potentially lethal weapons, ones that made his trusty old truncheon look pathetic and inadequate. He knew, too, that it wouldn't be long before every last one of those Morris men was drunk as a skunk.

In the middle of the square were half a dozen tractors paired with trailers, each one decked out with bunting and wot-not. No doubt the farmers driving the tractors would also be half-cut by the time the whole convoy hit the road. Good job he and his colleagues were under strict instructions to go easy on the law enforcement, apart from tackling the plague of pick-pockets. There'd be armies of them on the go already, no doubt about that.

The old cinema was off to his left and, if he wasn't mistaken, there was his sergeant, trying to keep a low profile amongst a small group of other people busy getting ready for their part in the day's entertainment. Dykeman set off at a modest gallop, a grin so big on his face that he was sure he must have looked like some sort of lunatic. Shapes saw him coming and made a feeble effort at hiding from his boss; an effort that was undermined by the sizeable outfit he was wearing.

"There you are, Shapes," declared Dykeman, keen that all and sundry knew who was hiding under the face paint. "I was getting worried you might have set off already."

Shapes muttered something inaudible, well aware that Dykeman knew exactly what time they were due to start out, which wasn't for another half an hour.

"All ready then, are we?" asked the inspector, affecting an entirely fake concern for the state of his sergeant's preparations.

More muttering followed. Dykeman started to laugh so much he came close to collapsing.

"Don't see what's so bloody funny," retorted Shapes.

In truth, he knew damn well what was so funny. The red and black make-up that covered most of his face and the Morris dancer clothes he had been forced into were bad enough, but the piece de resistance, the real cause of his humiliation, was the small, decorated wooden horse he was wearing. There was a big hole cut through the frame, so he could push himself up through the middle of the thing, which was then suspended from his shoulders by thick straps that were already biting into him. By the time they returned to the Market Place after their dance around town there'd be no bloody flesh left on his shoulders. And it had been made very clear to him that it was to be a dance around town, not a walk. What was wrong with a flipping walk, for God's sake?

Shapes wanted to blame Dykeman for this embarrassing predicament, but he knew he had in fact been set up by the Chief Constable. The man had been keen on the police taking an 'active part', as he put it, in this year's Hobby Horse Festival. Yeah, an 'active part' that didn't involve him wearing one of these stupid outfits. Unfortunately, it seemed the Chief Constable was still bearing a grudge against him for some misunderstanding involving the top man's car earlier in the year and had, therefore, volunteered Shapes and a couple of the beat constables for starring roles in the day's festivities.

Dykeman hadn't exactly put himself out to get the decision reversed. A request by Shapes to take the weekend as holiday, far away in Scotland, had been turned down flat, as had a proposal he feign a broken leg. Too risky, said Dykeman. For him, that was, not Shapes.

"You need to see things from my point of view, Shapes. Then you'd see what's so funny," replied Dykeman, trying to pull himself together. "Nice colour make-up you got there. Matches your eyes."

As Dykeman collapsed into another bout of side-splitting laughter, Shapes seethed. Revenge might take a while, but a coming it was. You could bet your last penny on that.

Dykeman struggled back into some sort of standing position, thinking he ought to give his sergeant a few encouraging words – not too many, you understand, just a few – but was disappointed to find another half-horse, half-man combo had started issuing instructions to the whole flock, or whatever it was you called a group of wooden horses, demanding they gather around him. Happily, a bald-headed bloke wearing a worn, brown, leather jacket, whom Dykeman knew to be a photographer from one of the town's newspapers, happened upon the scene. Wasting not a moment, Dykeman seized the snapper and started issuing instructions that seemed to involve ensuring every photo he took included Shapes.

As it turned out, it was a good job Dykeman made the most of this opportunity. As he stood by, making sure his instructions were filled to the letter, a familiar figure staggered to a halt alongside him, short of breath and red-faced.

"Hello, Nevin. What's up? You want to take part too, do you? Maybe Shapes can squeeze over and you can join him."

Constable Nevin, trying hard to get his breath back, shook his head as he leaned forward, hands on his knees.

"Better speak up soon, Nevin. Shapes is due off the starting line any minute now. I've got two bob on him to complete the course first."

"You're needed, sir," stammered Nevin. "There's been a murder."

"Do what?" Dykeman wasn't sure he'd heard the constable properly, what with all the wheezing.

"Murder, sir. At the Marlborough Hotel. Shooting."

Nevin stood upright and puffed out his cheeks. He'd not been able to get a car through the crowds, so had been forced to run most of the way from the police station, the breath of the Chief Constable hot on his back.

The Chief had not been the least bit impressed to hear a guest at the Marlborough had been careless enough to get themselves shot dead on the day of the Hobby Horse Festival. It wasn't good for business and the high and mighty of the town would be sure to point that out, often, until the horrid business had been put to bed. Nevin's instructions had been clear, find Dykeman and Shapes, and be quick about it. Or else. It had been a relief to Nevin to find Shapes hadn't yet set off on his little trip around town.

"The old man want Shapes too, does he?"

Nevin nodded. Dykeman felt all the fun of the fair leave him. You couldn't make these things up, could you? Talk about spoiling his fun. Perhaps things could wait until Shapes had carried out his civic duties, by completing his dance around the town wearing that silly outfit.

"Right now, I suppose?"

Nevin nodded a second time.

"Definitely can't wait a while?"

This time Nevin shook his small head.

"This is going to ruin Shapes's day, this is. He's been looking forward to this all week. Reckons it's the best thing he's done in years. He even went so far as to say he might join a Morris dancing troupe. Look at his face. That's the look of a deeply disappointed man, that is."

Dykeman and Nevin watched as Shapes dismantled his outfit with a remarkable turn of speed, the hobby horse landing on the floor with a clatter. He was free of the contraption in the blink of an eye and setting about wiping the worst of the make-up off his face with a hanky that was clearly nothing like new and unused.

"Thank Christ for that," growled Shapes, as he spat a second time into his hanky before wiping off more of the thick colouring that clung to his skin with impressive determination. "Where d'you say this murder is, Nevin?"

"Er, the Marlborough Hotel, Sarge." Nevin took in the strange outfit Shapes was wearing. "You got any more clothes here? Want me to fetch 'em for you?"

"Nope, just this lot. Had to get dressed at home before I got here."

Shapes eyed Nevin like a fox might eye up a newborn lamb, but had to admit to himself the man was a fair bit smaller than he was. His clothes wouldn't fit, not even at a stretch. Shapes turned towards the gloomy-faced leader of their Morris troupe, who was clearly disappointed at losing one of his happy band.

"Here, Bob. The Chief Constable wouldn't want to let you down. Nevin can take my place."

"What? But..."

Nevin's face was an instant picture of panic. Bob, a big man with hands the size of plates, wasn't slow to seize the opportunity. He had Nevin under his wing before the terrified constable could do a runner. There was no escape now.

"I'll put in a good word for you, Nevin, don't you worry about that," sniggered Shapes.

As he and Dykeman exited the scene, heading for the High Street, Shapes was laughing like a drain.

Chapter Two

Five minutes later, Dykeman and Shapes stood outside the Marlborough Hotel, looking up at the three-storey building that occupied a large site all of its own part-way up the Oxford Road. The sun's rays gave the limestone it was built with a warm, comforting glow, thought Dykeman, as it did with most of the older, stone buildings scattered across the town.

"Nice-looking place," remarked Shapes. "Not been here before."

"I like these old stone buildings. A damn sight better looking than any of that rubbish the Victorians put up."

"Isn't your house Victorian, sir?"

"It's one of the better ones," Dykeman wrinkled his sizeable nose. "I came here once, what, four years ago, I reckon. Round Table charity do, it was. Posh place then. Don't suppose it's any different now, not by the look of things. Did a nice cheese and ham sandwich, if I remember rightly."

Food, thought Shapes. Must be time for his mid-morning cuppa and biscuits by now. Shouldn't be much trouble getting his hands on some in a place like this. Maybe he could have a go at those cheese and ham sandwiches too. He couldn't be expected to work properly on an empty belly.

"Not the kind of place you'd expect to get yourself murdered," suggested the hungry sergeant.

"Happens in the best of places. Any place, any time. Come on, we ought to get on. The old man's probably pacing up and down his office already, wondering when our report is going to land on his desk."

"Reckon you'll have to pay him a visit for this one," smirked Shapes, knowing how much Dykeman hated having to give the Chief Constable updates on their cases in person. He always got more questions than he had answers for, which risked making him look stupid.

A short man, dressed in an immaculate two-piece black suit, his tie perfectly positioned and not a single hair of his close-cropped dark brown locks out of place, stood in the middle of the entrance hall. He was fiddling with his hands and a frown was drawn across his middle-aged face. He looked, decided Dykeman as soon as he set eyes on him, ill at ease. He turned to face the two policemen as they walked towards him and a beacon of hope lit up his eyes.

"Are you Inspector Dykeman?"

He sounded hopeful, as if a heavy burden was about to be lifted from his shoulders. Shapes noticed the man was sweating; little beads glistening on his temple.

"That's me," replied Dykeman. "And this is Sergeant Shapes. You the manager of this hotel?"

"Yes, yes. Reginald Plowright."

Plowright looked at Shapes, bemused at first by the sight the sergeant made. He wasn't wearing the kind of clothes you'd normally expect on a policeman, not even a plain clothes one. The remaining make-up suggested he might have had some sort of role in the Festival, but the hotel manager decided not to enquire. Other matters were more pressing.

"Don't think you were the manager the last time I was here," suggested Dykeman, shaking Plowright's hand.

"Only been here just over a year. Moved up from Oxford. I used to be deputy manager at the Athenaeum. You might have heard of it?"

"I have. It's a nice place. Wanted to run your own hotel then, did you?"

"You could say it was a dream come true when I got this job. Lovely hotel, established reputation and good staff. So many of our guests are regulars too."

Plowright stopped fiddling with his hands. He'd not been able to join the armed forces during the last war, what with his misshapen leg, but he'd signed up to the auxiliary fire service and seen plenty of bodies left behind by bombing raids. But somehow none of that could match the shock he'd felt at seeing the dead man here, in his hotel. Dead people during times of war was to be expected, but a killing here, in a nice, quiet little hotel in an equally nice, quiet little town in the north of Oxfordshire? No, that didn't seem right, not one bit. He'd got the shakes when he stood there looking at the body. That surprised him. The blood? The bullet wounds? Maybe. He'd ordered the staff to leave him, then locked the door behind and rushed down to his office to phone the police. His hands were still shaking when he made the call, the handset rattling against his ear. A murder. Here. In his hotel. He'd already started to ask himself if he'd be able to carry on as manager of the place. How could he walk into the building every morning knowing what had happened? He felt sick and had to bite back the phlegm that threatened to rise up from his throat.

"Right. Well, no time like the present, so they say," said Dykeman, keen to get cracking. "Where's the body?"

"This way. One of your constables is there now, keeping guard."

At Dykeman's insistence, they plodded up four flights of the wide, carpeted stairs that led off the entrance hall to the second floor. Sunlight flooded in through a tall, generous window at the top of the stairs, where a single hallway led off both right and left.

"How many rooms per floor?" asked Dykeman, as they turned to the right.

"Twelve. Thirty-six rooms in all."

"Fully booked, are you?"

"Very nearly. We've two vacancies, one a last-minute cancellation. Business is always good over the weekend of the Hobby Horse Festival."

"I thought you'd say that," responded Dykeman, a note of unhappiness in his voice.

A quizzical look appeared on the hotel manager's face.

"The more people are staying here," explained Dykeman. "the more people we'll have to talk to and the more suspects there are."

"Ah, yes."

Plowright's face changed, a little frown indicating fresh concern, thought Dykeman. The poor fella was probably already wondering how much money the place was going to lose as a result of one of the guests getting himself shot. Well, that couldn't be helped. First things first and that was tracking down the killer.

It was a short walk to room 215, the door of which was closed. A uniformed constable stood guard, visibly stiffening as the little party approached.

"Morning, Dartington. This the room is it?"

"Morning, Inspector. It is, sir."

Dartington noticed Shapes. It was the clothes that got his attention first. Definitely not his normal get-up. What really caught him off guard though was the state of the sergeant's face. He looked like he'd been in a nasty accident with a coal bunker, black stuff smeared all over his chops. Dartington looked away, before he caught Shapes's eye, and opened the door.

"What have we got in here, then?" asked Dykeman as he stepped into the doorway.

"Sir. One dead man. Shot twice, by the looks of it. He's stone cold, so likely happened a while ago. No sign of forced entry and, as far as I can tell, nothing's been nicked."

"Well done, Dartington. Now then, let's see what's what."

Every light in the room seemed to be switched on, the overpowering glare causing all three men to squint. The faint whiff of coffee tickled at Dykeman's nose.

"My God."

Plowright couldn't stop the words escaping from his mouth. Even though he'd seen the corpse earlier, unable to believe what his overwrought maid had wailed at him, it was still a shocking sight now. It looked so... so obscene. Was that the word? He'd didn't know. He didn't know what to think or what to say at all. Confusion began to overwhelm him.

"Well, Plowright," demanded Dykeman, who had seen the colour drain from the hotel manager's face and acted as quickly as he could to pull the man's attention back to him. "Can you confirm the name of the deceased?"

"The deceased?"

Plowright was quivering, playing with his hands again.

"That's right. Was he a guest here at the hotel?"

"Oh, yes."

"His name?"

"Ah, yes. His name. Puncheon. Mr James Puncheon."

Plowright steadied himself, placing a hand against the nearest wall, and felt the light-headedness begin to pass. Maybe it was having the police there that made the difference, made it all so much more real. Earlier he could have pretended Puncheon was just asleep. Not now.

"Was he booked in on his own? No wife?"

"Er, no. There's no wife. Well, not booked in with him. I mean, he could have a wife, but she's not staying here, at the hotel. He's staying here with some friends, from Leamington Spa. They've stayed before."

"We'll need a list of his friends, in that case. Shapes will pick that up when we've finished here."

"Yes, of course, Inspector. Quite a sizeable party."

"I'm told one of your maids found the body. What time was that?"

"I suppose it was about eight-thirty, or thereabouts. The maids try to clean as many rooms as possible while the guests are downstairs having breakfast. It helps them get a little ahead of the day."

"And this is exactly how she found things? Nothing's been moved?"

"Yes, exactly how it was. Nothing's been touched. Well, not by us."

"And by that you mean, what?"

"There was no one here for a while once the maid ran off to fetch me. She left the door open, I'm afraid."

"That'll be the shock. How long between her leaving and you arriving on the scene, would you say?"

"Oh, five minutes, I suppose. It wouldn't have been any longer."

Dykeman paused for a moment, before deciding there was nothing more he needed to ask the hotel manager there and then.

"Well, that will do for now, Mr Plowright. We'll speak to you again later and if you could draw up that list of guests in Mr Puncheon's party right away that would be a big help."

"Of course, Inspector."

"Dartington here will see you back downstairs."

With the room to themselves for the first time, the two policemen spent a minute or two casting a careful eye over the scene. Both had found from long experience that it helped not to go rushing in when you first arrived. Take a little time to look around. Acclimatise yourself to what's there, right in front of your eyes.

"He's made a right mess of that mattress," observed Shapes, nodding at the corpse sprawled across the double bed.

"Eagle-eyed as ever, Shapes."

"You noticed the blood on the wall here and on the floor?"

"I have." Dykeman paused, giving the situation some further thought. "Looks like he was probably shot standing here, by the door. Must have opened it, only to find someone pointing a gun at him."

"I'd hazard a guess he was trying to reach the phone there, on the bedside table," added Shapes.

James Puncheon was lying face down, arms sprawled either side of his body, almost plumb in the middle of the bed. His white shirt was stained heavily with blood. It appeared to Dykeman that Puncheon can barely have taken half-a-dozen steps before falling on to the bed. At least death appeared to have come to him quickly. That was something Dykeman anticipated the delightful Dr Sheila Delph, the resident town pathologist, would be able to confirm, once she'd had an opportunity to put her skills to good use.

"I don't suppose there would have been much chit-chat before the killer pulled the trigger. Too much chance of being spotted or Puncheon making a bid for freedom," said the inspector.

"You'd have thought someone would have heard the shots," suggested Shapes, fidgeting in his uncomfortable trousers. "Suppose the killer might have used a silencer."

"Possible. Would make sense if you wanted to improve your chances of getting away unseen."

Dykeman stepped in closer to the body, careful not to tread on any of the blood soaking into the carpet. Puncheon was a tall man, six foot at least, and well-built. Maybe too well-built; there was flab round his cheeks and a podgy belly peeked out at the world where his shirt had been pulled from his trousers. Late forties, maybe early fifties, thought Dykeman, noticing the man's brown hair had started to recede and was greying at the temples.

"Nice watch he's got there," pointed out Shapes. "Bet that cost a few bob."

"He'd need to have a few quid to be able to afford to stay at this place. Too pricey for the likes of you and me, Shapes."

Still taking care where he placed his feet, Dykeman stepped away from the bed and crossed to the far side of the room, where he'd noticed a jacket hanging over the back of a chair.

"Let's see what we've got here, shall we?"

Pulling his hanky from a trouser pocket, Dykeman eased open Puncheon's jacket and began to explore its inner pockets. A small red booklet was brought forth first. He opened it and perused its contents with interest.

"Driving licence. Name of James Puncheon. Date of birth February 12th, 1913. Born in Cheltenham"

Dykeman closed the licence and handed it to Shapes, who had taken up station at the foot of the bed. He gave it a cursory glance, holding it in his own, somewhat dirty, hanky then placed it on the bed.

"Something else here," added Dykeman, slipping a second, equally small booklet, out of the same pocket. "Golf membership card. Leamington Spa Golf and Bowls Club. Same name."

That too was handed to Shapes, who, for reasons he couldn't himself fathom, found it necessary to sniff at the booklet. It didn't help matters at all.

"No doubt about the name then. That's a start," sniffed Shapes.

"Nothing else here," reported Dykeman.

Shapes handed both booklets back to Dykeman, who placed them back where he'd found them. A search of the outer pockets on the jacket produced nothing.

Dykeman pulled a face. "Where's his wallet? It's not in here."

Looking around, the inspector spotted a small drawer in the top of the bedside cabinet. He stepped across and opened it, though only after he'd given the damn thing several good wiggles.

"Here we go."

The inspector plucked a brown leather wallet from out of the drawer, unclipped it, then emptied the contents on to the edge of the bed, before working his way through them.

"Lot of cash here," noted Dykeman, before counting out the notes. "That's ten, eleven, twelve, thirteen pounds. Chequebook too. Here have a look through that. See if there's anything interesting in it."

He handed the chequebook to Shapes, who began flicking through the stubs. Dykeman went back to the drawer, but all he came up with this time was a small Bible, of the sort found in most hotel bedrooms. Its near mint condition suggested few guests had paid it much attention.

"Doesn't look like there's anything in here that's going to help us," announced Shapes. "He's paid his green-grocer and butcher a couple of times. The garage too. Some small cheques to other people. No biggies. Nothing I'd say looks suspicious."

"We'll take it back to the station all the same, in case any of the names in there mean something to us later. Anything in that suitcase?"

Shapes turned to his left, where a brown leather case sat on a wooden rack set up in front of the wall. He reached out and undid the two chunky clips that held it closed.

"Empty. Oh, hold on, there's something in this here pocket."

He reached down and pulled a small white envelope out of a thin, elasticated pocket than ran along the front inside edge of the suitcase. Inside was a single, folded piece of paper.

"It's a letter," he muttered, as he began to read.

"Let me know if you need any help with the big words."

Shapes chose not to respond to the insult, though his fingers squeezed the sheet of paper a little more tightly.

"It's just something about an order for some new furniture. Parkins and Hartman in Leamington. Been a delay. Problem with the material." Shapes looked at the envelope again. "Postmarked yesterday."

"Probably didn't have time to read it before he left for Banbury, so shoved it in the suitcase. That all?"

"Yep. That's the lot."

Shapes put the letter back where he'd found it and closed the suitcase.

Dykeman turned his attention once more back to the room. There wasn't, it seemed, anywhere for guests to keep their valuables secure. It seemed likely the hotel would have a safe for that sort of thing.

"What's up? I know that face, something's bothering you," prompted Shapes.

Shapes and Dykeman had worked together long enough to be fully capable of interpreting one another's body language; those tell-tale little ticks and odd behaviours that said so much about their true thoughts or feelings. Dykeman, as he well knew himself, had a habit of twitching his nose when something was bothering him; something, that is, that he couldn't quite put a finger on. His nose was twitching now.

"If you brought something valuable with you, you'd keep it in the hotel safe, not in your room, wouldn't you?"

"Suppose so. Unless I didn't trust the staff."

Dykeman rubbed the fingers of one hand over his large, fleshy chin.

"Makes you wonder what Puncheon might have kept here that someone would think worth killing him for."

"Seems fair enough."

Dykeman went silent again, his fingers still playing over his chin. It was some little while before he spoke again.

"Well, can't go standing around here all morning," he announced, in a lively manner, the suddenness of which made Shapes flinch. "Best get on with speaking to these friends of Puncheon. Going to be our best way of finding out more about him." He looked down once more at the corpse. "Once Dr Delph has done her thing, get Dartington and another of the uniforms to go over this room, top to bottom. We need to start thinking about a motive and I want to know if there's anything missing. Since they left behind the wallet and that watch you reckon is worth a few bob, it means if this was all the result of a robbery gone wrong then the thief was after something else."

A low, quiet rumble arose from somewhere in the room.

Dykeman sighed. "Don't tell me that's your stomach, Shapes."

"What do you expect. Should have had my mid-morning tea and biscuits by now. I'm hungry."

23

"Don't know where you put all that food you eat. It never seems to make any difference to the size of your belly."

"Nervous energy. I'm on me toes all the time, poised to strike. Burns off the fat like nobody's business."

"If you say so, Shapes. Come on, let's find a room to do our interviews in and someone to sort us out a cuppa and a plate of biscuits, before you pass out from hunger."

Chapter Three

"I think this will suit your purpose, Inspector. Desk, chairs, reasonably clean and tidy, and well away from prying ears and eyes."

Reginald Plowright had initially been afraid the two policemen would insist on taking his own office when they announced they had need of a room in which to hold interviews. Although that had indeed been their initial thought, when they saw how inconveniently located it was, directly behind the reception desk, they agreed they needed somewhere less public and without the potential for them to be overheard by sundry nosey-parkers. That had been a relief to Plowright. It would have been difficult managing the running of the hotel without ready access to all the paperwork that he kept in his office and such access would have been difficult if the policemen had taken up residence there.

The room to which he had just opened the door was towards the back of the hotel, round the corner from reception. Big enough to comfortably accommodate half a dozen people, not overlooked, warm and free of unpleasant smells, it would, decided Dykeman, do very nicely indeed.

"Excellent," declared the inspector. "We'll not waste any time. Can you ask the maid who found the body to join us. Oh, and a pot of tea with a few biscuits would be great, if you don't mind."

"Not at all, Inspector," replied Plowright. "And it's Clare Hurling, the maid who found Mr Puncheon. I'll ask her to come through right away."

CLARE HURLING HADN'T been able to get the image of James Puncheon out of her mind. All that blood. And his eyes, still open, looking at her as she tried to work out if he was dead. She didn't stay around long enough to decide. Her heart was beating so fast she thought she was going to have a heart attack.

She had knocked, got no response, walked into the room and almost reached the bed before she saw him. For a second or two, she thought he was sleeping. Maybe he'd been drinking heavily the night before and was sleeping off a hangover. She'd heard the people he was with had drunk a lot of booze at dinner last night. Imagine that, sleeping on top of the bed in your clothes all night.

But then she'd noticed the deep red stain that seemed to be coming from his belly. She'd gasped in horror and stepped back, away from the bed. She wanted to run away, there and then. Tell Mr Plowright and let him sort it all out. But she forced herself to stay, to make the effort to see if the man on the bed was still breathing. He wasn't.

By the time she fled, she was shaking, tears beginning to well up in her eyes. If she could have run any faster, she would have. She nearly fell down the stairs, then had trouble blurting out her news to the hotel manager, before the sobbing started in earnest.

As she stood now, waiting outside the old office, digging her thumbnails into her fingers, she began to feel a little stupid. Why hadn't she phoned down to reception when she found Mr Puncheon? That would have been the sensible thing to do and she had always thought of herself as sensible. Other people did daft things, wasted their time trying to do the impossible, or spent all day dreaming about some wonderful life in another part of the world. She didn't. She kept her head and got on with what needed doing. Being practical was how she'd been able to cope since her husband, Harold, had done his back in and she'd become the one who had to earn enough money to put food on the table and buy the boys their clothes.

Now she was starting to feel a bit foolish. She's lost her head and panicked. The thought annoyed her. What would these policemen think of her? A silly woman who'd lost control and couldn't tell them a single thing that would help. She wasn't even sure she could remember everything she'd seen or done. Nerves gnawed at her wobbling confidence.

The door to the room opened and what an odd sight it revealed. Standing there was a man, older than herself, short and, well, ugly, wearing... what was he wearing? It came to her. She'd seen that sort of outfit before; it was what those Morris dancers wore. Why on earth was a policeman wearing an outfit like that? And as for his face, well, she was glad he wasn't related to her. What a mess. The nerves that put her off-balance almost entirely disappeared at the sight of this strange policeman.

"Mrs Hurling?" asked the odd-looking man.

"That's me."

She wasn't keen to own up.

"Sergeant Shapes. In you come. We won't keep you long."

She hesitated to follow the policeman into the room, but reminded herself this was all about a murder and stepped forward.

"Ah, Mrs Hurling," Dykeman sounded full of beans. "Do take a seat."

The nervous maid, half an eye on the unsettling sergeant, who had followed close behind her, sat on the lone chair in front of the old desk, straightening her skirt as she did so.

"I'm Inspector Dykeman and I'm leading the investigation into the murder of Mr James Puncheon. Shapes here is my sergeant." Dykeman glanced again at Shapes. "You'll have to excuse his appearance. He was supposed to be trotting around town in one of those hobby horse outfits. Mind you, I've seen him looking worse."

The inspector's friendly manner, sense of humour and explanation for the peculiar look of the sergeant made her feel a little more relaxed. It seemed the eccentric sergeant wasn't some sort of mad man after all. She managed a feeble smile.

"I was wondering why he looked so odd," she replied. "It's not every day you meet a policeman wearing make-up and clothes like that."

It would have helped, she thought to herself, if the sergeant tried smiling, but maybe he wasn't very happy about having to miss out on the Morris dancing. As it was, his face reminded her of one of her neighbour's dogs; ugly and snarly.

"We'll just have a few questions for you, Mrs Hurling. Won't keep you long. Shapes there will take a few notes as we go along."

She nodded, attempting to compose herself, to be the type of person she believed she was. She definitely didn't want the inspector thinking she was a silly woman who screamed when she saw a drop of blood or something as harmless as a spider, as so many women seemed to do.

"I understand, Inspector. I don't think there's much I can tell you that'll help, but I'll do my best."

"Excellent. Now then, I hear you were the one who found Mr Puncheon. Dead in his room, I mean."

"I was."

"And what time was that?"

"I can't say for sure, but it must have been about nine-fifteen. I was doing my rounds, changing the beds and the like."

"Was the door locked when you got to the room?"

"It was. We have our own keys, you see, so we can let ourselves into the rooms. I had to use my key to get into Mr Puncheon's room."

"The lights were on when we went into the room a little while ago. Were they already on when you opened the door?"

"Yes. It was very bright. I think every light in the room must have been on. Some people are like that, they switch all the lights on and leave 'em on when they go out. Very wasteful."

She wondered if the fact the lights were on was a clue. Did it mean anything? And they were all on, weren't they? Yes, she was sure about that. All the lights were on.

"And can you describe to me what you saw."

"Well, it was Mr Puncheon, laid out on the bed. I didn't know he was dead, of course, not right away. Thought he must have been drinking, last night, you see. Sleeping it off. Then I saw the blood, all over the bed. Awful, it was. I touched his hand. It was cold. That's when I knew he must be dead."

Saying those words left her feeling distinctly uncomfortable, but worse still was recalling what it felt like when she placed her fingers on the back of Puncheon's right hand. That sent a shiver up her spine. It was touching his cold and lifeless hand that had set her off, running away like a little girl.

Before he asked his next question, Dykeman gave the woman a moment to breathe. It was clear from the look in her eyes that recalling what she had seen was not an easy thing for her to do. No surprise there. His next question was an important one and he didn't want a nervous, unsettled witness blurting out the first thing that came into her head just so she could get it all done, as quickly as possible.

"Was Mr Puncheon alone?"

"Of course he was," she answered, wondering why the silly man had asked her a question like that. She would have noticed if there was anyone else in the room. She wasn't blind.

"You're sure about that? I only ask because there's an en-suite bathroom and it's possible someone could have hidden in there before you got the door open."

Oh, my God. She felt faint and placed a hand on the edge of the desk to steady herself. She hadn't thought about that. The bathroom door, was it closed? It was, she could remember that clearly. The door was definitely closed. She could have been there, in the room, all alone while the killer was hiding in the bathroom. What would have happened to her if she'd gone in there? She felt sick and a little light-headed.

"You alright, Mrs Hurling? Can Shapes get you a drink of water?"

She shook her head. She'd be alright. Give herself a moment or two, then she'd be right as rain. Breathe in deeply and slowly, that's the thing to do. She swallowed away the taste of sick and forced air right down into her lungs, deep, slow breaths. There we go, the blood was coming back to her head now.

"It's fine, Inspector. It's just, I hadn't thought about that. The killer being in the bathroom. The door was closed, you see. I didn't go in there. So there could have been someone else in the room."

"Excellent, Mrs Hurling. You're doing a great job. Remembering the bathroom door was closed is really helpful. Now, thinking some more about what you saw, were there any signs of someone else having been in the room? A coat or a jacket on a hanger, perhaps? Maybe there was more than one used coffee cup? Anything at all that might point to someone having been there with Mr Puncheon."

She took her time. It was important to get this right. She had been the first one on the scene of the crime, so it was really important she got things right. Oh, but who was she kidding? She'd barely noticed anything except for Mr Puncheon, dead on the bed. Silly, silly woman. But it was too late now. She shouldn't be guessing at these things. Best to be honest, even if it made her look hopeless.

"I'm sorry, Inspector, I was such a mess, I didn't really notice anything else. I ran for help as soon as I knew Mr Puncheon was dead."

"That's nothing to worry about. It's the shock. It kicks in before you even realise it. Same for everyone who stumbles on a corpse, eh, Shapes?"

"It is that, sir. Some people can't remember anything useful. Some even forget their own names."

"One last question, Mrs Hurling. Were any of the other rooms on the same floor still occupied or had everyone gone down to breakfast?"

"Well, I hadn't got to them all, you see. Only done 211 and 213. The guests in those rooms were down here, I suppose, having breakfast. Don't know about the other rooms."

"Excellent. You've been a great help, Mrs Hurling. If you should happen to think of anything else then you'll come find me or the Sergeant, won't you? Sometimes things come to you later, when the shock has properly worn off."

"Yes, Inspector. Oh my, I'm so glad I've been of some use. It's such a terrible thing to happen."

As the peculiar-looking sergeant closed the door behind her, the maid felt tears well up in her eyes. Poor Mr Puncheon. Who'd want to murder another human being? And here, in their hotel. Then she realised she didn't know if the poor man had any children. Oh dear. The tears began to trickle down her cheeks.

"WHAT D'YOU RECKON THEN, Shapes? Think the killer could have been hiding in the bathroom?"

"What, standing behind the shower curtain, holding his weapon in his hand, ready to strike if the maid stuck her head in there?"

"Something like that, Shapes," Dykeman ignored Shapes's attempt at humour, as he often did. "It's a thought, though. People don't go murdering folk without a reason and suppose our killer wanted something from that room, something he hadn't found when Mrs Hurling showed up. Wouldn't be anywhere else in the room to hide yourself. They could even have slipped out while she stood there staring at the body, not aware of anything else going on around her."

"Yeah, we've seen that happen before. Not going to know though, are we? Least not yet. I thought the old dear was going to fall off her chair when you told her the killer might have still been in the bathroom."

Shapes smiled. Things like that always amused him. The job had to have its upsides.

"Well, I reckon if the body was cold then Puncheon must have been dead a while. Doubt the killer would have hung around that long, even if they were looking for something."

Shapes opened his mouth, but it wasn't his words they heard next; it was a knocking sound. Knuckles on wood, thought Dykeman. Shapes stepped across the room and opened the door. Standing there was a beautiful, brown-haired woman, in her mid-forties, he guessed. Bit overweight, which was how he liked them, and her horn-rimmed glasses made her lively brown eyes look a bit bigger than they probably were. He should have said something, but his mouth had lost its ability to move. Instead, all he could manage was to step aside and gesture for her to enter the room.

Laura Sinkling had fallen to pieces when she heard about the death of her former husband. Although she wouldn't admit it to another soul, the strength of her feelings had surprised her. After all, their hadn't been particularly warm since she had left him; not that he had anyone to blame but himself for their divorce.

It was one of her friends, Sally Dingle, who'd told her the news. Sally had overhead two of the staff talking in an excited whisper about the murder. She imagined it was always impossible to keep a lid on these sort of things for very long. Scandal had a way of escaping any attempt at confining it.

Sally had admitted that, at first, she had been rather reluctant to say anything to her, but decided she would be better off hearing it from a friend rather than some official.

She was still in the restaurant with the others when Sally returned and pulled her into a quiet corner near the terrace. The poor woman was a bag of nerves. The odd thing was, although she heard Sally say the words, they didn't really sink in. It was as if they simply floated over her head and away. Such a peculiar feeling. It was her own tears that brought her back to the here and now; they tickled her skin as they slid little by little down her cheeks. She sat there with Sally, her friend holding her hands so tightly she began to lose feeling in them. It was, perhaps, a full five minutes before she could manage to say anything herself. By then, she could see from the look on their faces that everyone else in their little party now knew what had happened. So, in all likelihood, did everyone else in the hotel. There was no possibility of hoping it was all a mistake.

She'd been sitting in the bar with the others when the news reached them that the police had arrived; not, she felt, before time. Her husband, Frank, and Sally had tried their best to persuade her to wait, to let the police find her when they were ready. The police would, the others insisted, have a good deal to do, not the least of which was visiting the scene of the crime. It wouldn't help them if she went barging in there. She had managed to sit on her hands for a while, but eventually all that waiting simply became too much. She had to speak to the officer in charge and do so at once.

"And who might you be?" asked Dykeman.

Laura Sinkling looked at him, relieved to see he was properly dressed and his face devoid of make-up, unlike the peculiar individual who had opened the door.

"I'm Laura Sinkling," she replied, her voice unsteady. "I used to be Mrs Laura Puncheon."

The bushy brow over Dykeman's left eye arched. This was a turn-up for the books. Don't say she'd been staying at the hotel as the same time as her former husband.

"In that case, Mrs Sinkling, you'd better come in. I'm Inspector Dykeman and this is Sergeant Shapes. I'm guessing you didn't show-up here by accident?"

"No, my husband and I are staying here. The hotel manager told me where to find you. Please don't blame him if he did anything wrong in telling me; I was rather forceful."

"No problem, Mrs Sinkling. Please, take a seat."

As Laura Sinkling sat down and Shapes closed the door, Dykeman pondered for a moment how best to approach this new opportunity; for opportunity it certainly was.

"I, erm... were you still on friendly terms with your former husband?"

Dykeman rubbed the side of his nose. He'd have to tread carefully here. Sitting opposite him was both a prime witness and a minefield, through which he would need to step with more than his customary care. Put one foot in the wrong place and the resulting explosion might prove fatal to the investigation. On the other hand, if he navigated a safe course, the reward might be great. Who else, other than his parents, could know James Puncheon better than his former wife?

"Well, perhaps cordial would be the best way to describe it," began Laura Sinkling. "I'm sure you can understand that things between the two of us could never be expected to be anything more than that. But we were on much better terms than we had been not so long ago. I think we'd both come to accept that, if we wanted to continuing seeing all our friends, and we did, we'd have to be civil towards each other."

"Very commendable. Most married couples who split up wouldn't give each other the time of day. Would be better for all concerned if more would take a leaf out of your book."

"I can't pretend it's always been easy, you understand, but we are adults and really ought to be capable of being civil towards one another."

"Mrs Sinkling, I have to tell you that it does appear your former husband has been murdered. There seems little chance of it having been an accident or suicide." Dykeman paused, aware it must all have come as a shock to Laura Sinkling. He took a little nod of her head as his prompt to continue. "Can you think of any reason why someone would want to kill him?"

Laura Sinkling hadn't anticipated the question, despite it now seeming such an obvious one to ask, and she was momentarily taken aback.

"No, of course not. Why would I ever think anything of the sort?" she hesitated, realising the implication in the question. "Are you suggesting his death was planned? Surely not. Why?

Laura Sinkling looked aghast, shocked, thought Dykeman, at the suggestion her former husband's death might have been premeditated. That was fair enough. Murder was rare; something that most people don't have to get to grips with. He wondered if she might silently be piecing together possible suspects. If she was, she ought to realise pretty quickly that an ex-wife would most definitely be on any police list of suspects. But there were a lot of 'ifs' there and right now all he wanted to do was establish a few facts.

"We have to consider all the possibilities, Mrs Sinkling. Until we're able to exclude anything and anyone, Shapes and I will have to keep an open mind."

"But it's absurd," she said, adamant in her opinion. "What reason could anyone possibly have for killing James? He, me, the rest of us, we're all just, well, normal people. We don't mix in criminal circles, Inspector."

"Sad to say, Mrs Sinkling, there are criminals in all areas of life. Even the best of us can't be sure we're very far from someone who's up to no good, eh, Shapes."

"True enough, sir. Look at that Lord Wishbourne last year. Pillar of the Establishment. Didn't stop him from smashing his wife's head in when he fancied moving in with his sexy secretary."

"But... well..."

Laura Sinkling wasn't really sure what to say in response. The inspector's line of enquiry was troubling. No, it was more than that, it was awful.

"But, let's not go getting ahead of ourselves. It would be unusual, but it could be a gutless thief who'd brought along a gun, panicked and shot Mr Puncheon." suggested Dykeman.

Laura Sinkling looked about ready to collapse in a heap. Best to get her back on to firmer ground, decided the inspector.

"What sort of man would you say Mr Puncheon was?"

"Well, I suppose most people would tell you he was a hard-working and friendly man. He was..."

"But that's most people, Mrs Sinkling," cut in Dykeman. "How would you describe him?"

Laura Sinkling attempted to compose herself, a little irritated at Dykeman's stance.

"You have to understand, Inspector, although I was once very much in love with James, after he... well, once I found out about his affair, I no longer saw him in quite the same way. I'm sure you can understand."

"That's fair enough, Mrs Sinkling. Something like that is bound to change your opinion. All the same, you'll know better than most what sort of a man he was."

Laura Sinkling took a breath and did her best to focus on describing her former husband as plainly and fairly as she could.

"He was quite a sociable animal; happy to mix with most people. And he could be very caring and considerate. At least, he was to me, despite what he got up to later in our marriage." She paused for a moment before continuing. "I did used to tell him that he worked too hard. Long hours sometimes, especially when they were trying to complete a new marketing campaign. And I know he could be very demanding at work. His view was that if he was prepared to put in the hours then so should everyone else."

She was about to add further to her description, but Dykeman cut in again.

"Would you say he was ever a violent man?"

Laura Sinkling shook her head. "No. Absolutely not. He did sometimes have a bit of a temper. If things weren't going the way he wanted them to, he'd get very impatient. But he never threatened me in any way and I never heard of him engaging in violent behaviour towards anyone else."

"That temper never got him into any trouble?"

"Not that I'm aware. He wasn't the kind to resort to violence, if that's what you mean. It was more a case of shouting and desk banging. Apparently he was the same at work."

"You say he worked hard. What about outside of work, what sort of things did he like to do?"

"Cricket mostly. At least in the summer months. He used to play a lot when he was younger and still played the occasional game, although these days he was mostly a spectator. And he liked his wine. We had a wonderful cellar at our old house and James did his best to fill it with bottles of the best wine we could afford. We usually spent at least one week a year touring France or Italy, so he could track down vineyards he'd heard about from friends. Sometimes we brought so many bottles back with us, I feared the car would buckle under the weight."

Dykeman paused a moment, waiting for Shapes to catch up as he scribbled notes in his pad. The man's writing was bad enough at the best of times and the last thing he wanted to do was make him write any faster. He'd made that mistake before, when they'd first started working together, and hadn't been able to read a word the man had written. It also gave him a moment or two to consider his next question. Normally he would have given himself time to prepare for such an interview. It was an important one, given the circumstances, and not one he wanted to mess up. Laura Sinkling showing up as she did had robbed him of his chance to get himself ready. He knew already he'd need to speak to her again, in which case it was probably best to keep things simple for now. Focus on some of the basics.

"Did the two of you have any children together? Is there anyone we should be contacting?"

Laura Sinkling looked away for a moment, a pained expression on her face that Dykeman couldn't fail to notice.

"No, it wasn't something that was meant to be."

Her voice wobbled a little, causing Shapes to glance up from his notes. Dykeman hesitated. This wasn't the time and place to press her on what appeared to be a difficult topic, but he was curious, all the same. Maybe he could get Shapes to do a bit of digging.

He was about to ask if Puncheon's parents were still alive when a loud rapping at the door interrupted them. Shapes stepped across the room and opened the door.

"Oh, it's you, Fry. What's up?"

PC Fry peered into the room, not much good at hiding his curiosity.

"Thought you and the Inspector would like to know, Sarge, that Dr Delph is here. She's on her way up to Room 215 now."

"We'd best meet her there right away, Shapes," replied Dykeman. "I'm keen to hear what Sheila, er, Dr Delph has to say. I'd like to have her opinion as soon as possible. Could be very useful."

At least, that's what he told Shapes. And it was true, in part. In reality, he never could pass up an opportunity to meet the local pathologist and bask in the glow of her charming company. It was a shame there weren't more murders in their neck of the woods; if there were, there'd been even more opportunities for the two of them to bump into each other, so to speak.

"Will there be news you can share with the rest of us, Inspector, do you think?"

There was a note of hope, bordering on expectation, in Laura Sinkling's voice; something Dykeman knew he couldn't possibly meet. For one thing, he couldn't go around sharing sensitive information with the witnesses and possible suspects. For another, if Sheila Delph was to have anything useful to tell him then it would most likely come from the full postmortem examination and that would take time.

"Maybe, Mrs Sinkling, but I wouldn't go getting your hopes up too much. This will just be an initial assessment. We'll know more once the full examination has been carried out."

Laura Sinkling's shoulders sagged and she looked all of a sudden rather tired and run down. That would be the stress and her nerves, noted Dykeman. What she needed now was some rest and a bit of peace and quiet.

"Fry, can you escort Mrs Sinkling back to her room. I think she could do with a bit of peace and quiet. I'm sure this has all been a terrible shock. We can call for a doctor, Mrs Sinkling, if you'd like one. He might be able to give you something to calm the nerves."

Laura Sinkling shook her head, but he was right, she did feel as if the life had been drained out of her.

"My husband will take care of me. I imagine he's waiting impatiently now, wanting to quiz me; to find out what you've told me." She managed a rather feeble smile.

"Well, you take care and we'll speak to you again later, when you've had time to rest."

Dykeman watched the woman leave the room. He couldn't help wondering who would benefit from James Puncheon's will, given there were no children involved.

"What d'you reckon to that one, then sir? Heartless, cold-blooded killer is she?"

Shapes closed his notepad and dropped it on the desk. He'd seen far too many grieving husbands and wives, current and former, to be stupid enough to take anything they said at face value. Humanity was, he considered, a sordid affair, filled with liars, cheats and, sometimes, killers. There was bound to be more to unearth where Laura Sinkling's relationship with her former husband was concerned and, sure as eggs was eggs, some of it wouldn't look any too good for her. All the same, he had to admit that right now the suggestion she might be a cold-blooded killer did seem a bit of a stretch.

"Who knows, Shapes? Right now, as far as I'm concerned, the hotel manager could have shot James Puncheon. And so could the maid who found him."

Shapes smiled. He liked a decent line up of suspects, so long as it didn't stop them from fingering one of them for murder, eventually. Should be alright, too, spending a few days knocking around a hotel, what with the food and drink and, if he was lucky, a sexy maid or two for him to chat up. There were far worse places to find yourself.

"Anyway, Shapes, I think it's about time you got yourself properly cleaned up and into some grown-up clothes. People keep looking at you in an odd way, like you've got leprosy or the plague."

"It don't bother me. I'm used to people looking at me like that."

"That might be so, but off you go. Get yourself off home and cleaned up, then meet me back here as soon as you can."

"What are you going to do, sir?"

"Speak to Sheila, I mean Dr Delph, to see if she's found anything helpful. Then I'm going to have a bloody good lunch, in the hotel restaurant, and with any luck they won't charge me."

Dykeman grinned and tapped his tum.

Shapes wasn't happy. His heavily-lined face took on a petulant look, the sort of thing a young child would roll out when it's feeling unhappy about not getting its own way.

"I should have some grub too, before I go home. The restaurant might be closed by the time I get back and I'm starving already."

Shapes knew full well there was little chance of the restaurant being closed any time soon, since it had most likely not yet even opened for lunch. But he recognised the look of glee on Dykeman's face. The selfish git was going to stop him from tucking into a free feast and not for any other reason than that he could.

"Nope, can't have you going into the restaurant looking like that. You'll put people off their food. There'll be complaints. No, you get off home, get washed and changed, then make yourself a cheese and pickle sandwich. I'll keep an eye on things here."

Muttering followed. Dykeman struggled to hold back a bellyful of laughter. That was one-nil to him for the day, though he'd better be on his guard. Shapes was bound to be sniffing around for a chance of revenge. He would be, if the boot had been on the other foot.

"Wonder if they do a steak and kidney pie..."

Chapter Four

Sheila Delph was jotting down a few notes when Dykeman walked back into Room 215. She looked radiant, as she always did to the inspector. How someone so beautiful could end up working with dead people was anyone's guess, but it just didn't seem right to him. She was too full of life to be working with death, or maybe that was why she was able to cope with it. One thing was for sure, it never seemed to bother her much, not even the worst cases. Mangled bodies pulled from vehicle wrecks or charred corpses dragged from the ashes of burnt-out buildings gave him nightmares for days afterwards. He shuddered at the thought.

"Hello, Leslie. I thought you might have got here sooner."

She smiled at him. She never could resist teasing Dykeman, especially when it was so easy. It was true to say that Leslie

Dykeman was not one of those men who were naturally comfortable in the company of women. How lucky for her.

"Only just heard you were here. Came as soon as I could."

"No Shapes?"

"Had to send him home. He was attracting attention; of the wrong sort. Probably had something to do with the make-up and Morris dancer's outfit he was wearing."

Dykeman grinned. He'd be taking the mickey out of Shapes about that for years to come.

"I heard. Such a shame. I was hoping to see for myself. Did he get to put on one of those wooden horses?"

"He did and I made sure the photographer from the newspaper got a few good snaps. Wouldn't want Shapes to go without a memento or two."

"The poor man. I imagine you've been teasing him something rotten. I know what you two can be like."

"He'll get over it, eventually."

Dykeman couldn't help noticing that Sheila Delph was wearing an open-necked blouse, green, with a floral pattern, that exposed a goodly amount of her ample bosom. God, the woman was blessed. A familiar tingle ran through him. One day, yes, one day he'd do something about it. If only he could be sure how she felt about him. The bloody woman was impossible to read properly. Every time he thought he knew where he stood, she'd say something that left him filled with uncertainty. Was he the only man who had this kind of trouble with women? There was no way he was going to ask Shapes for his view. For one thing, he didn't want Shapes knowing how he felt about Sheila and, for another, the man was a lecherous old git whose advice on women would be sure to do nothing except get him into trouble. Why couldn't life be plain sailing, for a change?

"Penny for your thoughts."

"Eh?"

"You look like you're miles away. Wondering who might have done this?"

"Er, yes, that's it. Lots of people involved. Going to be a messy one. What can you tell me, then? Anything useful?"

"He was shot?" She smiled.

"You sure? I thought he was suffocated and the bullet wounds are there to distract us."

"Nothing much I can tell you yet. I would say he's been dead around six hours. I'll be able to say more once I've got him to the morgue. Can he be moved yet or do you need me to wait?"

"He's all yours, Sheila. Six hours. Definitely killed some time this morning and not last night, as far as you can tell?"

"I'll go as far as saying he wasn't murdered before midnight. Did no one hear the shots?"

"Not as far as we know. The place is packed, too, but the killer could have used a silencer. I doubt even someone in the next room would have heard if that was the case, especially if Puncheon didn't get chance to shout for help."

Dykeman wondered what else he could talk about to make it look like he had a proper reason for prolonging his stay, but his mind had gone blank, as it so often did when he was alone with Sheila. Well, alone, as in no other living people present. Why didn't the woman just take pity on him and say something, anything, that would keep the conversation going.

"Well, I'd best get on. I'm supposed to be in Oxford, attending a meeting at the Radcliffe Infirmary, later this afternoon, so if you want my examination results before then, I'll need to start right away. Do you want me to phone them through to the station?"

"Might as well. I'm not sure where I'll be. Oxford, eh? Should be nice on a day like this."

"Sadly, I won't get to see much of the outside world as I'll be spending all my time stuck inside. Maybe I'll sit on the sunny side of the train on the way there."

She smiled again and Dykeman felt a sense of abject hopelessness fall over him. Thank God he had a murder case to take his mind off things.

THE RESTAURANT WASN'T officially open for dinner until twelve, but the hotel manager hadn't needed much persuading to agree to Dykeman's request for an early meal. In fact, as the hungry inspector had hoped, Plowright had even offered to provide the meal free of charge. After all, there was a murder to be solved, one that had taken place in the hotel, and it was important the inspector wasn't distracted by pangs of hunger.

Dykeman had chosen to sit at a table set for two, near the entrance to the restaurant, which was a modest-sized room containing twenty tables, most laid out for four diners. It overlooked the small garden at the rear of the hotel. The low ceiling made it feel cosy when it was empty but, Dykeman thought, probably made it quite oppressive when it was busy.

Anyhow, he had a decent view of any comings and goings as members of staff went about their business.

He ran a finger over a length of the table-cloth that hung down over his legs. It was so white it had the appearance of snow, or, it did until he spilled gravy on it. So thorough had the staff been in setting up the tables, they'd wiped away the spots of pepper and salt that might normally be found decorating the tops of each pot. No chance of finding any such thing in his own home.

"How was your pie and mash, Inspector? To your taste, I hope."

Joseph Pearling, the waiter who'd been looking after Dykeman at the hotel manager's instruction, had returned. Stealthy bugger, thought the inspector, creeping up on him like that. Probably a skill you developed on the job, he mused. It would be called being unobtrusive. Might be a handy skill for a policeman to pick up.

"Best pie and mash I've had in years, Joseph. Tell the chef to pop a dozen round to my home when he's finished here for the day. There again, best not. I'd only end up getting into trouble with the Chief Inspector if he thought I was accepting gifts from someone working at the scene of a crime.

"There's a fine-looking apple and blackberry crumble on offer, if you'd like a pudding, Inspector. Custard or cream to go with it?"

Joseph Pearling swept up the dirty plate and cutlery, along with the half-empty gravy boat, as Dykeman weighed up the pros and cons of having a pudding. It was tempting. He liked crumble. Cream too. The trouble was, he'd never get through the afternoon without falling asleep if he added crumble and

49

cream to the pie and mash that was already sitting heavy in his stomach. Maybe he could nip back later for an afternoon snack. Bound to be some crumble leftover, once lunch was all done and dusted.

"I'd best not, thanks. Need to keep my wits about me."

"No problem, Inspector. Tea or coffee?"

"Coffee would be good, thanks. Maybe a biscuit or two, if you can manage it."

They would be a poor substitute for crumble, thought Dykeman, but at least it would be something sweet to go with his coffee.

"I think we can rustle up a few biscuits, Inspector."

Pearling was back a few minutes later, carrying a tray loaded with a pot of coffee, milk, cup, spoon and a dozen biscuits of various sorts. Dykeman was impressed. As Pearling went about his business, transferring the contents of the tray to the table, Dykeman noticed the waiter had lost the end section of the little finger on his left hand. Odd he hadn't noticed it earlier. Probably focused too much on that pie and mash to spot it.

"What happened to your finger?"

"Accident when I was a young boy. Got it stuck in the cellar door. Nasty thing, that door. My gran always told me I'd lose a finger if I didn't take care. She was right, as always."

"My sergeant shut a finger in the door of our police car last year. Swore like a trooper, he did. But he was lucky. Some nasty bruising and bleeding, but he kept the finger in one piece. I told him he should be more careful, but he didn't reckon I was being much of a help saying that after he'd done it."

Pearling poured some of the coffee into the cup, the sweet aroma filling Dykeman's nostrils.

"Milk and sugar?"

"Milk and two sugars, thanks."

"Terrible news about Mr Puncheon. We can't believe it's really happened. The staff, I mean. It just doesn't seem real, a guest getting murdered. Am I allowed to ask if you have any idea why?"

As he spoke, Pearling poured the milk, added two cubes of sugar, then set the spoon on the saucer so Dykeman could stir as he saw fit, before brushing a fragment of biscuit off the tablecloth and into his gloved hand.

"Early days, yet. Very early. I think we're going to need to speak to a good few people before we can start putting together a picture of what happened."

"They say it's always about the motive in a murder case. Is that right?"

"It is. But that's the same for any crime. If you can work out what the motive is, then you've got a fair chance of tracking down the culprit. But that can be easier said than done some of the time. The motive can be so obscure it takes a month of Sundays to work it out. I've been on cases where people have wreaked their revenge on someone who upset them years ago, sometimes for the most ridiculous of reasons. But it's eaten away at them all that time, until one day they've decided to do something about it. You'd be amazed."

"Well, I hope you find them soon, Inspector. Makes us nervous knowing there's been a killer on the loose in the hotel. Don't know who might be next on their list."

"Sensible precautions should be enough to keep you safe. We don't even know yet if the killer's someone who has anything to do with the hotel. They might have slipped into the building, done what they needed to, then legged it."

"I hope so. I wouldn't feel so afraid if I knew that was the case." Pearling cast an eye over the table and decided all was as it should be. "Will there be anything else for you, Inspector?"

"No, that's your lot. Thanks Joseph. Think I'll read the newspaper while I have my coffee. Enjoy a few more minutes' peace and quiet before my sergeant gets back."

As Pearling made his way back to the kitchen, Dykeman let out a little sigh. It was a West Country accent, he declared to himself. It had been bothering him since Pearling had first spoken. The accent was so slight it had almost disappeared. Probably not lived down there for years, decided the inspector. Happy he'd finally solved another problem, Dykeman picked up the copy of *The Times* he'd grabbed on his way to the restaurant and set about perusing the front page. Life was good for the moment and he was going to make the most of it. Such moments of peace and quiet could be few and far between when you were working on a murder case.

"THAT'S BETTER, SHAPES. You look almost human again. At least you shouldn't go scaring the living daylights out of anyone else."

Shapes had returned to the hotel, he'd washed his face and was wearing his usual work-a-day clothes. He was feeling all the happier for it. One thing was for sure, he was never again going to put on one of those stupid outfits he'd been forced to squeeze into earlier that morning. He'd rather resign from the force than do that again. Sod the Chief Inspector. Which reminded him, "Chief Inspector says hello and he wants an update on progress before the end of the day. A personal update. Face-to-face, like," emphasised Shapes.

"I shall look forward to it. Can hardly wait," groaned Dykeman.

"Thought you'd be happy about that."

Shapes grinned. He knew full well Dykeman would rather do pretty much anything else than spend time with the Chief Inspector, who always seemed to think they should have any new case wrapped up within twenty-four hours and all without upsetting a single member of the public, whether they deserved it or not.

Dykeman noticed there was something not right about his sergeant. At first he couldn't put his finger on it, despite the persistent nagging feeling that, whatever it was, it was staring him right in the face. Not much ever varied about Shapes. He was as predictable as they come. Same grumpy attitude, terrible jokes and lecherous behaviour. He seemed to wear the same clothes every day, too. Ah, then it dawned on him.

"You've got a new pair of shoes, Shapes. I didn't know we paid you enough to go around splashing the cash like that."

Shapes glanced down at his shiny brown shoes. They had him feeling quite chipper.

"You don't. It's my first new pair in three years. Truman and Hymns. Got a proper good price out of them, I did."

"Truman and Hymns?" Dykeman was genuinely surprised. "How d'you afford that? The Chief Inspector shops there. Don't let him know where you got them from, or he'll stop you wearing them to work. Won't put up with the riff raff wearing shoes from his favourite outfitters."

"Yeah, I know. I got them cheap because the tongue on the left one isn't quite right. Got messed up when it was stitched in place. But I'm not fussed. You can't see it when I've got the shoes on. Good, aren't they? Might even polish these ones."

Dykeman wiped his napkin across his lips, then dropped it on the table next to the almost empty coffee cup. Enough of this chit chat, it was time to get back down to business.

"I'd offer you some coffee, but there's only the one cup and, anyway, we need to get cracking. I want to speak to all the other people in the Puncheon party as soon as we can. You got that list I asked for earlier?"

Shapes pulled a single sheet of paper from one of the pockets in his jacket.

"They're all on here. Names and room numbers."

"How many?"

"Including Laura Sinkling, there's seven of 'em. All couples, except one, a single woman."

"Good. Shouldn't take too long to get round them. What about the rest of the guests and the staff?"

"Dartington and Humphries are on to that. Some of the staff work nights, so we'll have to wait for them to come in later, or go and hammer on their front doors."

"When we've finished up here, I want you to do some digging into Puncheon's past. I don't really have any time for the idea his murder was a bit of thieving gone wrong. He's upset someone, somewhere. Bad enough for them to want a bit of revenge and we need to find out what that upset could be."

"I can get on with that while you're talking to the Chief Inspector." Shapes picked up the discarded coffee cup. "I don't mind using your cup. I ain't fussy."

"What?"

"The coffee. I don't care if there's not another cup. I can use yours."

"Not now, Shapes. Think of the impression it'll make on the staff. Come on. Who's first on that list?"

Dykeman was damned if Shapes was going to share in his little treat. It was his, all his. Letting Shapes in on it would stop it feeling special. He could make himself a coffee later. When they were back at the station.

"There's one of 'em in the bar. Frank Sinkling. Hotel manager told me just now. We could start with him."

"Indeed we could, Shapes, and if he's been imbibing he might be a little freer with his answers than otherwise." Dykeman looked around. "Where is the bar?"

"Through there," replied Shapes, nodding in the direction of a set of double doors on the far side of the room.

"Should have realised you'd know where the bar is."

FRANK SINKLING WAS perched on a bar stool, peering into a small glass. He was, observed Dykeman as they entered the room, a tall man, his short, closely clipped hair flecked grey at the temples. An equally well-maintained moustache covered the width of his top lip. It was all indicative of a man with a military background. Hardly unusual, given most men in their forties or fifties would have seen active service in the last world war. Most, however, had done their best to throw off this link to the past, intent on getting on with their lives.

His suit looked expensive and, despite the outsize feet that Dykeman almost gawped at, he was a man most ladies would no doubt consider handsome. A little frisson of envy played at the edges of Dykeman's mind. Sinkling hadn't noticed the two policemen heading his way.

"Mr Frank Sinkling?"

He turned a little to see who was talking to him. The voice wasn't one he recognised.

"That's me," he replied. There was little doubt what these two men did for a job. He'd encountered their sort in the Army. They had that same sense of self-confidence and officialdom you found in policemen everywhere. "And I'd hazard a guess you're the police officers investigating James's murder."

"We are." It always irritated Dykeman a little when he and Shapes were so quickly fingered for the officers of the law they were. He didn't really like being so easy to spot. Might as well have it tattooed on their foreheads. "I'm Inspector Dykeman and this is Sergeant Shapes. We'd like a word, if you don't mind. Somewhere more private."

"Happy to tell you all I can, Inspector, though I doubt I'll be of much use to you."

Dykeman glanced around the room, with its low ceiling and dim lighting. Apart from the barman, it was empty.

"Let's use one of those tables over there."

He led them to a small table by the far wall. If anyone else did come into the room, they'd be hard pushed to overhear him and Shapes talking with Sinkling.

"It was a pretty big shock, I can tell you, Inspector. I saw plenty of death during World War II; you get used to it, after a while. But this is different. You don't expect something like this to happen to one of your friends in a hotel in a quiet little town like Banbury." Sinkling shook his head. "Do you have any idea who might have done it or why? I'm damned if I can think of any reason why someone would want to kill James."

Sinkling possessed, noticed Dykeman, the archetypal Home Counties accent, every word pronounced as near to perfection as any school teacher could ever wish for, though with just a hint of military snap thrown in. A lot of people think murder and mayhem only affects your working class folk, in dark alleyways or pub fights, but experience had long since told him otherwise. It didn't matter how well off you were or what people you mixed with, everyone was potential fodder for such a despicable crime.

"Had you known James Puncheon long?"

"God, yes, years. We first met in, what was it, '46, I'd say. Mutual friend introduced us during a meeting of the Leamington Chamber of Commerce. We were both in the marketing business. Got on like a house on fire, right from the start."

"And you say you can't think of any reason why someone would want to kill him?"

"I wish I could, Inspector. I really do. We've all been trying to think why someone would do such a thing, but it just doesn't make any sense. I've even wondered if it might have been a case of mistaken identity. You know, someone knocked on the wrong door and pulled the trigger before they realised it was the wrong man. Do you suppose that could be what happened?"

"Can't rule out anything yet, Mr Sinkling. It's too early to do that."

Shapes was, as usual, scribbling away in his notepad. He glanced up, a dark look on his face. It a look Dykeman recognised. His sergeant was irritated. Mistaken identity never did for Shapes and mere mention of it was enough to annoy him. Hard luck. Right now, anything was possible.

"When was the last time you saw Mr Puncheon?"

"That would be at dinner last night. In there," he nodded in the direction of the hotel restaurant. "Not bad, really. Better than you'd get at most establishments of this size. We were all there."

"When you say 'all', who do you mean, precisely?"

"There was my wife, Laura. I think you met her earlier."

"We did. Nice woman. Understandably upset at what's happened."

Sinkling frowned, deep lines creasing his forehead.

"They didn't always get on too well, you know. Not surprising after what he did. But she never could bring herself to completely dislike him. I've always thought it was mighty impressive of the two of them to be able to keep things civil, so they could carry on with their lives more or less as they were before the divorce."

"What was it he did? Your wife didn't elaborate."

"Ah, yes, Laura still finds that part of things difficult to discuss. I think it's always been an embarrassment to her. Can't really blame her. He had an affair, with a woman in London. Been going on for quite some time, by all accounts, when Laura found out. His work took him down there fairly often. Often enough, as it turned out, to keep a mistress on the go. I know he's not the only chap to have made that mistake, but Laura was never keen on forgiving and forgetting. She kicked him out on the spot, by all accounts."

"And you were friends with the Puncheons when all this was going on?"

"Oh, yes. It was me that persuaded James to come and work for our firm, Marsh and Wallow. We're marketing specialists, based in Leamington, and James had been working in marketing for years, acquiring a very impressive reputation for himself. Took me the best part of eighteen months to persuade him to jump ship. The pair of them were already married by then."

"Happy couple, before the divorce, I mean?"

"Always seemed that way to me. Bit of a shock to find James had a mistress. I asked him about it, just the once, and he said he just fell into it. Didn't get the impression he'd ever thought much about what he was going to do if Laura found out. I don't suppose you do when things are going along so nicely and your bit on the side is about a hundred miles away from the wife at home."

"What happened to the mistress?"

"Oh, he got shot of her right away. Hoped it might persuade Laura to change her mind. It didn't, of course."

"I see. And who else was in your dinner party last night?"

Sinkling swirled what little remained of the ice cubes in his glass before knocking back what was left of his gin and tonic. Perhaps he'd have another when the two policemen had finished with him.

"Harry and Lisa Kindleman. James and I met Harry in a pub, the Royal Oak, one evening about five or six years ago. You'll soon find out for yourself that Harry has, as they say, the gift of the gab. He talked his way into our friendship, not that I've ever had any reason to complain. He's good company. Bit of a looker, is Lisa. Lucky man, Harry, so long as he doesn't mind other men letching at his wife. Nice woman, unless she takes a dislike to you; then she can be a right bitch."

Sinkling looked at his empty glass again and decided he didn't want to wait for another drink. All this talk of murder was unsettling. He held his glass up in the direction of the bar. The barman nodded and set to work.

"How about yourselves, care to join me?"

"Best not, thank you, what with us being on duty."

Shapes's face, noted Dykeman, darkened further. In fact, if it darkened any more you wouldn't be able to see anything of it. Mind you, that wouldn't necessarily be a bad thing.

"You were saying," prompted the Inspector.

"I was, wasn't I. There's also Bernard and Sally Dingle. She's a friend of Laura's, from Dr Barnardo's. They're volunteers there, help run the home in Leamington. Bernard played the occasional round of golf with James, though he's not really the sociable type. Prefers to be reading his collection of books on Anglo-Saxon England. Something of an expert on the subject, or so Laura tells me. Sally is an odd little woman, always nervous. Makes you feel uncomfortable at times just being in the same room as her."

The barman arrived, clearing away the empty glass and replacing it with a new one. The large, rectangular ice cubes clinked against the sides of the tall, glistening glass. Shapes underlined the same sentence several times, digging deep into the paper, blunting his pencil considerably.

"Then there was Lucy. Forget her surname. Friend of Sally's. Think I met her once before, at some do or other. Likes her drink. Sally rather obviously brought her along hoping to pair her up with James, but the poor woman was trying too hard. Made herself look rather desperate. In any case, for what it's worth, I don't think she's James's type. Too... plain."

Dykeman noticed a little twitch of the eyebrows from Shapes, a man forever drawn towards the opposite sex but without any success; or, at least, that's how it had been for as long as he's known his sergeant.

"How did the evening go? Any disagreements or such like?"

"No, it was all very civilised. Most of us have known each other long enough not to be knocked out of shape by one another's little peculiarities. As it happens, I spent quite a sizeable part of the evening talking to James and Harry. Bernard was there, too, but he's not what you might describe as a talker."

"Do you all get together like this on a regular basis?"

"Once or twice a year. We were here for the Hobby Horse Festival last year. No Lucy. And George and Annie Luckman were here then. Nice people. They had other plans this year."

Sinkling pulled a silver cigarette case from out of one of the inside pockets of his jacket and flipped it open, before holding it out to Dykeman.

"Cigarette, Inspector?"

"No thanks."

"Do you mind if I do, only I've not had one all morning?"

"Don't let me stop you, Mr Sinkling. I think, in any case, we're almost done."

Sinkling produced what Dykeman took to be a rather fine silver-plated lighter from another of his jacket pockets and lit up a cigarette, drawing the smoke deep into his lungs. The inspector wouldn't have considered the other man to be tense, but all the same he relaxed visibly, his shoulders dropping and the muscles in his face loosening. Dykeman wondered if it was the stress of the interview or the killing of his friend that had Sinkling apparently on edge. Maybe it was both. The murder was bound to have an impact on everyone in the party.

"You didn't see Mr Puncheon this morning, then? Not for breakfast, perhaps?"

"No, not at all. Thought it rather odd, as the idea is supposed to be we all eat together. Mind you, Harry didn't make it down until the rest of us had pretty much finished. Difficult nights sleep, by all accounts. Indigestion, he said."

"There was no word from Mr Puncheon? Nothing to say he'd be having his breakfast in his room?"

"No. I think we assumed he'd show up sooner or later or, as you say, have his breakfast in his room. You know, if that maid hadn't found him, it would have been one of us. We were supposed to be going into town for the Festival not long after we heard the news. Can't imagine what it would have been like to find him there, stone dead. I suppose we should be thankful for small mercies."

"Not sure the maid sees it like that, but I get your point," responded Dykeman. He had no doubt at all the maid would have been far happier if one of Puncheon's friends had found him.

"There is one other thing, Inspector."

Sinkling hesitated, studying his cigarette.

"Probably best to tell us, sir, if there's any chance at all it might have a bearing on matters. Chances are we'd find out sooner or later anyway."

Sinkling scratched the small dimple in his cleanly-shaven chin.

"I might be wrong about this, Inspector, though I'm pretty certain I'm not. I think James was having an affair... with one of the women in our little group."

Chapter Five

"Well, there aren't many women to choose from, are there?" pointed out Shapes, still grinning. He always enjoyed a bit of scandal. It brightened up his day. "You can't think he's been seeing his ex-wife again..."

"You sure about that, Shapes? What if Laura Sinkling had decided to forgive and forget. Maybe they were planning to get re-married."

Dykeman didn't really believe that, but they had to consider all the options and, anyway, he rather enjoyed teasing Shapes, especially if it helped keep the man on his toes.

"No chance. Doesn't happen. And, anyhow, there's no way Puncheon's been jumping into bed with his former missus and Frank Sinkling doesn't have a clue about it. Don't believe it. You can cross her off the list here and now."

"Very forthright of you, Shapes. Don't you think it's a little bit too soon to go writing anyone off our list?"

"If she killed Puncheon, I'll hand in my cards."

Dykeman was amused, as he often was when Shapes had made his mind up about something and was determined to stick to his guns. He might well be right this time, of course, but he really ought to keep more of an open mind.

"What about this Lucy Proud woman? Think we can cross her off the list too? After all, Frank Sinkling was pretty clear that Puncheon hadn't take a fancy to her and she's not married, either."

"We don't know she's not married, do we? We haven't checked yet. She might be going around telling her friends she's still a virgin, when she's really knocked out half-a-dozen kids and has a different husband in half-a-dozen towns."

Dykeman looked at Shapes for a moment, wondering how it was his sergeant could jump to two such extreme conclusions so quickly. Shapes had no inhibitions about expressing his views, whatever sort of case they were engaged on, be it a petty theft or a horrific murder. His little grey cells always seemed reluctant to spend much time mulling over possibilities before reaching a conclusion. It was as if he felt there were more pressing matters. Oddly, though, it invariably seemed to result in their working better together as a team, since he, Dykeman, was pushed into a more vigorous analysis of the alternative possibilities.

"By all means take a look into the woman's background, Shapes. Now, what about the other two women? By the sounds of it, I'd rather be warming my toes with Lisa Kindleman. Sally Dingle sounds like she's a bit too domestic."

"We should speak to them next. Give 'em a good grilling. See if we can make the guilty party crack."

Dykeman wished it could always be so easy. Shapes seemed to be in a somewhat optimistic mood, perhaps the result of escaping from that hobby horse costume.

Frank Sinkling's parting snippet had changed things considerably. Prior to that, what Sinkling had told them about James Puncheon had been run-of-the-mill stuff, helpful background but not much use in working out who might have killed him. Now, though, things were different. Now they had a potential motive; one that featured often when it came to cases of murder. Jealousy, sex, revenge might all have had their little part to play here. Of course, they couldn't know yet if that's what lay behind the killing, but it gave them something solid to work with.

"Yes, we might as well get on with it. Let's speak to Sally Dingle first. I'd say she's the least likely of the two to be hopping into bed with anyone but her husband, so let's get her out of the way. See if you can find her and bring her back to our little cubbyhole of an office. While you're doing that, I'm going to have a word with the hotel manager."

"What's that about, then? Didn't like his food, even though it was free?"

"The pie was top drawer, Shapes. Worth stretching out our investigations into a second day just so I can have another one tomorrow. No, I want to know if there were any messages left for James Puncheon at reception. We're focused on the other guests right now, but shouldn't forget the killer might be someone from outside the hotel, even if that's not what we're expecting."

"You reckon it's someone on the premises then who did it? If you ask me, it's a woman. Revenge. It's written all over this one. He probably had his bit of fun, made all the usual promises, then dumped her when things started getting a bit too cosy."

"You might not be a million miles off the mark there, Shapes."

DYKEMAN STOOD IN FRONT of the reception desk, his forearms leaning on the smooth, polished marble top. It was so bright you could almost see your face in it. The hotel manager was out and about on his rounds, ensuring everything was ship-shape and the restaurant ready for lunch to commence. No problems there, thought the inspector, if his test run was anything to go by.

The receptionist on duty was Anita, a young woman barely out of her teens most likely, with pale, flabby skin and a mass of jet black hair. She couldn't seem to make up her mind whether to be excited at being asked to check on something related to the murder or to be scared at any kind of involvement, even if it was only to see if there were any messages for Puncheon.

It turned out there were no such messages and, no, she hadn't seen any waiting for him since she came on duty at seven that morning. Oh well, mused Dykeman, he could hardly expect to find a note from the killer owning up to the deed.

His latest encounter with a member of the hotel staff prompted Dykeman to consider another possibility, namely that the killer could be from their ranks. That was a thought. What might cause a member of the hotel staff to stick two bullets in one of the guests? Sex? Money? He made a mental note to follow up on that thought.

He was about to ask Anita a question or two when a familiar figure stepped off the main stairs and joined him at the desk.

"She's too sick to come down here, says her old man," moaned Shapes, annoyed at having been given the brush off. It wasn't as if Sally Dingle was the one who'd been shot, nor even her husband. In fact, it wasn't even her who'd found the corpse. "It's her nerves, apparently. Such a horrendous thing to happen," he added, complete with a hopeless attempt at an exaggerated upper class accent.

"And you didn't force your way into the room? Must be getting soft, Shapes. Come on, if she won't come to us, we can still go to her. I don't want her husband in the room, though, when we speak to Mrs Dingle."

Shapes smirked.

"You mean, in case it was her Puncheon was knocking off?"

"Precisely."

"Well, her old man don't exactly come across as being a barrel full of laughs, so who knows. Maybe she went looking for something a bit more exciting."

BERNARD DINGLE WAS a tall, slim man who, thought Dykeman, looked rather stern. Something along the lines of a school headmaster. The thin black moustache that decorated his top lip didn't help. A moustache suits some men, but Dingle wasn't one of them. He stood in the doorway to their room, reluctant to let them anywhere near his wife.

"My wife's not at all up to a grilling from the police, Inspector. Her nerves are in pieces. Can't we do this later, once she's recovered herself?"

"I can assure you, Mr Dingle, it won't be anything like a 'grilling'. We just need to ask a few questions, so we can start building an accurate picture of the deceased and the events of the last twenty-four hours. This is a murder we're talking about here, not some petty crime."

If it should come to it, Dykeman wouldn't have any qualms about heaving Bernard Dingle out of the way, or, more accurately, asking Shapes to shift him out of the way. But that might end up with a complaint landing on the Chief Inspector's desk and they weren't so desperate, yet, to go down that particular road. Tact and persistence were the order of the day.

"Well, I doubt very much there is anything she could tell you that you couldn't get from the others in our party. I really must..."

"Bernard, darling, it's alright. It really is. I don't mind answering the policeman's questions."

"It just won't do, Sally. They can come back later. It won't do any harm."

"No, Bernard, dear. I'm fine. It's just a few questions, that's all. We must remember poor James has been murdered and if we can help find the killer then we should do so."

It was a timid, nervous voice that reached the ears of the two policemen. Shapes thought it sounded more like a little girl than a grown woman. Maybe Bernard Dingle liked 'em young.

Dykeman waited. Dingle half-turned, towards the room, his hands clamped to either side of the doorway.

"I don't know, dear. It's all very well you trying to be helpful, but I don't want you ending up in hospital with nervous exhaustion or wot-not."

If Dingle sounded uncertain, it was because he was. He cared deeply for his wife and he wasn't about to let anyone, not even the police, put her health at risk. She could be too accommodating at times, when she ought to think more about herself.

"Please, darling, I'll be fine. I'm sure these policemen will be gentle with me. After all, I haven't done anything wrong, have I?"

Dingle glanced back at Dykeman, before accepting what seemed to be the inevitable. "If you start to feel faint or nauseous, you're to put a stop to the interview right away. Is that clear?"

"Of course it is, Bernard. Now, don't worry, please. I'm sure everything will be fine."

Dingle turned back towards Dykeman, his face set like stone, his voice a deep rumble.

"If you do anything to upset my wife, Inspector, anything at all, I'll see to it your days as a police officer come to a swift end. Do I make myself perfectly clear?"

Dykeman was unimpressed at the threat, though appreciated the man's concern for his wife. He continued with the tactful, understanding approach, maintaining a calm demeanour as he sought to set the man's mind at ease. "I can assure you, Mr Dingle, we will be entirely mindful of your wife's delicate state. It's only run-of-the-mill questions we need to ask, so we can continue building up our understanding of events. There won't be anything that's likely to upset your wife."

"There'd better not be." Dingle let go of the door frame. "I won't go far, dear. Call me at once if you feel unwell, won't you?"

"Of course, darling."

"Perhaps you'd like to wait at the end of the hallway, Mr Dingle," suggested Dykeman. "There's some seating there, I believe. That way you won't be far from your wife."

Dingle looked at Shapes. For a moment Dykeman wondered if all his good work was about to unravel. Shapes had that effect on people. He made them feel many things, but rarely entirely comfortable. Dingle seemed nonplussed and simply ignored Shapes; an occurrence that gave Dykeman cause to question the man's judgement.

With Bernard Dingle evicted and the door to the room closed, Dykeman got his first clear view of Sally Dingle. She was a short, plump thing with pale skin, which didn't do her any favours, whereas her deep green eyes and short red hair, cut in a bob, caught him totally off-balance. It gave her an appeal which, it occurred to him, might very well be enough to tempt many a man into a clandestine relationship. She wasn't entirely the plain woman, lacking in sex appeal, that he'd been expecting.

She was sitting on one end of a small settee, wrapped in a blanket, a glass of what looked like sherry in one hand and a cigarette in the other. The little metal ashtray on the sideboard next to her was heaped high with butts, all clearly stained with pink lipstick.

The Dingles had booked themselves a small suite. Through a partially open doorway to their right, Dykeman could glimpse the bedroom, a long, silk robe in bright pink draped over the end of the bed.

"Do take a seat, Inspector, won't you. You'll make me feel uncomfortable standing there."

"Thank you. Don't mind if I do."

The space they were in was something like a sitting room you'd find in someone's home; nice plain carpet in deep green, a pair of landscape paintings on one wall, one of them a view of Blenheim Palace, if he wasn't mistaken, and two armchairs that matched the settee. All very civilised and, no doubt, on the pricey side. He sat on the armchair furthest away, so Shapes could take the nearer of the two. He would have had a view out of the window, except for the fact the heavy cotton curtains were pulled shut. They kept the light out so effectively it was impossible to tell if it was day or night outside.

"Good of you to talk to us, Mrs Dingle," came Dykeman's opening remark. He wanted to get things off on the right foot. Civilised, like the room! "Can't be easy for you, under the circumstances."

"It's such a shock, Inspector, don't you think? Who would want to... well, you know, kill James?"

Sally Dingle placed her glass on the sideboard, then drew heavily on her cigarette, blowing a long arm of smoke up towards the ceiling. Her other hand began to play with the edges of the blanket.

"I understand you're a friend of Laura Sinkling's. You've known each other for quite a while, is that right?" Dykeman proceeded to business with a simple question.

"Yes, that's right. We both volunteer at the Dr Barnardo's home in Leamington. That's where we first met. We both feel it's important to do something for the less fortunate members of society." She hesitated for a moment, then added, "It was such a shame when James and Laura separated. They made such a lovely couple. Always seemed so happy together. It makes you wonder if anyone's marriage is ever safe these days, don't you agree?"

As Shapes scribbled down notes, he eyed up the woman with the busy hands and nervous-sounding voice. She was no looker, as far as he was concerned; not his cup of tea. Mind you, she did have a fulsome bust and that hair was enough to get most men's attention. He wondered if she dyed it. It was hard to see her having what it took to get herself a bit-on-the-side, not unless the bloke was desperate. Mind you, who knows, maybe Puncheon had drawn a blank elsewhere. He could very well understand that particular problem himself.

"Did they always seem to be a happy couple? Didn't ever fall out or argue?"

Sally Dingle went to rest her cigarette on the ashtray, then changed her mind and stubbed it out, a half-hearted effort, observed Dykeman, that left it still smouldering. Her lips seemed suddenly very thin, almost non-existent.

"Don't all couples argue sometimes, Inspector? I'm sure you and your wife must disagree on some things, don't you?"

"I've never had the dubious pleasure of being married. Not sure I can afford it. Every married man I know always seems to be broke."

"Oh, such a shame. Not being married, I mean."

There was a bowl of red apples on the sideboard. Sally Dingle reached across and picked one up, looked at it, then put it back where it had come from.

"But things didn't turn out too well for them, in the end, did they?"

"So very sad," she answered, reaching for another cigarette. "They always seemed so happy. Poor Laura was devastated. To be treated like that. It isn't right, is it? Not at all."

She lit the new cigarette, filled her lungs with smoke, then stubbed it out. She began to fidget, as if, thought Dykeman, she might be sitting on a nest of ants. It didn't escape his notice that she'd developed this symptom of discomfort when he'd moved the discussion on to the subject of the Puncheons's failed marriage.

"I understand you all went to dinner together last night?"

"We did. It's one of my favourite parts of our little weekends away. I'm sure everyone else would agree. It's so nice to be able to talk together, away from other things."

Other things, wondered Dykeman. Just what other things might they be?

"Were you all at dinner? No laggards showing up half-way through or only making it in time for coffee and mints?"

"Oh, no, Inspector, we all make a point of getting down to dinner on time. It would be so rude not to, don't you think? Anyway, Bernard is a bit of a stickler for these things. He doesn't like arriving late for anything, no matter what."

Shapes couldn't help noticing that Sally Dingle didn't seem half as nervous now as she had done a short while ago. Dykeman asking her about their dinner had perked her right up. Maybe she liked her grub. If only he could get a chance himself to try out the food on offer at the hotel, then he might be able to make a better informed judgement about things.

"Shapes all over, that is," said Dykeman, nodding towards his sergeant. "Can't stand anyone being late. One time I fell down a well and finished up over an hour late meeting him back at the station. Gave me stick for that for days afterwards. Kept banging on about having better things to do with his time. Eh, Shapes?"

Shapes ignored the taunt, even if there was some truth in it. At least, as far as the part about the well was concerned.

"You fell down a well, Inspector?" Sally Dingle's eyed widened and the hesitancy in her voice disappeared. "How on earth did you manage to do that? Were you hurt?"

"I was looking for clues. Didn't notice the brickwork at the top was loose until it was too late. Some of it gave way and down I went. Luckily for me it wasn't a deep well. Felt a right twit, I did. But happily all I got for my troubles were a few cuts and bruises. Not that Shapes showed me much sympathy."

"Oh, dear, you poor man. I imagine you could have been very badly hurt. I'm so glad that wasn't the case."

She glanced at Shapes as she spoke, wondering what kind of man could be so heartless as to show no interest in another person's misfortune. He certainly didn't look the sort to show anyone else much sympathy. Such an ugly little man.

"Thank you for your concern, but let's not get bogged down with my little accident. I don't suppose you can remember who sat where at dinner?"

"Oh, that's easy, Inspector. We always do things properly; man, woman, man, woman and so on. I sat opposite Frank, with Harry next to me. He was sat opposite Laura. Lisa and Bernard were sitting opposite each other at the far end. At the end nearest me, we made sure James and Lucy sat together. I'm afraid I was rather hoping they might ... get along together, if you understand me."

Dykeman was impressed at the way the woman had perked up once he got her talking about the previous evening's dinner. Did it matter? Maybe she was simply glad not to be talking about death and divorce any more. On the other hand, she might just like a good gossip and there was bound to be some of that on offer when you got a group of people together and started plying them with booze.

"Anyone leave the room for more than a minute or two?"

"No, not until we'd finished our meal. The men went to the bar. The women had drinks where we sat."

"And nothing cropped up in conversation that might have suggested there was anything wrong as far as James Puncheon was concerned?"

Sally Dingle visibly stiffened at this reminder of Puncheon's sad demise. She shook her head.

"No, nothing. Do you think we might have been able to do something to help if he had spoken up?"

That nervous, thin voice of hers had returned. Dykeman was annoyed at himself. He should have steered clear of Puncheon for a while longer. Got her talking freely about the rest of them.

"Oh, dear, Inspector, I'm starting to feel very tired. Will you be much longer?"

Dykeman couldn't see anything be gained from upsetting her at the moment. He knew where to find her if he had more questions. Just a couple more for now and then he'd leave her alone.

"What did you and your husband do after dinner?"

"We came back here, to our room. Bernard doesn't like to stay up very late. It gives him a headache, you see."

"And had anyone else left before that?"

"I don't think so, no."

Dykeman glanced at the bowl of apples, silent for a moment, wondering how best to move the conversation on without fraying Sally Dingle's sensitive nerves any further.

"We all have our secrets, Mrs Dingle. I know I've got mine." Dykeman deployed what he hoped was a disarming smile, though he feared it looked rather forced.

"I'm sure you're right, Inspector." Sally Dingle's voice betrayed her uncertainty as to where such a comment was leading.

"I don't suppose you ever had any suspicions that James Puncheon was hiding a secret or two? Something that might be pertinent to our enquiries."

"Oh." Sally Dingle's eyes went wide for a second or two. So that was where the policeman was heading. He was right, of course, almost everyone had a secret they hoped would remain precisely that. She certainly did, but she absolutely wasn't going to say anything about that. As for James, well, if he did have any secrets, then she for one would like to know about them. "I'm afraid not. I can't even begin to imagine what sort of thing he might want to keep hidden away. It's the British thing to do, isn't it? Not to pry."

"I suppose it is," replied Dykeman, wondering if that was really true. In his experience, most people were perfectly happy doing all the prying they could, so long as they could do it without anyone noticing. "And what about his relationship with Frank Sinkling? There must have been some room for a bit of tension there."

"It was a little difficult when Laura and Frank first went public with their new relationship. I suppose it was to be expected, wouldn't you agree? But everyone has been very sensible about things since then."

Dykeman couldn't help noticing that Sally Dingle seemed to be flagging, her voice having tailed off to something approaching a whisper and if her shoulders drooped any further they'd be in her lap. If she'd been more the sort to engage in gossip he would have pressed on regardless; who knows what little gems someone like that might unearth for him. But gossip didn't seem to be her thing, in which case he might as well let her get the rest her husband was so keen on her having.

"That's very helpful to know, Mrs Dingle. Now then, I'd better not keep you any longer or I'll get myself into trouble with your husband. We'll have a quick word with him, then leave the two of you alone."

"I do hope I've been of some help, Inspector. It's so awful, what happened to James."

"Every little bit of information helps us to build up a picture, Mrs Dingle, have no doubt about that. Ready Shapes?"

As the two policemen said their goodbyes and turned to leave, Sally Dingle wondered if she should have said more. Perhaps she had information that would help the police track down the killer. One thing was for sure, she knew full well that James Puncheon had left his failed marriage well behind and was enjoying a relationship with another woman. How could she not?

Chapter Six

As the door closed softly behind them, the two policemen turned to face each other, their toes almost touching they were so close, and began to exchange their initial thoughts, in hushed voices.

"I reckon if Puncheon was jumping into bed with her then he must have been desperate," was Shapes's opening observation.

"Sitting on the fence, as ever, eh, Shapes? I don't know, she's not the worst I've ever seen, though I reckon she's one of those there hypo-whatsits, always making out she's ill. Probably gets her a bit of extra attention."

Shapes lifted an eyebrow, but left it at that. He had other things on his mind, like the way his boss was going about the investigation.

"Why you going so soft on this lot? You're all tip-toeing around the place."

Shapes always had a preference for more of a full-frontal assault when it came to questioning, something he knew Dykeman was more than capable of. Pussy-footing around just wasted everyone's time. Get in there, get what you need and move on.

"Alright, grumpy, keep your hair on. We don't know yet that any of Puncheon's friends had anything to do with this murder. We're just fact-finding. If things change, then we can alter our approach, but until then, we'll be respectful."

"If you say so."

"I do." Dykeman glanced up, towards the end of the corridor, where movement had caught his eye. "Hold on, here we go. Her old man has seen us and he's heading this way."

Bernard Dingle had tried his best to sit quietly and patiently while the police spoke to his wife. But he'd found it almost impossible, twice getting to his feet and walking part of the way back towards their room. He'd been surprised at his lack of composure, never normally one to get so anxious when under pressure. After all, what did they have to be concerned about? But that wasn't the problem. He was genuinely worried about his wife's health. She'd been on edge, fretful and nervous, even before they'd arrived at the hotel. That wasn't necessarily anything unusual, but he was sure he'd been able to detect a steady decline over the course of the last month or two, despite her protestations to the contrary. Her nerves had been worse and her smoking had become almost continuous. So often when he tried to speak to her, she babbled incoherently, then brushed him aside. It wasn't behaviour he was used to from her.

And now this business with James Puncheon. It was barely believable. Who on earth would want to kill him? And for what? A theft? Seriously? As far as he was aware, there wasn't anything of real value that James had brought with him. Or was there? Had his friend brought something the rest of them didn't know about? Maybe he had. For all he knew, there might have been a side to James that he'd never glimpsed, one far removed from the man he knew.

He breathed deeply and slowly, conscious of the tension in his chest. Stress, that's what it was. He didn't like to acknowledge it, let alone admit it to anyone else, but he'd never been the same since he'd been shot during the war. The two bullets that had left their mark on both sides of his left shoulder had also left their mark inside him, in his head. His confidence had been almost literally blown away. So close to death, was it any real surprise? He'd sobbed in his bed during the nights he was in hospital. He'd not been the only one. Everybody on that make-shift ward was there because they'd been shot or blown up, some of them with the most appalling injuries.

But, after that initial spell of depression, he'd been determined not to let it undermine the rest of his life and he'd worked hard, bloody hard, to build a wall around this new weakness. He didn't want sympathy for it and he wasn't going to let it stop him getting on. The trouble was, those negative feelings never fully went away and at times like this they had a habit of pushing towards the surface, threatening to undermine his self-belief and composure.

He took another long, slow breath in an effort to restore his composure. Slow and deep, that was the trick. Get himself all calm before speaking to those two police officers. No need for them to think there was anything wrong with him. Now, off you go, Bernard, firm, steady steps. Let's see how things go.

"Mr Dingle, there you are."

Dykeman tried to sound upbeat. There was no need to do otherwise, despite Shapes's prompting to get tough on these people.

"Inspector. Sergeant. How did it go? Is my wife alright? Her health's very delicate right now. Really is quite a concern."

"Mrs Dingle was very helpful, sir, and she's just fine. It was only a few routine questions. The sort of thing that helps us to build up a picture of the deceased. Always an essential part of an investigation like this."

"A murder, you mean. Yes, I can imagine it is. Motive, isn't it? That's what you need to work out. If you can establish why someone might want to commit a murder, then you're well on your way to tracking them down."

"You're quite right, sir. Motive is everything and getting to know the deceased helps a good deal in identifying what the potential motives might be."

Dingle shook his head. At only five foot four, he had to look up to Dykeman, as he did most men. Even the odd-looking sergeant was a little taller than he was. He'd been tall compared with other boys at school, but somewhere in his late teens he'd simply stopped growing, much to his own annoyance.

"Your wife said you and the other gents in the party retired to the bar after dinner last night?"

"Yes, that's right. Well, I did for a while, but I'm an early-to-bed man myself. Sally and I didn't stay up late."

"So your wife said. How did James Puncheon seem at the time?"

"Fine, I would say. No different to usual. Nothing seemed to be bothering him, if that's what you mean."

"He didn't say anything at all that might have sounded odd or been a matter for concern?"

"No, nothing. Perfectly ordinary evening, I'd say."

The truth was, he couldn't remember much of the detail from the previous evening. Who said what, when and to whom were all things that held little interest for him. That was more Sally's department. She liked a little gossip every now and then. Lisa Kindleman had been genuinely interested in his recent purchase of a pair of fine Saxon coins, that much he could recall. Made a pleasant change to be able to talk to someone about his favourite hobby. The others usually looked like they might be about to fall asleep whenever he mentioned numismatics.

"Harry teased him about Lucy Proud. I told Sally, I didn't think it was a good idea bringing her along." He leaned in a little closer to them and lowered his voice, "Sally thought she might be able to pair them off, Lucy and James. I told her, you can't force these things, but she was very determined."

"Did it bother Puncheon?"

"He didn't really say, but I didn't get the impression he was much interested in Lucy."

"And there's not been any other time recently when Puncheon said anything to you about being in some sort of trouble?"

"Never. Played golf with him week before last and he seemed right as rain. It seems complete madness to me, Inspector, to think that anyone would have a reason to kill the man. Complete madness."

"Just one last question Mr Dingle. Did you see anything of Puncheon after you returned to your room last night?"

"No, I didn't." Dingle shook his head and looked glum. "Terrible, isn't it, to think I left him there in the restaurant, not knowing I'd never get to speak to him again. Makes you realise how quickly things can change in life."

"THEY'RE AN ODD COUPLE," proposed Dykeman as he and Shapes made their way along the corridor, heading for their temporary office. "She's a bag of nerves and I bet he's about as exciting as an old pair of socks."

"Cares about his wife, though."

"Looks like it. Probably worried no other woman would take him on if anything happened to her."

They stepped off the stairs and into the entrance hall, where they found the hotel manager, Reginald Plowright fiddling with a display of white roses on a small, low table. He saw them and left off fussing over the blooms.

"Inspector, how goes your investigation? Any progress?"

It's started already, thought Dykeman, familiar as he was with this sort of thing. Whenever there's been a crime committed on commercial premises, like a hotel or pub, it's never long before the manager or owner starts trying to find out when you might be clearing off out of their way, so they can get back to making money, unmolested by the police. The best course of action when this started happening was to avoid said individual as much as possible, but that was often easier said than done.

"Early days, Mr Plowright. Lots of people still to speak to, which will take time, of course, but we're getting there."

Dykeman noticed the somewhat pained look on the face of the hotel manager. He was sure another question was heading his way, once Plowright had worked out how best to ask it.

"Do these things normally take very long? A day or two, perhaps? I'm not familiar with such investigations. Don't really know what to expect."

"It's hard to say, I'm afraid. Sometimes it's twenty-four hours and other times it's days or even weeks."

The hotel manager's face dropped, his mouth ajar.

"And sometimes they get away scot-free," chipped in Shapes, sounding far too cheery for Dykeman's liking.

"Oh," was all the hotel manager could muster by way of a response, looking down at the carpet.

Fully expecting that more questions were bubbling towards the surface, Dykeman decided to act first by removing himself and Shapes from the hotel manager's presence, forthwith.

"Well, must be getting on. Plenty to do, eh Shapes?"

"Sir."

"Ah and there's the very man. Constable Dartington. Come on Shapes, I want an update from him on how he's getting on with the rest of the interviews. Chin up, Mr Plowright, I'm sure we'll have the killer locked up in next to no time."

Though, added Dykeman to himself, you're not going to hold me to that. He'd made that sort of promise in the past, when he was new and hopeless. Fell flat on his face, he did. Unhappy people all round. There was no way he was making that mistake again. And, truth be told, right now he hadn't the foggiest idea who they might end up arresting.

"Hold up, Dartington," commanded Shapes, his voice so loud it made Dykeman flinch.

PC Dartington had just left their temporary office and was heading away from the other two policemen, whose presence he had not initially noticed. He stopped and turned towards them, a startled look on his face. Loud, assertive commands from Sergeant Shapes always made him jump; the man would make the perfect army sergeant-major.

Ensuring the three of them were safely behind the closed door of their office, Dykeman wasted no further time getting down to business.

"How's it going then, Dartington? Anything useful cropped up yet?"

"Afraid not, sir. Most of the rooms have been booked by couples here for the Hobby Horse Festival. Mainly old people," by which he meant people older than himself. In fact, he considered anyone over forty to be getting on a bit.

"And let me guess, they were all tucked up in bed by ten o'clock? Never left their rooms until breakfast and have cast iron alibis?" suggested a cynical Shapes.

"That's about the long and short of it, Sarge. Of course, we've not spoken to all the guests yet and there's the rest of the staff to go through before we're done."

"Any you've spoken to know Puncheon?" asked Dykeman.

"None. Well, not before this weekend. There's one couple who spoke to him in the bar before dinner last night." He flicked through his notebook until he found what he was looking for. "Mr and Mrs Stein. Retired couple from Winchester."

"Maybe Puncheon made a pass at the old man's wife, then the old fella topped him in a fit of pique?" quipped Shapes.

"I think we'll pass on that one, Shapes. Nothing else, then?" Dykeman asked the constable.

"People are starting to get restless, sir. Some of them are worried the killer might be a mad man who'll strike again. One old fella said he's going to stay up all night so no one can sneak into their room and murder himself and his wife. Didn't look to me like he could stay awake much past his teatime."

"I suppose it's fair enough that they getting the jitters. You'd best arrange for someone to be on duty here through the night, Shapes. And let the hotel manager know. Might help calm him down a bit."

"Will do, sir. You don't reckon there will be another murder, do you?"

"Who knows, Shapes? Best not make things easy for them, eh, if they are set on striking again. And there's something else for you to sort out. Get someone back at the station to see if there's any pattern of thieving from hotels in the area in recent months. If there is, then have them take a look through the guest registers to see if they can spot the same name or names cropping up."

"Good idea, sir. Might take a while, but we might get lucky."

"Right, off you go, Dartington," said Dykeman. "Let's get the rest of those interviews done and dusted before the end of the day."

"Sir."

As the door closed behind the departing Dartington, Dykeman dropped himself into the nearest chair and stretched out his legs and arms.

"We need to find the gun, Shapes. Can't be all that hard, if it's still on the premises."

"If," replied the sergeant, sitting on the edge of the loaned desk. "If the killer's managed to smuggle it out, then it could be anywhere by now."

"It could, but let's not give them any longer to shift it if they've not already done so. I'd also like to know who gets their hands on Puncheon's loot."

"Not his ex, I shouldn't imagine. If he's been killed for his money, that ought to put her bottom of the list of suspects."

"Unless he hadn't amended his will and she'd found that out."

"That's true. Get in there before it's too late, you mean. We ought to find out who his solicitor is."

"Add it to your list, Shapes."

"Will do."

"We also need to know more about these people..."

Dykeman found himself cut off by a loud knocking at the door.

"Come in."

"Sorry, sir." The concern in Dartington's voice was clear. "Thought you'd want to know; Harold Kindleman has disappeared. Left the hotel around eleven, by all accounts, and hasn't been seen since."

Dykeman's initial response was nothing more than a raised eyebrow, followed by a moment's silence, before he replied, "In that case, I think it's pretty clear who we need to speak to next."

Chapter Seven

Lisa Kindleman was nervous and, as far as she was concerned, with good reason. James's murder had been unwelcome and unfortunate, but he was gone now, no longer there to face the inquisition the rest of them were being subjected to. And there were things she had no desire whatsoever to share with anyone else, let alone the police. Everything had been going along so very nicely. Not one of their little group seemed to have the slightest idea what she was up to. And why would they, when she'd taken such care? Poor, dear James had been so easy to manipulate.

The last thing she needed was the police nosing around her affairs. That could prove very awkward indeed. As for Harry, he could be so bloody self-centred. Why she covered for him so often, she really couldn't say. The same stupid mistake over and over. Fool. It was time to stop doing that. He should explain himself, not leave it to others to clear up after him.

Despite it being both too small and too rigid for the purpose, she had draped herself over the chair, her long legs stretched out in front of her, ready to be admired. With practised ease, she shook out the long, luxurious hair she lavished so much time and attention on. Women needed to make the most of what they'd been given. Men had things so much to their own advantage, it left little in the way of options for women like her; ones with a desire to be something other than the little lady at home. These two desperate-looking old men would be putty in her practised hands. Especially the older one, whose eyes were already fixed on her.

Let them ask their questions, their nosey, rude little questions, if they had to. She'd let them have just enough to satisfy their curiosity and nothing more. A little care and a lot of distraction and it would all be over and done.

DYKEMAN WAS NOT IMPRESSED. In fact, he'd taken a disliking to Lisa Kindleman the moment she walked into their temporary interview room, oozing arrogance and vanity from every pore. Festival enough, she was a bit of a corker, beautiful and sexy, but it was obvious she reckoned she would have him and Shapes wrapped around her little finger. One glance to his left told him she was right about his sergeant. No surprise there. But he was made of sterner stuff.

He had to admit those legs were pretty impressive. It wasn't fair, not really, some women being blessed like that, while others had legs that looked like they'd come straight off the rear half of a donkey. Mind you, her clothes were pretty decent too. Didn't look like she skimped when it came to trips to the shops.

He wondered, for a brief moment, how Harold Kindleman might feel about that, then decided he'd probably seen that as part and parcel of the package he took on when he asked her to marry him. Some women were higher maintenance than others.

He was a bit surprised to find a woman like her in the Puncheon party, as he was now referring to it. The others were what you might call plain, not in the least bit exotic. Lisa Kindleman looked totally out of place. Perhaps the rest were more her husband's friends and she tagged along; the dutiful wife, or something like that.

Pleasantries over, Dykeman decided to crack right on. He needed to get to the point, so he did.

"Mrs Kindleman, we hear your husband's left the hotel. Seems to have been gone for at least an hour, as far as we can tell. Any idea where he might have gone? Only, we did make it clear no one was to leave the hotel until further notice, what with there having been a murder."

He tried to adopt a stern tone, but found it difficult when the woman looked so alluring. And that, he had to admit, irritated him. Next, if he wasn't careful, he'd start getting annoyed that he was irritated. He couldn't let her get to him like that. It was pathetic.

"I'm hardly my husband's keeper, Inspector. He doesn't have to ask my permission to go out. Well, not normally."

She smiled and, she made sure, her deep blue eyes sparkled.

Shapes wanted to weep. It wasn't fair, being expected to interview a woman like Lisa Kindleman. His mind wasn't on the job, that was for sure. It was occupied with other, more basic, thoughts. He coughed against the back of a hand, then tapped the tip of his pencil against his notepad, trying game-fully to regain some focus.

"Meaning he didn't say where he was going?" persisted Dykeman.

"Indeed, Inspector."

"Could you hazard a guess at where he's gone? Did he mention anything earlier in the day, perhaps?"

"I should imagine he's found himself a nice little pub somewhere in town where he can impress the locals with his endless supply of stories. He likes doing that sort of thing."

"Is he likely to be gone long, in your experience?"

"Possibly. Hard to say. Probably depends on how willing people are to listen to him. He gets bored if there's no one to talk to. I imagine that's why he went out in the first place. The poor little thing needs constant entertaining."

Cold, thought Dykeman. Hardly the kind of thing a loving wife says about her husband.

"Let's get someone checking out the local pubs, Shapes, when we've finished up here."

"Sir."

Dykeman remained silent for a moment, wondering what sort of woman Lisa Kindleman really was. One thing was already clear, she was more than just a pretty face. It seemed they were dealing with someone who benefited both from being very beautiful and blessed with a strong personality. Blonde bombshell was entirely inappropriate, it seemed.

"How would you describe the relationship between James Puncheon and Laura Sinkling?"

Lisa Kindleman didn't so much as hesitate. "You do know they used to be married, I assume?"

"We do."

"They didn't get on very well at all. They tried to make it look like everything was wonderful, no hard feelings and all that, but they weren't fooling me with that. They were always having little digs at each other, snide comments about one another's short-comings. Not really surprising, I suppose."

"Why did they get divorced?"

Lisa Kindleman smiled, but not in a pleasant way. It made Dykeman think he'd better not turn his back on this woman if ever he was alone with her.

"James had an affair. He'd been knocking off a younger woman he'd put up in a flat in London. I'm sure they have a name for that sort of thing, providing sex in return for money. Laura found out, eventually. She kicked him straight out and wouldn't let him back in the house. Very sad, but good for her, standing up for herself. Don't know why so many men think it's alright to do that kind of thing."

"It's been suggested James Puncheon was having another affair," Dykeman left the suggestion hanging in the air.

"Have Laura or Sally been talking to you?" She smiled, a kind of pitying number, thought Dykeman. "They can be such gossips when they want to. And just who would he be having an affair with? His ex-wife? Or Sally with her nerves? Or could you see me jumping into bed with him?" Dykeman said nothing. Lisa Kindleman continued. "If he was seeing a married woman, then I very much doubt it was one of us, Inspector. You'll need to cast your net wider."

She didn't lack confidence, mulled Dykeman. Unlike Sally Dingle. The two women could hardly be more different. Was a wonder they had anything in common. Maybe they didn't.

Maybe it was the husbands who had things in common. Interesting thought.

"I also hear you all went to dinner together last night. How did that go? Anything seem odd or out of character about Puncheon?"

"I wish it had. Would have made things more interesting."

"You don't sound like you much care for your friends, Mrs Kindleman?"

"They're not my friends, Inspector, they're Harry's.

He noticed Lisa Kindleman had three small freckles clustered together on the skin of her neck, under her left ear. He didn't know why, but they seemed out of place on such a beautiful woman.

"So, Mr Puncheon didn't seem upset or worried about anything?"

"Not that I noticed. But, there again, the men all ran off to the bar once we'd finished eating. If James did have something on his mind, maybe he told them."

Dykeman looked at the far wall and scratched the back of his head, silent for a moment, before turning his attention back to Lisa Kindleman.

"And how would you describe your own marriage, Mrs Kindleman?"

Take that, thought Dykeman, pleased he'd managed to deliver the question without warning, keen as he was to knock her off balance. She was far too comfortable. Some might even say she was the one in control of the interview. She needed reminding this was a murder investigation; one he was leading, not her.

There was a barely discernable flare in her nostrils and, Dykeman noticed, a tightening of the skin around her eyes. But he had to give her credit, she kept her composure.

"Is that anything to do with you, Inspector? I thought you were investigating a murder, not offering marriage guidance."

Shapes was grinning, noticed Dykeman. It left him feeling quite pleased with himself. His sergeant hadn't seen that one coming, either. It was a just shame it hadn't made more of an impact on their interviewee.

"It's important for us to get as thorough an understanding of the dynamics involved here as possible, Mrs Kindleman. You never can tell what will and will not be relevant to an investigation."

Excellent, he congratulated himself. That sounded about right. Guff, of course, but passable.

"Harry and I are the model of married contentment."

Ooh la la, thought the inspector. There was a real edge to that. Married perfection, my wotsits. He wondered if their marriage might possibly be rather more one of convenience than real substance. Pure speculation, of course, but a thought all the same. The urge to speak to Harry Kindleman was growing by the second. What kind of man had what it took to live with a woman like this?

"I'm pleased to hear it." He glanced at his watch. In fact, he really would like to speak to Mr Kindleman. The man already had some explaining to do. Now, though, Dykeman was just as keen to find out what it took to share a life with such a wife. "We'll leave it at that, for now, Mrs Kindleman. I appreciate your help, though you should expect we'll have more questions for you as the investigation progresses. That's the way these things tend to go."

Lisa Kindleman showed no outward sign of relief at the interview coming to an end, noted Dykeman, still feeling a little miffed that he'd not been able to maintain his usual degree of control over proceedings. He couldn't make his mind up about the woman, though he was inclined to think that if she really was as cold and arrogant as they'd just seen then she might very well have what it takes to commit murder; that is, if she had a motive for doing so.

"Well?" he asked, as the door thumped closed behind the departing Mrs Kindleman.

"Bloody Nora, they don't make many like that," drooled his sergeant. "No way I'd clear off down the pub and leave her all alone."

"You're too predictable, Shapes. We need to find you a woman desperate enough to take you on before you make a fool of yourself."

"What d'you mean, desperate?"

"Then blind, maybe."

Shapes sniffed, irritated at the accusation he was desperate for any woman he could get his hands on. Just because it might be true, that was no reason for Dykeman to point it out like that. Happily, he had an ace tucked in his back pocket and now seemed the time to play it.

"You're not doing so well yourself on the woman front. A little bird told me, Dr Delph has a friend visiting; a man friend."

He gave a little roll of the head, the implication of what he'd just said as clear as could be.

Dykeman rubbed ones side of his nose. No, he hadn't heard Sheila had a man friend visiting. Maybe it was professional. Nothing for him to be bothered about. But, damn it, he was bothered and, worse still, Shapes knew he would be. The git had probably been sitting on the news, waiting for the right moment to speak up. It was nothing to worry about, it really wasn't, he said to himself. But he wasn't fooling anyone, least of all himself.

"We all have friends, Shapes, even you, don't you? Not illegal, you know, to have friends. Anyway, what about that woman? Can we believe a word she says?"

"Nope. Leggy blonde with a nasty attitude like that? The way she slated her husband. It's not what you'd call loving."

"She didn't go much on the notion of James Puncheon sleeping with a married woman, or any woman for that matter."

"Maybe she's got something to hide."

"You serious, Shapes? She almost laughed in our faces."

"Just saying. Anything's possible. Well, almost anything."

"I've got a feeling if she was going to engage in a bit of the old extra-marital then the bloke would need to look like Errol Flynn or have a couple of million in the bank and Puncheon doesn't fit the bill on either count."

"I want to see what her husband's like. He must have something about him to have persuaded her to marry him."

"Yes, I agree with that observation, Shapes. I think we need to speak to the man as soon as possible. See if you can round up a uniform, better make it just the one, and take a look in the nearest pubs. Getting on for closing time, so I doubt he would have gone far. I'm going to take a look at whatever statements we've got from the other guests and the staff."

"Can I drag Kindleman back in cuffs if he won't come quietly?"

"Better still, offer to take him down to the station in cuffs. That ought to do the trick."

Shapes left the room with a veritable spring in his step, noted Dykeman. The chance to slap a pair of cuffs on a suspect didn't come along anywhere near as often as his sergeant would like. Every opportunity was gleefully accepted.

SHAPES HAD DESPATCHED Dartington to look in the clutch of pubs that populated the High Street, leaving himself to check out those scattered along the roads closer to the hotel. Given the hordes of tourists in town for the Hobby Horse Festival, that wasn't going to be an easy or quick thing to do, although it was almost closing time. If getting chucked out of whatever pub he'd gone into would persuade Harry Kindleman to head back to the hotel, then all well and good, but if he decided to find somewhere else to while away the time then Christ knew how long it would take to find their missing witness.

There were people everywhere, including large numbers of children. He didn't like children, they got in the way and seemed to think the whole world revolved around them. They were worse than... well, pretty much any other sort of human being he could think of. There were exceptions, like Nelly Squirrel's two little 'uns, Daisy and James, who clambered all over him whenever they got the chance and made him laugh like a good 'un. But they weren't normal. Most kids were a pain in the backside and to be avoided at all times. He needed to keep his wits about him, otherwise he'd find himself being ambushed by grabbing hands demanding sweets and chocolate.

Despite his natural inclination to affect an air of all round grumpiness, Shapes couldn't quite stop himself from feeling good, happy even, as he ambled down the road from the hotel. The sun was out, people were smiling, some of them laughing, and a man had been shot dead in the Marlborough Hotel. What more could he ask for, apart from a beer, a woman and a steak and mustard sandwich.

A flat-bed truck rolled past at little more than walking pace, heading towards the Banbury Cross. Half a dozen members of a brass band were standing in the back, playing a tune he didn't recognise. People waved at them and those band members with a hand to spare waved back. On a small patch of open land to one side of the Cross, watched by a good-sized crowd of spectators, a troupe of Morris dancers were doing their thing, bashing sticks and jingling their bells as they hopped from foot to foot. They were probably drunk by now, if previous experience was anything to go by.

He arrived outside the ancient structure of the Saracen's Head, a sixteenth-century coaching inn. The last to finish their drinks were stumbling out of the door, temporarily blinded by the bright sunlight. Shapes looked in through one of the small lead-panelled windows, but it was too dark to see much; he'd have to go inside.

The landlord, Adam Rightly, noticed him straight away and tried to shove a pint in his hand. The familiar beery smell that percolated up Shapes's nose made it tempting to accept the landlord's offer. It wouldn't have taken him long to knock back a pint of bitter. But the sensible part of Shapes's personality prevailed and he opted against accepting the proffered drink, albeit with a good deal of reluctance. It wouldn't look too good getting back to the hotel whiffing of booze.

He described Harry Kindleman to Rightly as best he could, but the landlord had been far to busy to notice one customer from another. Anyway, it wasn't much of a description, pointed out Rightly. Could be half the men in town. With that, Shapes left and made for the Fox and Hounds on the other side of the road.

In fact, he hadn't got all the way across, dodging a tractor pulling a trailer-full of smelly, noisy sheep, when he spotted two men by a bench outside the Fox and Hounds. One of them he instantly knew. George Stunt was one of the town's regular dossers, doing odd jobs here and there for cash in hand, most of which he spent in his favourite pubs, before falling asleep in the doorway of one of the town centre shops. He was known to favour those with an easterly prospect, as they caught the early morning sun, which helped warm him up. Shapes also recalled that Stunt always reeked of booze and other, more disgusting, things.

The other man, Shapes didn't know, but he was pretty certain who he was. Tall and handsome as any fella Shapes had ever seen, Harry Kindleman, if that's who it was, was wearing what must have been an expensive, snappy blue jack and trousers, with an open-necked white shirt. His wife had described his clothes to a T. He was leaning on the back of the bench with his elbows, chatting away happily with Stunt, apparently not bothered by the stench coming from his new friend. Shapes could see why most women would find Kindleman attractive. The sod had been dealt a bloody good hand by the man upstairs, unlike himself, who had to make do with whatever had been left in the tool box at the end of the day.

Shapes watched the conversation for a while, standing in the lee of a telephone box. Stunt took regular gulps from what looked like a bottle of vodka, in between laughing and nodding at whatever it was Kindleman was saying. If this exchange was anything to go by, thought Shapes, Kindleman must have an endless supply of jokes and amusing anecdotes and certainly didn't appear to lack the confidence needed to deliver them. More difficult to judge was his suitability for the role of killer. Did he look like the sort who could shoot a so-called friend stone dead? Hard to say, without talking to him. Shapes stepped out from the shadow of the telephone box and walked towards the other two men.

DYKEMAN'S CURSORY LOOK through the growing pile of witness statements provided precious little by way of useful information and PC Dartington was of the opinion they had yet to interview any serious contenders for chief suspect. The staff seemed harmless and too busy to find time to put two bullets in one of the guests. Plus the hotel's clientele were hardly of the dubious sort, let alone downright dodgy. Many of them were scared witless they might be next to be killed and the rumour mill was already in full flow, including one story involving a Russian spy and a double-crossing agent. Lord knows, thought Dykeman when he heard that one, he hadn't even begun to think about such possibilities. The Chief

Inspector would have kittens at the merest suggestion the murder was down to anything of the sort.

With no sign of Shapes and the absent Harry Kindleman, Dykeman wandered aimlessly around the hotel for a while, before ending up in the garden at the rear of the property. He felt the need for some quiet thinking time. There were a lot of people at the hotel and already a ream of information to process. He sat down at a small, round, metal table, in the shade of a large tree towards the bottom of the garden, and closed his eyes. Thoughts of Sheila Delph began to fill his head. He tried, without much success, to think of something else.

"Hello, Inspector. You look thoughtful. Are you having a Hercule Poirot moment with the little grey cells?"

The waiter's interruption came mere seconds after Dykeman had closed his eyes. Some might have got a little grumpy but the policeman took it on the chin. There was, after all, little point in complaining.

"Oh, it's you, Pearling. No, nothing to do with the case. I was thinking about... a friend. Take them for granted sometimes, don't we?"

"I think we sometimes do, sir."

Joseph Pearling was carrying a tray loaded with all the necessaries for afternoon tea and cake. He placed it on the edge of the table and began transferring the contents.

"Mr Plowright asked me to make sure you and your sergeant were being properly looked after. We do a top notch afternoon tea here. Best Battenberg and Banbury Cakes in town, or that's what the chef always says."

Dykeman liked what he saw. Battenberg was a favourite and this one looked seriously good. It helped that Shapes was off elsewhere for the time being. Less competition.

"That's very good of you, Pearling. Think I'm ready for an afternoon cuppa."

The sun, which had been hiding behind a bank of thick, fluffy cloud, moved out into a patch of deep blue sky, its rays reaching down into the garden, making everything seem so much more vibrant, thought Dykeman.

"Sir, I hope you don't think it's out of place, but, you see, one of the maids, she saw something, well heard it more like, but she's afraid to speak up, in case it gets her into trouble. She reckons Mr Plowright will think she's been spying on the guests."

"Something that might be of relevance to our investigation, you mean?"

"Could be, sir. Don't rightly know, but I guess that's for yourself to decide."

Pearling brushed a stray leaf off the table and folded the now empty tray under an arm.

"What did she hear, do you know?"

"Two of the guests arguing. I told her she should speak to you in case it had anything to do with what happened. The dead man, I mean."

Dykeman looked longingly at the Battenberg, concerned at the prospect of Shapes returning before he'd had time to tuck in. The pink and yellow quarters were especially vibrant, something he took to be a sign of quality.

"Is she here now, this maid?"

"She is, sir."

"Do you think you could ask her to join me here? I won't bite, you can promise her that. Oh, and what's her name?"

"It's Daphne McDonald. She's not the sort to mess about, so I'm sure you can believe what she says."

"I'll see about that."

As Pearling made his way back inside the building, Dykeman grabbed a knife and cut a huge slice from the Battenberg. If there had been anyone watching, they would have thought he consumed it with remarkable, perhaps even unnatural, haste.

"DAPHNE, IS IT?"

The maid looked nervous, holding back a little way from where Dykeman sat. She was short and thin, a small thing with brown hair and a pointy nose. Dykeman found it hard to imagine she had the strength to do the work of the average hotel maid. Appearances, he had often observed, could be deceptive. For all he knew, she had the strength of an ox, just like Gladys in the police station canteen. Gladys was just as small and several decades older, yet hauled around vast containers of stew and whatnot like they weighed no more than a feather. He'd once shifted a pot of stew and dumplings for her and he'd had to have two goes at picking it up, it was so heavy.

"Yes, sir," the maid replied, sounding as timid as she looked.

"It's alright, I won't bite," smiled Dykeman. "Look, I've just eaten."

She smiled back and walked slowly across to where Dykeman was sitting, her hands held together in front of her skirt.

"Fancy a bite yourself? Too much here for me to eat all on me own," said Dykeman, waving a hand at the cakes on the table.

"No, thank you, sir. Mr Plowright don't like us to eat any of the food, least not 'til it's back in the kitchen. Then the chef lets us have a few bits and pieces."

"That's a shame, I'll have to share it with my sergeant now. He's a greedy so and so. Probably whoof down the lot. Do take a seat and try to relax. You're not in any trouble here."

"Thank you, sir."

She sat down so lightly that Dykeman wasn't sure she actually made contact with the chair. It was probably a good thing it wasn't windy. Anything more than a breeze might blow her away.

"So, I understand you heard two of the guests arguing. When was this?"

She nodded her head slowly.

"Yesterday. Here, in the garden. I wasn't spying. I was cleaning the tables, on the patio. They were down there, at the end of the garden."

"And who were they? Did you recognise them?"

"Yes, it was the dead man and a lady."

"James Puncheon? Are you sure about that?"

"Yes, I'm sure."

"You got a clear look at his face?"

"Yes."

"Good. And who was the lady, do you know?"

Dykeman's hesitant witness described a woman he soon recognised as Laura Sinkling. There seemed little possibility of it being any other woman he'd yet seen at the hotel and it made sense the two of them would be seen together.

"And I don't suppose you happened to overhear what they were arguing about?"

"No, they were too far away, but they were definitely arguing. The man, Mr Puncheon, he was very angry, he was. Wagging a finger in the woman's face. But she didn't seem bothered. She pushed his hand away."

"What happened after that?"

"He walked off. He was in a right huff. But I didn't wait to see any more. I didn't want to get into trouble for spying on the guests. So I went back in the building and took some dirty glasses to the kitchen."

"Was there anyone else around, anyone who could have heard them?"

"No, not in the garden."

Dykeman rubbed his chin, taking a moment to consider what the maid had told him. Did it really mean anything, the former married couple arguing? No big surprise, as least not as far as he was concerned. But, there again, a man had been murdered and someone had done it. The gun didn't pull the trigger itself. And there needed to be a motive, a reason for someone to kill James Puncheon. Money? That was a possibility. It was certainly the sort of thing two formerly married people could fall out over. But was money an issue for Laura Sinkling? Didn't her current husband have enough of the stuff for the two of them? On the surface, at least, it looked like he did.

"Well, you've been very helpful, Daphne. I'm very grateful to you for taking the time to come and speak to me. I hope I've not risked getting you into any trouble with Mr Plowright."

The young woman stood up, went to leave, then stopped and turned back towards Dykeman, a look of concern on her face.

"I don't like to be a gossip, sir. Only Joseph said you'd want to know what I'd seen. Said it might be important. I don't want to get in any trouble."

"And he was quite right about that. It might be nothing, but, there again, what you've told me might turn out to make a considerable difference to our investigation. It helps just being able to cross something off our list."

That was what he and Shapes spent a great deal of their time doing; crossing things off their list. But right there and then, Dykeman was more inclined to think something had just been added to their list, not crossed off it.

HARRY KINDLEMAN HADN'T made any trouble when Shapes asked him to accompany him back to the hotel. Kindleman had handed Stunt a pound note before they left, a very generous handout, thought Shapes, who wasn't in the habit of giving Stunt's sort so much as a halfpenny whenever the begging bowl came out. Mind you, someone like Kindleman probably pulled in more money in a month than a copper like himself earned in a year.

On the way back to the hotel, Kindleman had got Shapes into a conversation about horse racing, a subject close to the policeman's heart. It occurred to Shapes later than Kindleman had worked out remarkably quickly what interests he had and done so without seeming to be in the least bit nosey. Quite amazing, really. Maybe Kindleman was the one who should have been asking questions of their witnesses, not him and Dykeman. It only took three minutes to get back to the hotel, but by then Shapes felt like he and Kindleman were already old mates. Odd feeling.

Having failed to locate Dykeman in their temporary interview room, Shapes had a hunch he'd find his boss in the garden on such a nice day. He liked a decent garden and would really like to spend more time pottering around his own.

"Ah, Shapes, you return. I thought you'd be gone a lot longer." Dykeman stood up and offered his hand to the man standing alongside Shapes. "And you must be Harry Kindleman, I'd hazard a guess."

"Inspector." Kindleman had a solid handshake and Dykeman got the distinct impression the other man was consciously weighing him up in the couple of seconds their hands were locked together. It unnerved him a little. He was there to weigh up Kindleman, not the other way around.

"You were asked not to leave the hotel, Mr Kindleman. The instruction slip from your mind, did it?"

"It's such a decent day, Inspector, and the beer here at the hotel isn't up to much. Never is at a hotel, is it?"

Kindleman smiled warmly, his deep, engaging voice immediately starting to roll back the senior policeman's defences. This, thought Dykeman, was going to be a tricky interview. The man seemed capable of making friends with just about anyone, if he put his mind to it. His wife's more confrontational style had been easier to deal with.

"If it happens again, you'll likely find yourself studying the inside of a police cell, is that clear?"

"It certainly is, Inspector. Clear and understood."

Kindleman and Dykeman sat down. Shapes remained standing, detached a little from the others. He found it easier to write his notes when there was a bit of distance between him and the witness or accused.

"So, why don't we start with you explaining where you've been for the last hour," ordered a visibly irritated Dykeman.

"Needed to get out of this place for a bit. I'm sure you know what it's like, being cooped up in one place for too long. It starts messing with your head. So, I had a look outside. Didn't go far. Put my head in the first pub I came to. The Saracen's Head, I think it's called. Bit too busy in there for me. So I moved on to the next one, the Fox and Hounds and that's where Sergeant Shapes found me. Had a drink in there. Decent pint of Brakspear. When they kicked us out at closing time, I found myself chatting with a homeless chap, Lester Stunt. Nice man. Good conversation."

Shapes nodded his agreement, at least to the bit about where he'd found Kindleman.

"What about the rest of the day? What were your movements this morning?"

"Nothing exciting, I'm afraid. The alarm went off at seven-thirty. Would prefer to stay in bed longer myself, but Lisa's an early bird, you see. We got washed and dressed, then went down for breakfast with the others. They were all there. I think the Dingles were the first. They're normally up with the lark."

"You said they were all there. Everyone? You're sure about that?"

"Well, yes." Kindleman paused. "Ah, no, not quite everyone, of course. No James. He didn't show up at all. We thought he must have decided to have breakfast in his room. Got that one wrong, didn't we."

"Didn't anyone suggest checking on him, in case anything had happened?"

"No, I don't think so. It's not a three-line whip, showing up for breakfast, Inspector. We normally all do, but no one's going to take offence if you decide you'd rather have a quiet start to the day."

Dykeman wanted to remain annoyed at Kindleman, who'd flouted a clear and important instruction to remain in the hotel, but the bloody man's charm and good humour was already starting to wear him down. It was a knack he no doubt found very useful in life. The trouble was, there was now an hour or so of Kindleman's day they were unlikely to be certain about. Even if they were lucky enough to find one or two people who could confirm what he'd said, that still didn't mean he'd not met up with person or persons unknown, who might have a bearing on the case. The worst of it was, if it was Kindleman who'd shot Puncheon, he'd now had all the opportunity he needed to get rid of the gun. Damn it, why couldn't the man have simply done as he was told? It wasn't as if the hotel was a hovel you'd want to escape from as soon as possible.

"I understand you all had dinner together last night," prompted the Inspector.

"That's right. Damn fine meal it was, too. And a decent red wine, despite what Bernard thought about it."

"He didn't like it, did he, the wine?"

"Considers himself a bit of a connoisseur. Got a pretty decent cellar, to be fair to the chap, but always expects the very best wherever he goes. Not really fair to think a place like this, nice though it is, is going to have the same sort of cellar as the Ritz."

"How did the evening go?"

"By which you mean, were there any disagreements, especially anything involving James?"

Kindleman glanced at his watch.

"Got an appointment to keep, have we?"

Dykeman had intended to sound sarcastic but immediately realised he'd probably overdone things.

"I told Lisa I'd only be gone an hour and it's an hour-and-a-quarter now. She'll be wondering where I am."

"I shouldn't be concerned about that, she knows we were looking for you. So, did anything happen last night that we should know about?"

"Frank started talking shop again. He always does. Reckon that man has sales and marketing running through his veins. Laura had to tell him to put a sock in it. I don't think the rest of us really mind all that much, but she does worry he'll bore us all to tears. But, seriously Inspector, that's as bad-tempered as it got and there was nothing I saw or heard that even suggested James had any kind of problem. It just doesn't make any sense to me. Surely if you were in some sort of serious trouble, you'd speak to your friends about it, ask for their help, wouldn't you? I know I would."

"It probably depends on what sort of trouble we're talking about. Puncheon might have been trying to keep the rest of you out of it for your own good. So, you were surprised when you heard he'd been killed? You didn't have any idea something was wrong?"

"I was bloody shocked, Inspector. Who the hell would want to kill James? And what I can't begin to fathom is, what for? That's what gets me most of all; what would anyone want to kill him for?"

For the first time since they'd started interviewing him, Kindleman looked and sounded perplexed and uncertain, something that was lost on neither policeman.

"You've no ideas what that might be?"

"No, nothing. Believe me, if I had the foggiest idea I'd say so."

Dykeman leaned back, stretching his hands across the worn, pitted top of the desk in front of him. Surprise was his weapon of choice and it was time to deploy it now.

"It's been suggested that Puncheon was having an affair with one of the women in your party. Is that something you're aware of?"

Although not sure what reaction he'd get, Dykeman hadn't expected Kindleman to burst into laughter, but that was precisely what he did, after the shortest of pauses. It took a moment before he was able to answer the question.

"James? Seriously? You must be mad, Inspector. Who the hell has been telling you things like that?"

"You don't agree, then?"

"James, having an affair? I'm telling you, that's nuts. He got his fingers burned so badly doing that in the past I'd say he'd rather have spent the rest of his life living in a monastery. No way. Stupid idea. And one of the women in our group, you say?"

Kindleman smiled and shook his head.

"Like you say, he'd done it before. He's got the form and, of course, he's single now, so he has no one to betray. Why wouldn't he do it again?"

"He had a hard old time of it when Laura left him. Knew he'd messed things up, but her kicking him out was the last thing in the world he wanted. Really hit him hard. He's spent a bit of time with a couple of other women since then, but there was nothing he regretted more in his life than losing Laura. There's no way he would have done something like that again."

Dykeman stood up and began to walk with small steps round the side of the desk. Kindleman seemed very sure about Puncheon. Could he be right and everyone else wrong? It didn't seem likely. Might that have something to do with Lisa Kindleman? If Puncheon had been seeing her, then the one person they'd work the hardest to keep it from would be her husband. But, there again, wouldn't one of the others have done something, dropped a hint to Kindleman or had it out with Puncheon? People were complicated, that was the problem. Complicated and, far too often, untrustworthy; liars even. Someone here was lying, but who?

"An interesting thought," said Dykeman. "I'll take that into account. Well, thank you for your time, Mr Kindleman. That'll be all for now. And let's have no more trips to the pub, eh?"

"WHAT D'YOU THINK?" asked Shapes, having seen Kindleman out of the room.

"I think he could shoot a man in cold blood, if he had a reason to."

"A man messing with his missus, you mean?" Shapes grinned.

"They're an interesting couple. Not sure which one I trust the least. Certainly wouldn't put it past the wife to find herself a bit of extra-marital entertainment. Same goes for him. Wonder, though, how he'd take it if he found out one of his friends was jumping into bed with her."

"So, you reckon he was?"

"No idea, Shapes, more's the pity. Just a thought."

Dykeman checked his watch. It was nearly two o'clock. That was more than half the day gone and what had they found so far? Hard to say, if he was to be honest about it. But there was something not right. It was there, lurking under the surface, out of sight but registering with his copper's intuition. But what about the motive? That was one thing they still hadn't got the foggiest idea about.

"I'm sticking to a botched robbery. Can't see any of this lot killing one of their own. I bet there's someone out there right now, keeping a low profile, waiting for the storm to blow over before they try and sell on whatever it was they nicked. All we need to do is keep our noses close to the ground and, bingo, we'll have them as soon as they surface."

"Wish I could say it seemed that easy to me, Shapes. But I have a feeling there's more to this one than that."

"What about the maid who found him. Maybe it was her. He caught her helping herself to the cash in his wallet and before she knew what she'd done, there he was, lying dead on the bed."

"And she happened to be carrying a gun with her dusters, did she?"

"Well, maybe. Or how about the gun was Puncheon's? We hadn't thought about that. Maybe he kept it with him for just such emergencies, but she got hold of it before he did."

Shapes, recognised Dykeman, was on a roll. He had been known to go on for hours in the past, one mad-cap idea leading to another and another. He needed cutting off at the pass, before things got out of hand.

"Talking of the murder weapon, you'd best track down Dartington and see how they're getting on with the search. It won't help things at all if we don't find the gun today. By tomorrow morning it could be anywhere."

"Big hotel this. Lot of places to hide something as small as a pistol. I wouldn't bet on it turning up, not if the killer did a decent job of hiding it."

"All the same, let's do out best. I'll have the old man on my case if I can't tell him we've found it and you know how much I don't like that."

WITH SHAPES SCAMPERING off in search of Constable Dartington, Dykeman went looking for something himself; in his case a fresh pot of tea. All this talking they'd been doing had left him parched and there was no better solution for that than a nice cup of tea, preferably with a biscuit or two.

As it was, he'd not got far from their interview room when Carol the receptionist spotted him and called across. There was a message for him, something the woman was obviously excited about, given the wide-eyed look on her face as she handed him a folded piece of paper.

The message was from Sheila Delph. She had news for him and was requesting his presence at the hospital mortuary. Excellent, thought Dykeman, even if he did then tell himself not to get too carried away. What constituted good news for Sheila didn't always match his own idea of good news, as in the sort of thing that made it easier for him to collar a criminal.

"You take this message yourself?" he asked the receptionist, his voice low.

"Oh, yes, sir. No one else has seen it. Dr Delph phoned," she glanced at her small, leather-strapped wristwatch, "eight minutes ago. Do you think it will be good news? Something that will it help you catch the killer?"

The woman looked and sounded far too excited for Dykeman's liking. Before he knew it, half the people in the hotel would have acquired the very distinct impression he was on the verge of making an arrest. Then they'd start grumbling and slagging him off when it turned out he was nowhere near doing anything of the sort. That kind of thing had happened to him and Shapes far too many times in the past. A little lowering of expectations was in order. He folded the paper and put it in a pocket.

"Carol, isn't it?" asked Dykeman. The receptionist nodded. "I wouldn't go jumping to too many conclusions, Carol. More often than not, there's not a great deal Dr Delph can tell us in these situations."

The receptionist suddenly looked a little deflated.

"It probably just means that Dr Delph wants to present me with her official findings, even if all she has to say is confirmation of the cause of death."

"Oh, that's a shame. I was hoping we'd be able to see you arrest the killer here in the hotel. That would be so exciting."

Carol still sounded hopeful, noticed Dykeman. More water needed to be poured on the flickering fire of her enthusiasm.

"Well, we wouldn't want to go giving the game away, would we? Wouldn't want the murderer to know we're on to them. If they were to find out what's going on, they might abscond and, before we know it, they could be on a boat to foreign parts. So, I'll have to ask you to keep this information to yourself, Carol. It'll be just the two of us that know for now, eh?"

Carol smiled and leaned across the desk, replying in a soft whisper, filled with conspiracy, "Just you and me, oh, and Dr Delph, of course. You can trust me. I'll not say a word."

"Excellent. I knew you'd understand. Not everyone does, you know. You'd be amazed."

"Oh dear, that's terrible. Well, I'm trustworthy. I won't even say a thing to Janet and I normally tell her everything."

Dykeman avoided the obvious temptation to ask who Janet was. He had a feeling Carol was keen to let him know, but he didn't want the distraction of what might end up a long and drawn out answer. Mind you, Carol might have other uses. Receptionists were well-placed to see what was going on in a hotel.

"You noticed anything odd in the hotel over the last couple of days? People behaving strangely, for example."

Carol gave herself some time to think, which pleased Dykeman. Many people would have said the first thing that came into their head, then probably approached him a day or two later to say something different.

"No, I don't think so. We're so busy on Hobby Horse weekend you don't get much chance to notice what's going on. People coming and going all the time. When they don't know the town, they ask for ideas where they should go to see everything. Of course, there's all the checking in then all the checking out and people lose things all the time. You wouldn't believe what they can lose. Last year, one man lost his wife. He left her at the train station. How do you do that? Wouldn't you notice before you got here?"

His time with Carol, decided Dykeman, was done. She was wittering on now and time was pressing. Best he get moving, so he did, having first reminded Carol of her commitment to silence on the matter of Sheila's note.

Dykeman paused outside the hotel entrance and looked up at the sky. The hospital wasn't far. Close enough, he decided, for him to walk, especially when it was such a nice day outside. It couldn't possibly take more than a few minutes, could it?

Chapter Eight

The greater part of the walk from the hotel to the hospital was up a lengthy and decidedly steep hill, something Dykeman had neglected to take into account before he set off, and, by the time he'd made it to the medical establishment, he was sweating heavily, dark, damp patches in the armpits of his shirt and a film of perspiration all over his face and most of the rest of his body, for that matter. Damn sun. He definitely wasn't going to be looking his best when he met Sheila and that bloody so-called friend of hers. He was still muttering away to himself when he walked in through the main hospital entrance.

The place was, he quickly found, busier than usual, no doubt the result of the heaving masses thronging the town centre in search of entertainment. He knew from previous experience there was always a big increase in crime during the Festival, so it made some sense if there was also an increase in the number of people requiring medical attention as the result of accidents and over indulgence. Funny thing was, he hadn't ever really given that any thought before, despite it seeming obvious now.

Mind you, as far as he could tell, the extra workload didn't seem to be bothering the nurses much. They were going about their business as calmly and efficiently as ever, which always brought forth a sense of admiration on his part.

The morgue was at the back of the main building, down a short flight of steps that took you into what Dykeman considered to be a rather small room for the purpose. With a low ceiling and stupidly bright lights, as usual he found himself squinting as he pushed open the double-doors and entered. Mind you, although he usually found the place too cold for comfort, on such a warm day as this, it made for a welcome change; especially if it put an end to his unwelcome sweating.

Sheila was a bit of a stickler for cleanliness, even by the standards of the average medical practitioner. As usual when he entered the morgue, his nostrils were assailed by the whiff of cleaning agents. He couldn't imagine he'd be able to work somewhere for very long when there was such a strong and, to him, unpleasant smell about the place.

Sheila Delph was tidying away a few of the less gruesome-looking implements of her trade. In Dykeman's mind, the woman had a questionable fascination with her large collection of knives, saws and pliers. If pushed, he might even go so far as to say it was an unnatural level of interest.

She looked up as she heard the doors swing open.

"Leslie. Perfect timing, I've just finished cleaning up."

"I won't complain about that."

He felt himself sag as she ran her eyes over his sweat-soaked figure.

"Warm out, is it?"

"Just a bit. I walked. Should have jumped in the car."

Damn it, even when she was teasing him those green eyes of hers got him every time. They were little gems, sparkling with life. Made him wonder what it was she saw when she looked into his own eyes. Muddy pools of stagnant water, he shouldn't wonder.

He was about to ask if she had any plans for the evening, hoping he might be able to persuade her to go out for drink with him, when, out of the corner of his eye, he noticed something move, away to his left. He half-turned and, this time, he didn't so much as sag inside, but slump. Sitting on small wooden chair was a sickeningly good-looking man.

"This is an old friend of mine, Leslie, James Hardyman. We've known each other since our student days."

To his despair, Dykeman found himself starring at a tall, well-built man with the kind of chiselled features that gave him something of a rugged, manly appeal almost all women, in his experience, found attractive. The thick, dark hair with a race horse lustre didn't help. The shoes looked hand-made and, no doubt, his shirt and trousers had been made by a tailor, not a machine. The git probably had a brand new MG sports car and spent most of his summer weekends smashing a ball around a cricket pitch with friends called Julian and Tristan.

Sheila continued with her introduction, but Dykeman was already barely aware of what it was she was saying. An unfamiliar emotion began to take an increasingly firm hold of his insides and to tie his innards in knots. Jealousy. For the briefest of moments, the thought entered his mind that a second murder in two days wasn't altogether out of the question.

Unaware that the gap between the two of them had closed, Dykeman found himself shaking the other man's hand and exchanging the usual pleasantries. It felt, however, as though he was having some sort of out-of-body experience, watching what was happening rather than taking part in it. Hoping it looked accidental, he deliberately kicked his left shin against the leg of an adjacent table, the resulting pain bringing him back down to earth with a satisfying bump.

Perfect James, as Dykeman immediately thought of him, was asking a question, something about the case.

"Sheila tells me you're busy tracking down whoever shot this chap she's just carried out an examination on. Quite the job to have. I suppose you often get to see the worst of people?"

It took Dykeman a moment or two to fashion a response. It was hard having a conversation with someone you'd prefer wasn't there.

"No one's perfect and, if you ask me, if push comes to shove, most people are capable of doing anything they reckon they need to do, including murder."

How about accidentally-on-purpose pushing someone down a big flight of stairs, wondered Dykeman.

"Don't you think some people are simply born bad, Inspector? They're bad eggs and there's nothing anyone can do about it?"

"Rubbish," the word came out of his mouth with more aggression than he'd intended. Oh, well, he couldn't take it back now. "I'll grant you, some people seem determined to be bad 'uns, whatever you do for them, but when a person gets desperate enough they'll resort to all sorts of things. I've seen decent parents steal so they can put new clothes on their children's backs and we had a case year before last when a woman killed her husband because he'd been beating her for years and she couldn't take any more. Sad case that one. No one knew what had been going on, not even their family."

"What do you think the motive was for killing Puncheon? Sheila says you're looking at the possibility it could be related to an attempted theft. Bit extreme, isn't it, killing someone because they catch you in the act?"

Dykeman glanced across at Sheila Delph. He was surprised she'd said as much. He'd got used to being able to say whatever he liked to her, safe in the knowledge she wouldn't say a dicky-bird to anyone else. No doubt it was an indication of her feelings towards Mr Perfect.

"We're still trying to work out the motive, though a botched burglary is a possibility. There are a lot of people to account for and I should imagine it'll be a while yet before we've got all the statements together and gone through them. It'd be best not to say anything about a burglary to anyone else, if you don't mind."

"Ah, yes, of course, Inspector. I won't say a word."

"I don't like to interrupt," cut in Delph, "but I think, Leslie, you're here to listen to my report."

The two men looked up at her.

"Sorry, Sheila. I couldn't resist asking Leslie a question or two."

Hardyman held up his hands as if to emphasise his apology. Delph smiled. Dykeman groaned inside.

Having steered things back on course, Sheila Delph proceeded to give Dykeman a detailed run through her findings, which failed to provide the policeman with anything new that might help him progress his case. There weren't, noted Dykeman, many occasions when she was able to give him a really juicy bit of information, so her failure to do so this time didn't much disappoint him. It definitely didn't even come close to disappointing him as much as the sight of James Hardyman did.

"So, you don't think he'd been dead more than six hours, eh? Sure about that?" asked Dykeman, as Delph concluded her report.

"I am. There is no doubt in my mind he died some time during the morning, but I'm afraid I can't be any more specific than that, Leslie."

He murmured something indecipherable and scratched his head. Normally this would have concluded the business part of things and he'd be free to move on to a little chit-chat; not that he was much good at that sort of thing. But Hardyman's presence put a block on that and now Dykeman didn't know what to say or do. He didn't want to leave so soon after arriving and, in any case, if he did that would leave the field open once again for Sheila's so-called friend. The trouble was, he found himself floundering, searching for some excuse to prolong his stay, yet coming up empty. Sod it, this seriously risked ruining his day.

"Nothing else, then, apart from the bullet wounds, I mean?" It was pretty feeble, but all he could come up with.

"I'm afraid not."

Sheila wasn't helping matters, felt Dykeman. Least she could do was show him some pity. She ought to be making jokes at his expense by now or foisting her theories about the crime on him. And the whole time, there was Hardyman, all puffed up and so sure of himself, just because he was so damn good-looking and bound to be able to offer Sheila everything he himself couldn't. He began to wish he hadn't bothered making the trip. Should have insisted on sending Shapes.

Succumbing to the feeling that he would be taking on a battle he couldn't possibly win, Dykeman decided to leave the other two to it. It wasn't a happy prospect, leaving the two of them together, but what could he do? With any luck the case would take his mind off things, until it was too late and Sheila was ringing him up to tell him all about her forthcoming marriage. Dr Hardyman; it had a horrible ring to it.

"Well, I suppose I ought to get back to it. Lots going on. And can't leave Shapes on his own too long, or he's likely to start complaining about the responsibility being too much for him. Puts him off his food, it does."

"I'll send over my written report this afternoon, Leslie." Sheila both looked and sounded far too happy for Dykeman's liking.

"A pleasure to meet you, Inspector. I must say, I hadn't banked on so much excitement when Sheila asked me over for the weekend. Well, good luck with the case. I think we'll all sleep a little better when this killer is behind bars."

Hardyman shook Dykeman's hand firmly and, even though he sounded friendly enough, the inspector was sure there was a subtext to what he'd said, especially the bit about Sheila asking him over for the weekend. It was galling to think the man could just turn up like this, out of the blue as it were, and find Sheila was putty in his hands.

In the hallway, with the doors to the mortuary safely closed, Dykeman swore under his breath and kicked a trolley lurking by a wall. Indeed, he kicked it hard and immediately wished he hadn't. It hurt his toes something rotten.

JAMES HARDYMAN ALWAYS had been a handsome man, but, if anything, he'd become even better looking since she'd last seen him, contemplated Sheila Delph. The years had given him more maturity and more ease. There had been a time when she thought he seemed unsure of himself. Why, she never had been able to fathom. He had every reason to strut around like a peacock. Good God, there were plenty of men who behaved like that when they didn't have half the reason for it James did.

She'd been surprised at herself. Alright, she'd always found him attractive, but nothing like she did now. She even felt herself blushing a little at one point. It wasn't a feeling she had experienced in a long time and it had left her confused.

Hardyman had told her that he needed to get his car to a garage, so they could check out a slight misfire in the engine. It wasn't likely to be much of a problem, but, as his journey home the following day was a long one, he didn't want to take a chance on the misfire developing into something more serious. He'd noticed a small garage half a mile or so out of town to the north and wanted to get his car over there right away. He was so apologetic, Delph had to insist he not feel bad about disappearing for a while. In any case, she had her report to write up.

She followed Hardyman out to the tiny car park. The weather was wonderful, the sun warm and bright, a gentle breeze just strong enough to make the leaves on the trees lift and fall a little. Promising to be back as soon as he possibly could, Hardyman climbed into his green Triumph TR4 and exited the car park at a modest pace, Delph waving from under the shade of a large ash tree.

Although she was smiling, inside Delph was a bit of a mess. James's visit, welcome as it was, had taken an unexpected turn. He'd asked her to marry him. Just like that, no warning or subtle hints at what he was about to say. He just came right out with it. And now she was confused, a bubbling mess of uncertainty and indecision. Once upon a time she would have jumped at the opportunity like an excited schoolgirl. He had been everything she and most of her girlfriends had ever wanted in a man. But now, well, she wasn't so sure. In fact, she was even confused about whether or not she really was so unsure. Was it the thought of marriage that was really bothering her? She'd turned down an offer once before, but he'd not been the right man at all. No, that wasn't it, was it? Maybe.

One thing was for sure, there were other things or, more accurately, there was another person to take into account. As the Triumph disappeared out of sight, with a throaty roar, she turned and walked back into the building, her head a whirlpool of thoughts and her emotions a jumble of happiness, fear, trepidation and, worst of all, guilt. It was the guilt that bothered her most of all.

HAVING GIVEN DARTINGTON a proverbial kick up the backside, Shapes was on his way back to their temporary interview room when he quite literally bumped into a woman he didn't recognise as he made his way across the entrance hall. Not, he decided at once, that he had any complaints about that. None whatsoever. In fact, he considered it a bit of good fortune.

Gwen Jones was apologetic, insisting she should have been paying more attention, but Shapes was having none of it. It was all his fault. Wasn't looking where he was going. Was she alright? No broken bones or concussion? Maybe a whiskey would help settle her nerves.

As soon as he looked into them, her sparkling brown eyes held him transfixed and he went, temporarily, silent. A familiar sensation swept over him. For a moment there was nothing else in the world apart from the two of them, everything else seeming to have drifted off the face of the Earth. Her soft, floral perfume drifted up his nostrils and he felt a little light-headed. Maybe he'd better sit down, but not just yet.

Gwen Jones smiled as she reached out a hand to steady Shapes.

"Steady there," she said, her voice rich with the lushness of the Welsh hillsides. "I think you might be the one in need of a drink. Are you sure you're alright?"

God, what a woman, mused Shapes. A bit on the thin side, if truth be told, but she still had a decent figure. Plenty enough to please him. And the voice, well, that was just the icing on the old cake. Cherries, too. Been ages since he'd heard a Taff speak, face-to-face like. It made him want to just stand there and listen to her all the rest of the day. He'd already forgotten what he was supposed to be doing.

"All ship shape here," was all he could manage to get out.

"Well, if you're sure." She straightened up the collar of his jacket and brushed a hand lightly across his right shoulder. "There, that's better. I suppose you'll be one of those policemen what's been investigating the murder."

"That's me," started Shapes, who found his voice thin and wispy. He coughed, in what he considered a manly way. "I'm Sergeant Shapes. It's my boss, Inspector Dykeman, who's in charge. Good man, he is. We only get assigned to the top cases. Got a long track record of success, we have."

"Well, that's a relief to hear. I wouldn't like to think they'd put someone hopeless on the case. I wouldn't be able to sleep in my bed at night. No husband to look after me."

Shapes felt a little shiver of excitement run up his spine. Could things get any better? Never look a gift horse in the mouth, his mum had always told him. Yes, strike while the iron's hot and don't live to regret a missed opportunity. He began to wonder how he might persuade this Welsh beauty to agree to a drink or two, or perhaps even dinner.

"No husband, you say? I'd have thought someone would have snapped you up by now."

"Oh, some try, but I'm not ready to settle down, see. There's too many things I want to do and see first."

"So, you staying here long, are you, or just here for the Festival?"

"Nothing definite. I like to see how things go and stay or leave as I please. Depends what there is to stay on for."

Shapes couldn't make his mind up whether the woman really was flirting with him or he was simply imagining things, but those lips of hers were tempting enough for him to hope it was the former. The only drawback he could see to a potential dalliance was her height. She must have been an inch or so taller than him, a situation that never left him comfortable. Made him feel inferior, somehow, did looking up at a woman. But it wasn't much of a difference, was it?

"Well, if we get this here case all done and dusted before you head off home, I'd be happy enough to show you some of the sights hereabouts."

What sights, he wasn't quite sure. There were plenty of fields, sheep and cows. There were even a couple of nice-looking Victorian buildings just off the Market Place. Well, people told him they were nice. He wasn't so sure about that himself. They looked a bit, well, old and ugly. Anyway, he was sure, sort of, that he could rustle up a few interesting attractions. Enough to keep the woman entertained for a while.

"I wouldn't want to deprive the police force of their best sergeant," Jones replied, softly. "But if you have the time to spare, well, that would be just wonderful. I'm sure someone like yourself knows all the best places to take a visitor."

The smile she launched at Shapes left him all befuddled. Had his ship finally come in or was this going to turn out to be yet another addition to his long list of failed romantic encounters? Right now, he didn't much care; all that mattered was the woman had smiled at him and not run away in fright. Maybe there was a God, after all.

THE ONLY GOOD THING about the walk back to the hotel, decided Dykeman, was that it was downhill. The exercise didn't do anything to help relieve him of his growing bad temper and simmering frustration; neither of which he felt the slightest inclination to snuff out. Best to let these things run their course, he'd long ago decided. Try to keep a lid on them for long and they'd sooner or later blow up, right in your face.

Off in the middle distance, at the bottom of the hill, was the Banbury Cross and clustered around it were little groups of people, every one of them apparently having a good time. Dykeman found himself resenting their happiness. Why couldn't it rain? That would soon wipe the smile off their grinning faces. He stumbled on a bump in the pavement and swore in annoyance.

As he stepped into the hotel entrance hall, eager to track down his sergeant, he saw Shapes straight off, loitering near the reception desk. He was engaged in conversation with a tall, raven-haired beauty. Although slim, her bumps and curves were decent enough for the irritable inspector to know full well why Shapes appeared to find her worth an investment of his precious time. If he'd been a dog, Shapes would have been sitting there holding one paw up, hoping for a treat. The bloody man was more predictable than a rigged winner at a greyhound race.

"Shapes. Office, now."

The barked command snapped Shapes out of his trance-like state abruptly, almost painfully. For a moment there, he was confused, unsure where he was and why. For an equally brief moment the delightful look on the face of Gwen

Jones also disappeared, but he forgave her for that. Dykeman's summons would have knocked most people off balance.

"Better go," he muttered, filled with disappointment that things had been brought to an end just when they were getting so interesting. "I can tell, he's in one of his grumpy moods. Just been to see his girlfriend and she's probably not had anything useful to tell him. Always like that when he's not getting his own way."

"I'm sure it's a very stressful job, Sergeant. Maybe we can continue our conversation another time. We were getting along so well."

"We were, weren't we. I'll let you know when I've finished for the day. We could, erm, have a drink in the bar, maybe."

"That would be lovely."

Shapes purred with pleasure. The day was turning into a real corker. Sexy woman, drinks. It almost made him suspicious, but he quickly brushed away the thought. It was about time he had a bit of luck with the ladies. He wasn't sure how long it had been since he'd last snogged a woman; well, one that wasn't drunk. Alice Ralph had jumped on him last New Year's Eve down the Three Conies pub, but she'd been so drunk she'd passed out not half-an-hour later, so he didn't count that.

"Shapes."

Glass panels and smaller ornaments quivered as Dykeman's voice filled every last nook and cranny of the entrance hall.

"Close the door, Shapes," ordered Dykeman as he slumped into the chair behind the desk in their on-site office.

"I have," replied Shapes, who chose to remain standing.

A dark cloud hung over the inspector, so heavy-looking, thought Shapes, that a violent storm seemed to be looming on the horizon. He recognised the signs and the source of the unhappiness was easy to guess at. For once, he'd had better luck with the ladies than Dykeman. Shapes felt a smirk lingering on the edge of his mouth, but held it back. No point in giving Dykeman any more of a reason to take things out on him. Mind you, it was tempting, to make the most of things and wind-up Dykeman to the point where he would explode, volcano like.

"Good," snapped Dykeman. "Who's that woman you were slobbering over? Didn't recognise her."

"One of the guests. I was questioning her as to her whereabouts and plans."

"I bet you were. Got her room number did you?"

"No, as it happens I didn't."

Shapes felt a moment's concern, then realised he could always get Gwen Jones's room number from reception. Temporary crisis over.

"Well, I'm glad to see you have time to muck around trying to chat up the female guests. Suppose you must have found the murder weapon, in that case."

"Not yet. Dartington and the others are still searching, but it's like trying to find a needle in a haystack."

"So, what the bloody hell am I going to tell the Chief Inspector? No suspects, no murder weapon, no motive. Well done, Dykeman, he's going to say. Keep up the good work and we'll have you on traffic duty from Monday."

Dykeman climbed back to his feet and shoved his hands in his pockets, lines etched across his forehead.

"Been to see Dr Delph, have you?" ventured Shapes.

"Might have." Dykeman spoke to the wall.

"Things not go too well, did they? In which case..." It was then that the penny dropped. Shapes knew what had happened. "Her friend was there, wasn't he?"

Shapes couldn't hold back the smirk any longer. It was smeared right across his thin face. Oh, what a day this was turning into. He began to wonder how best to make the most of this turn of events.

"Damn man. Tall, good-looking, educated. Probably got a small fortune, flash car and homes all over the place," answered Dykeman in a voice thick with contempt.

"Fancy Dr Delph being attracted to a bloke like that," tutted Shapes. "You'd think she'd go for someone with a bit more personality. Someone a bit more... down to earth."

Shapes was sniggering by now. Harsh, perhaps, but Dykeman wouldn't have held back if the boot had been on the other foot. That was how things were between them.

"Shapes," Dykeman had his back to his sergeant now, staring up at the top of the wall. "Bugger off and find that damn gun before I wipe that smile off your ugly face."

LEAVING HIS BITTER and unhappy boss to fester, Shapes sauntered out of the office and into the entrance hall. Carol Stitch, the receptionist, was busy on the phone, but Shapes didn't want to pass up the opportunity of finding out what room Gwen Jones was staying in, so he waited in front of the desk, picking at his fingernails. Life could be a bag of spanners sometimes, he mused, but there were other times when it was

Heaven on Earth and that was precisely how things were starting to feel now. Mind you, it wasn't before time. He'd had more than his fair share of crappy days and missed romantic engagements. He began to hum a little tune.

"Sarge."

"Er?"

Shapes had slipped into a daydream without realising it. It can't have been long, because Carol Stitch was still on the phone. They had, though, been joined by PC Johnson, a big man who'd played front row prop for the town's rugby team in his younger days. He was blotting out a good portion of the available light.

"There's been a development, Sarge. A big one."

Johnson had a surprisingly high-pitched voice for a big man. Shapes still wasn't used to it. But there was no disguising the big man's excitement; for one thing he was grinning like the proverbial Cheshire Cat.

"What development, Johnson?"

"We found something. Something that belongs to Mr Puncheon."

"We found lots of things that belong to Puncheon, but a fat lot of good that's done us."

"Not this one, Sarge. It's different."

"Johnson, what 'ave you found and what's so bloody important about it?"

Shapes felt his good mood was in danger of being undermined, a situation he was keen on avoiding.

"It's a gold-plated lighter, Sarge, with an inscription on the bottom, *J.P. love L.P.*"

It took but a brief moment for Shapes's brain to whirr into action.

"James Puncheon and Laura Puncheon?"

"Has to be, Sarge."

"And I'm guessing you didn't find this in Puncheon's room."

"No, Sarge. We found it in a suitcase in someone else's room. There was other stuff too, watches and jewellery. It was all in a hidden pocket, but not hidden well enough so we couldn't find it."

Johnson's voice was rich with a tone of self-satisfied achievement, something Shapes thought the other man was taking for granted, so far.

"So, someone's been thieving stuff, you reckon?"

"Has to be, Sarge. What they doing with all that lot otherwise? We reckon Puncheon caught 'er nicking the lighter, so she popped a couple of bullets in him."

"Her?" An odd and unexpected sense of trepidation arose within Shapes, though he had not the slightest idea where it came from.

"That's right, Sarge. It's a woman."

Shapes starred at Johnson, who declined to add to his statement.

"And?"

"And what, Sarge?"

"What's her name, for God's sake?"

"Oh, sorry, Sarge. It's Jones. Gwen Jones. Welsh bird, she is. Dartington's got her in handcuffs in her room. Said I was to fetch you and the Inspector. Don't suppose you know where

136

the Inspector is? I should let him know. He'll do his nut if he reckons I've been slow telling him..."

Johnson might have said more, but, if he did, Shapes didn't hear any of it. His unexpectedly happy, even glorious, afternoon had just blown up in his face. Worse still, Dykeman was bound to make sure the egg remained stuck there for as long as possible.

Chapter Nine

Gwen Jones was sitting on the end of her bed, hands in cuffs behind her back. Her face was dark and determined, to the point where it left Dykeman feeling a little uneasy. PC Dartington stood alongside her in a pose most soldiers of the Household Cavalry would have been proud of. She was his trophy and he was showing her off, while trying to look for all the world as if it was an everyday occurrence to arrest a possible killer.

"Take the cuffs off, Dartington. I don't reckon Miss Jones is going to get out of this room with the three of us here."

Dykeman glanced around the room. It was like all the others, decent size, nicely decorated. There was a bunch of pink carnations in a glass vase on top of the bedside table. He wondered if there was any chance they might have come from his sergeant. A soft, floral perfume filled the room, even though one of the windows was open.

Gwen Jones inspected her wrists as she massaged them, now the handcuffs had been removed. She wouldn't admit it to Dykeman and Shapes, of course, but it wasn't the first time she'd felt the cold embrace of metal cuffs around her wrists.

"Better?" asked the inspector of their suspect.

She nodded. "Thank you."

Shapes looked down at her shapely calves. He was feeling confused. Hope was doing a bit of a double act with disappointment, whilst anger was loitering in the shadows. He was glad he wasn't the one to be asking the questions. Probably make a right mess of it.

"Seems you have a few things to explain, Miss Jones," began Dykeman, leaning back on his heels. "For starters, what were you doing with James Puncheon's gold-plated lighter?"

He bit back an urge to say something clever or sarcastic, sure the woman wasn't going to have even a half-decent explanation. She was up the proverbial creek without a paddle. The lighter was bad enough, but all those other items as well. Someone had been doing a bit of thieving. It had already crossed his mind it might not be her first time playing that game. They'd need to check police records, as soon as possible.

Jones looked up at Dykeman. It felt intimidating, what with him being only six feet away from where she sat. But then, she imagined, that was how it was supposed to feel. They weren't there to wish her a happy birthday. The inspector was a big man, a bit fat and chubby-faced. She suspected he lived alone. He had that untidy, unkempt look men who live alone had. Women who lived alone never had the same problem and she should know. What sort of man was he? His sergeant was easy pickings, so desperate for a woman to say something nice to him, she could have run rings round him. But what about his boss? Would he be a sucker for a little womanly charm?

She tried out a soft-faced look of innocence on the inspector as she answered his question. "James let me borrow it. I couldn't get my own to work and he was such a gentleman. I didn't realise I still had it."

Dykeman's eyebrows danced. Was he really meant to believe a load of old cobblers like that? Surely she could do better. Best, though, to tread carefully. There was something determined, fearsome even, in those deep, dark eyes of hers. Beautiful woman, no doubting that. He could see why his sergeant had been such a push-over. But there was more to her than just a pretty face, he was sure.

"You borrowed it, eh? And it just happened to end up in a pocket in your suitcase. That and a bunch of watches and jewellery."

"I suppose it did, Inspector. I can't really remember putting it there."

"And where were the two of you when he handed over such a valuable item?"

"I was sitting in the garden, early yesterday evening. I didn't realise he was there, but he happened to be walking up the path behind me and saw I was having trouble lighting my cigarette."

"And then he told you not to bother giving it back, just pop it in your handbag for later?"

"Not exactly. He told me I could borrow it until I'd had my own re-filled with lighter fluid. I'm embarrassed to find I still have it. If you'd asked me, before now I mean, I would have said I'd already given it back."

Dykeman didn't believe a word. Puncheon might not have been bothered it if had been a cheap lighter without any sort of emotional attachment, but this one had been a gift from his ex-wife and the fact he'd kept hold of it made it clear it meant something to him. Even the charms of a beautiful woman wouldn't have persuaded him to hand it over like that. The obvious question, therefore, was how did she get her hands on it? But one thing at a time.

"And all those watches and that jewellery. All yours is it?"

Her nose twitched and Dykeman detected a fleeting hint of uncertainty in those eyes. Her powers of creativity were going to be stretched finding a way out of this one.

"I don't know where they came from, Inspector. I've never seen them before. In fact, I haven't seen them at all."

"Someone else popped them in there for you, did they? Some mysterious admirer, leaving you a few gifts. Happen a lot does it?"

"I don't see what's wrong with having a few admirers. There's plenty of women would give their right arm for that."

Dykeman stepped across to the window and peered outside, looking at nothing in particular. Turning back towards Jones, his face was hard set, his manner determined. He didn't appreciate being messed about.

"You know what I think? I reckon you broke into James Puncheon's room, hoping to add to your haul of stolen goods, and you got unlucky. Puncheon caught you at it, probably with your grubby mitts on his lighter, and in a blind panic you shot him. You didn't fancy doing time. Decided it was worth a man's life to avoid getting sent down."

Dykeman fired the words at her full force, catching even Shapes momentarily off guard. But the sergeant knew his boss well enough to understand what he was up to. Trying to knock a suspect off balance was one of his favourite interviewing techniques. Pounce on 'em out of the blue and see how flustered they get. And it worked a lot. There were plenty of people not quick enough, thinking on their feet, to make something up without either giving the game away or collapsing in a sobbing heap. The problem was, it didn't seem to be working this time. Gwen Jones looked a bit startled, at first, and flinched a bit, but she didn't let it upset her.

"That's a disgusting thing to say," she snapped back. "I never went near his room. Like I said, he let me borrow the lighter and I forgot to give it back."

"I don't believe a word of it," Dykeman said, his voice dismissive now. "You'll be telling me next he asked you to marry him, too. What d'you reckon, Shapes, sound likely to you?"

Shapes tried not to let it show how awkward he was feeling. He'd have preferred it if Dykeman had kept him out of things altogether, just left him to get on with writing his notes.

"Doesn't sound too likely, sir, what with all that other stuff too. Some of those watches are gents' ones, not what you'd see on a woman's little wrist."

"Stop messing me around, Jones. I don't like it and when I don't like something life can get very unpleasant for whoever's involved," Dykeman was on the verge of shouting. Most people would have been intimidated. "Admit it, you broke into Puncheon's room and stole that lighter, just like you stole all those watches and the jewellery."

"I told you, I've never set eyes on those things. They're nothing to do with me."

Jones decided that she didn't like Dykeman. He was a bully. If he had any skill, he'd get what he wanted out of her without making silly threats he couldn't keep. He didn't have anything on her; not something he could really make stick. It was a pathetic performance. All the same, she still felt tense, nervous and a little worried about the situation she now found herself in and, if the policemen took the trouble to look into her background, things were likely to get a good deal worse.

"Father Christmas and his little elves put them there, did they? That's about as believable as your story. And I bet a jury would see it that way too."

Ah, things were warming up nicely, contemplated the inspector, and now to deliver a more telling blow; one he was confident would change her attitude. "I like a little bet every now and then, don't I, Shapes? And I'm willing to bet when we take a look in police records we're going to find your name there. I reckon you've done this sort of thing before. Could even say you're a professional at it. Wouldn't surprise me if we find things have been going missing from other hotels in the area. Just think about it, going down for a second or third offence. The judge won't look any too kindly on that. They never do, not with repeat offenders, even ones with a sweet smile. You could be looking at a long stretch inside this time. Fancy that, do you?"

"I told you, I did not kill James Puncheon and that's all there is to it."

Jones stared hard at the wall. What more could she say without giving herself away? A jury wouldn't convict her, would they, just because the police found those things in her suitcase? No one could prove she'd stolen them, just like they couldn't prove her story wasn't right. But her self-confidence was ebbing fast now. All that was standing between her and her police record was the false name she was using. It didn't seem much, not right there and then. It wasn't meant to be foolproof, just a little cover, but it was all she had. Maybe she ought to keep her mouth shut for now. Leave them to it.

"We'll see about that." Dykeman could see the fight draining out of the woman. She'd clam up now, like the pro he was almost certain she was. But that wasn't a problem. She just needed a bit of time to come to her senses. "Take her down the station, Dartington. She can spend the night in a cell. See if that doesn't improve her memory. And stick the cuffs back on. That's a murder suspect you have there."

Gwen Jones was bundled out of the room by Dartington and PC Smith, who he called in for support. The look she gave Shapes as she passed him made him shrink inside. Christ, what a near miss he'd had there. He probably wouldn't have survived a night alone with the woman, if things had got that far. Mind you, that wouldn't necessarily have been the worst way to leave this world.

"She's lying through her teeth, that one, Shapes. Nicked every bit of that lot, she did," Dykeman added, pointing at the loot that had been found in her suitcase. "You'd best get it all bagged up and down the station before it goes missing again. And we'll need to try and find owners for it all. My guess is most of it doesn't belong to people here, otherwise they'd have reported it missing by now."

"I'll get someone to phone the hotels hereabouts. Best speak to nearby police stations, too, see if they've had any reports of stolen watches and jewellery from hotels on their patches."

"Near miss you had there, eh, Shapes?" Dykeman was smiling.

"Don't know what you mean, sir." Shapes blushed.

"Promise to make you breakfast in the morning, did she?"

"She couldn't do that, I don't have anything in the fridge."

Dykeman slapped his sergeant on the shoulder.

"Surprised you fell for a Welshie. Didn't think you liked foreigners."

Shapes put his notepad away and studiously ignored the wind-up.

"Right, then. After that little bit of excitement it's about time I got back to the station and put in my report to the Chief Constable. He'll be getting ready to go home to Mrs Chief Constable soon for his dinner and he won't be happy if he's not heard from me before he does. You, on the other hand, Shapes, are going to stay here and make sure the rest of the staff and guest interviews get done. I want to go through those in the morning. Oh, and when you've done that, see about some background checks on everyone in Puncheon's party, him included. I want to know more about that lot."

"Don't reckon she did it, then, Jones?"

"Not counting any chickens just yet, Shapes. Women are tricky bleeders, as you ought to know."

Dykeman was chuckling to himself as he walked out the room. Shapes most definitely was not. He walked over to the window and looked outside, his shoulders slumped, an audible sigh leaking from between his lips. He'd had enough of living on his own. Years and years of waking up every morning to an empty bed and a cold house. It wasn't the life he'd expected to lead and he didn't really have a clue how things had turned out this way. God knows, he wasn't fussy. Any woman, well, almost any woman, would do. Surely to God there was one out there who'd be happy enough to walk down the aisle with him. There had to be, didn't there?

Chapter Ten

Dykeman's walk to the police station the following morning was a most pleasant one. The sun was out, the birds were singing and, it being a Sunday, the streets were all but deserted. He'd stood in his back garden drinking a cup of tea earlier, listening to the bells of St Mary's church in the town centre, the sound of which reached out across the rooftops. It had been many a year since he'd last been to church; voluntarily, that is. Police business sometimes made it a necessity, or so the Chief Inspector claimed on occasions like Remembrance Sunday.

As he'd left his house, he'd secretly laughed at old Fred Strimmer from number twenty-three, who could never take his collie for a walk without falling over the lead and, as often as not, his own feet. This time he'd not even made it to the end of his front path before finding the lead tangled around his legs. It was a clever dog, was that collie. Shame it didn't have a kennel down the station.

Walking into the small room he shared with Shapes, a fresh cup of tea in one hand, Dykeman was delighted, though not surprised, to find his sergeant already hard at work. Apparently Shapes had been there, nose to the old grindstone, for nearly an hour. Small piles of papers were laid out on his desk, ready for his attention, and Shapes was working his way through another batch of notes, cross-referencing them in the hope of spotting some helpful clue.

Shapes looked up, "Morning, sir. I got you a tea, but it'll be cold by now."

"That's alright, Shapes, I picked one up on the way. What you got here, then?"

Shapes, who was sitting behind his own desk, waved the papers he was holding. "I've got some lists of reported thefts, watches and jewellery, from the half a dozen stations nearest to us. Been going through them trying to match them up with what we found in Jones's suitcase."

"Any luck?"

"Yep. Looks like two of the watches and one necklace are a match for what's been reported as stolen. Still checking the others. Don't look any too good for her, I'd say."

"Well done, Shapes. You're not half bad when you've got your mind on the job and not other things," replied Dykeman as he sat down behind his own desk. "And what about this lot?" He waved his hand over the orderly spread of papers in front of him.

"They're some of the interview notes from yesterday. Those what might be of interest. Most of 'em were useless. Nothing in 'em to help us. I've put those in a pile down there."

Dykeman glanced down at a larger stack of papers on the end of his desk. Impressive stuff indeed. Maybe he'd stop taking the mickey out of Shapes now for his little indiscretion the previous day. Maybe.

"And the rest, they're worth a read, I take it. Anything good in them?"

Shapes grinned and tapped his pencil on the desk.

"I reckon there is. There's people at that hotel who've got some explaining to do. Been a bit remiss in what they've told us, you could say."

Dykeman's eyes widened and hope welled up inside him. The day, though still early, seemed to be getting better and better.

"Which ones? These?"

He laid a hand on the small set of papers right in front of him.

"That's them. You'll want to read the one on the left first."

Dykeman didn't say another word as he snatched up the papers and read through them as fast as he was capable of doing. Shapes waited, confident what he'd found was going to be of serious interest, even if it did complicate things.

"Bloody Nora, that sounds like Lisa Kindleman," remarked Dykeman, jabbing at the first paper he read. "Who's this Stanley Roundtree? Can we trust him?"

"An old fella, staying in a room two doors down from James Puncheon. Dartington's not in yet, so I've not been able to ask him what he thinks about the bloke."

"Well, that's a turn up for the books. Mind you, shouldn't go counting any chickens. Suppose it could have been someone else."

"A prostitute, you mean? Don't reckon there's any that good looking working around here."

"That's not exactly what I had in mind, Shapes, but I guess we can't dismiss the idea."

"Well, I don't reckon we've seen any other sexy blondes staying in the hotel."

"I'm sure if they were there, you'd have noticed them by now, Shapes."

Dykeman moved on to the next paper. What more did Shapes have to offer him?

"Well, well, Laura Sinkling and James Puncheon having a barney in the garden. Joseph Pearling? I've heard that name somewhere else..." Dykeman re-checked the witness details. "Of course, he's the waiter who brought me that tasty dinner. Knew I'd heard his name before. And he overhead them arguing on the Friday evening, eh?"

"It gets more interesting," prompted Shapes, now rolling his pencil between his fingers, with the kind of skill that came only from a lot of practice.

Dykeman's lips moved in silence as he continued reading and what he read proved to be explosive stuff.

"Well, would you believe it, Pearling heard her saying, 'Sometimes I could bloody well kill you'. You know what, Shapes? We've gone from famine to feast here. I don't know what to sink my teeth into first."

"There's more," prompted Shapes.

Dykeman picked up the single remaining sheet of paper and resumed his reading.

"Bernard Dingle didn't tell us he went for a walk after breakfast on Saturday morning," complained Dykeman. "Half an hour too."

"Odd thing is, sir, we haven't found anyone who can vouch for him. Even the receptionist can't remember seeing him leave the Marlborough, nor come back, for that matter."

"And half an hour is plenty enough time to pop a bullet in a man, if the mood took you."

"Could easily have shot Puncheon, then stepped out of the hotel for his walk. So long as no one saw him anywhere near Puncheon's room, there'd be no reason to get suspicious. Mind you, if he's our killer, I'd bet he was banking on being seen leaving the hotel. Surprised he didn't make sure. If I was him, I'd have made up a reason to speak to the receptionist, even checked the time while I was there, so they'd be more likely to remember it later."

"Mm," Dykeman murmured as he placed the three sheets of paper side-by-side in perfect alignment. "But what about a motive? We've not found any reason yet why Dingle might want to murder Puncheon."

"Maybe Puncheon was getting his leg over with Mrs Dingle."

"Come off it, Shapes. You met the woman. Would you, what with her being a hyper wotsit?"

Shapes coughed. Dykeman looked towards the ceiling.

"Don't know why I asked," added the inspector, with a shake of the head. "Right, I want to speak to this Stanley Roundtree first. Assuming we're right and the woman he saw was Lisa Kindleman, then we'll speak to her next; only this time we'll not be so friendly as we were before."

"Reckon our Welsh friend downstairs isn't the killer after all?" asked Shapes, wondering if that might make any difference to his chances of re-igniting their tentative relationship. If only there wasn't the small matter of all those stolen items.

"Doesn't change a thing where she's concerned. She's still got the best motive and I wouldn't trust a thing she said."

"Suppose you're right, sir. She is Welsh."

Dykeman eyed his sergeant with suspicion. Surely the man wasn't thinking there was still any chance of copping off with Jones? No, even Shapes had to have realised by now she'd been playing him for a fool, hoping to get some inside information on their investigation.

"Which reminds me, we need to find that damn gun, Shapes. I don't like running a murder investigation where we don't have the murder weapon. I want you to get together another team and go over the Marlborough with a fine tooth comb. Every drawer, every cupboard, every nook and cranny. That gun has to be somewhere."

Their discussion was, for the moment, interrupted by the sound of whistling, which appeared to be heading their way along the corridor outside their office. It was far too happy-sounding for either of them. The whistling stopped, followed by a loud rap on their office door.

"It's open, Johnston," barked Shapes.

"Just checking, Sarge," replied PC Johnston as he stepped into the office. "Didn't want to interrupt anything important."

"What is it, then?"

"It's that Welsh woman we've got banged up in the cells, Sarge. Says she wants to talk."

Dykeman and Shapes looked at each other, both their faces creased with a smile.

"Well, in that case," announced Dykeman, "we'd better get down there and hear what she has to say."

GWEN JONES HAD, DECIDED Shapes almost at soon as they stepped into the small, stuffy cell, lost some of her allure during the course of the night. Her make-up was largely gone, revealing skin that looked paper-white, and her eyes were circled by dark rings that suggested she'd not had the best night's sleep in her life. Sitting there on the edge of the thin, hard bed, she looked years older and nothing like the self-confident woman who'd sidled up to him so sexily the day before. He almost felt sad for her. Almost, but not quite. The sneaky, untrustworthy woman didn't deserve his attention. He'd moved on, as it were, and she wasn't going to play him for a fool a second time.

Dykeman, on the other hand, could hardly have been happier with what they found. The woman had obviously given her predicament some serious thought overnight and decided her situation was looking decidedly dicey. He was filled with a happy expectation she would now adopt a more helpful attitude than she'd done the day before, when her relationship with the truth had been a somewhat tenuous one.

"You don't look like you got much sleep last night, Miss Jones," suggested Dykeman, trying not to sound entirely unsympathetic, as he stood there in the middle of the room with his arms crossed behind his back. It wasn't so much that he really cared about upsetting her, more that he didn't want to unintentionally annoy her to the extent that she might change her mind about co-operating.

She looked up at the two of them, the chubby one in charge who looked serious and intent on extracting his pound of flesh, and the older, thin one, who reminded her of a rodent and stunk like one too. How on earth had she managed to summon up the strength the previous day to flirt with him? God knows how, but there was no way she going down that road again. She'd sooner eat her own kidneys.

"Might I have a cup of tea, Inspector? It's been a while since the officer with the big feet brought me my breakfast."

"I think we can rustle up a cuppa," replied Dykeman, nodding at Shapes, who opened the door just enough to place an order with the constable waiting outside. "That will be Constable Johnston, the man with the big feet. Size elevens, he tells us. Biggest at the station."

Dykeman pulled the single, battered, metal-framed chair into position opposite Gwen Jones and sat down. He was glad he'd kept his jacket on. The room had felt a bit on the cool side when they first walked in, but it was starting to feel distinctly cold, something that had no doubt contributed to Jones's restless and unhappy night.

He'd not noticed before how long and slender her fingers were. He couldn't think of another woman he knew, Sheila Delph included, who had such beautiful hands. It seemed a shame they were being put to criminal use.

"Men often notice my hands. Seems like they can't take their eyes off them sometimes."

Dykeman looked up to find Gwen Jones staring directly at him. He felt, for a brief moment, a little heat flush in his cheeks. Maybe Shapes hadn't been such an easy target after all. He'd better tread more carefully.

"You asked to speak to us, Miss Jones. I assume it's to tell us the truth about that cigarette lighter."

Jones shook our her hair, or at least tried to. It had become knotted overnight as she struggled for sleep and she disliked facing the man in front of her now when she was such a mess.

"I didn't kill James Puncheon."

There was a pause, left deliberately by Dykeman.

"So you said yesterday, but I don't see any more reason why we should believe you today than we did then."

Dykeman was intent on approaching things in just the same way as he would have if Shapes had not presented him with all that new information a short while ago. It was important not to let himself be swayed by other possibilities. Unless and until she proved otherwise, Gwen Jones was their number one suspect. She had both opportunity and motive, so it was up to her to prove them wrong.

"I admit I stole that lighter, but that's all I did."

"That's a good start."

Dykeman played the silent game a second time. The years had shown him what a powerful technique it could be.

"I didn't kill James Puncheon. What would I want to do that for?"

Jones's voice was, noted both policemen, tinged with frustration.

"Maybe Puncheon caught you stealing his property and threatened to call the police. I'm betting you've got history, might even have done some time in the past, and you couldn't face the prospect of going to prison again, especially as you'd be expecting to get a longer sentence, what with being a habitual criminal and all."

Jones remained silent, starring at the concrete floor.

"Why don't you start by describing just what you claim did happen, that way Shapes and I will have something we can start working with."

Jones returned her focus to Dykeman and straightened her shoulders as she tried to compose herself. This was, she realised, her opportunity to convince these two men that she was innocent. Innocent, at least, of murder.

"I saw Puncheon and his friends in the restaurant on Friday evening. Posh lot, they were. Snooty bunch too, if you ask me. Their sort are just the type I look for, rich enough to have some nice jewellery and so on. With so many people eating in the restaurant, it seemed a good time to do some exploring. Not much chance of getting caught, you know. I knew which rooms Puncheon and his friends were staying in. I made it my business to overhear when they checked in."

"So, you admit this was pre-meditated."

Jones remained silent for a moment, before continuing. "Puncheon's was the first room I went into. It's easy, you know, to get into most hotel rooms. Even your sergeant could do it, I should imagine. I like to find cash, if I can, what with it being so easy to spend, but he didn't leave any money in his room. In fact, the only thing I could find that was of any value and small enough to hide in my suitcase was that bloody lighter. I wish I'd never found it now, what with all the trouble it's brought me. That was it. I pocketed the lighter and left. The man never came anywhere near the room and I didn't kill him."

"So, what time did this happen?"

"A quarter to nine. I was only in the room for five minutes. It's too dangerous to stay any longer."

"And you're sure no one saw you go into the room or come out?"

"No one."

"That's a shame. Would help you a lot to have someone who could verify your claims. You see, Miss Jones, when someone commits a murder they need a motive for doing so and, right now, the only person we can see who has a motive for killing James Puncheon is you. So you'll understand why we're having a hard time believing you."

"Why would I admit to stealing the lighter if I thought it would make me look like a murderer?"

"I don't know, Miss Jones. Maybe you're hoping to get sent down for a minor crime rather than a major one. Better to own up to stealing if it might help us believe you didn't shoot James Puncheon. Wouldn't be the first time someone's tried that one on us, eh Shapes?"

"Certainly not, sir."

"Well, how about I don't own a gun and never have? How can I shoot a man dead if I don't have a gun?"

"We've only your word for that and, at the moment, your word isn't worth much."

"Well, haven't you got the gun? Can't you check my fingerprints to see they're not a match for those on the gun?"

"We've not found the murder weapon, yet. Seems you've hidden it too well."

Jones ignored the accusation. She was struggling to get her thoughts straight, what with the lack of sleep and Dykeman's refusal point-blank to believe her. For some reason, she hadn't expected it to be so hard, not once she owned up to stealing that bloody cigarette lighter. Maybe she'd made a mistake, should have kept quiet. Now she felt as though all she'd done was make things worse. What was the point of saying anything else?

"Come on, admit it," demanded Dykeman. "Puncheon caught you in the act, you panicked and shot him, scared stiff you'd get locked up for a long stretch. Then I suppose you stuffed the gun in some hidey-hole you're hoping we won't find and went about your business as if nothing had happened. I bet that's about it, isn't it?"

Jones remained silent, looking at her hands.

"Probably got a bit nervous yesterday afternoon, something we did must have spooked you, so you tried chatting up Shapes here to give yourself a way of finding out just how close we were to catching you. And I bet last night you came up with some scheme hoping if you owned up to a bit of thievery, we'd decide you wouldn't have told us that if you'd also shot Puncheon. But you don't fool me, not one bit. You had a motive and you had the opportunity and, so far, you've told us nothing that says you didn't commit murder. I bet when we do find that gun, and, take my word, we will, we'll find your fingerprints all over it."

He stood up and leaned in over their chief suspect, deploying his sizeable presence to best effect. A bit of intimidation could elicit an admission of guilt surprisingly often.

"Well, what have you got to say for yourself?"

Jones didn't even budge, let alone collapse into a tear-filled heap of regret and sorrow.

There was no need to rush, thought Dykeman. They had other people to speak to and different avenues to explore. Jones could be left to stew in the cell while they were busy. Perhaps by the time they returned to speak to her again, she might have more to say or, better still, they might have got their hands on the gun. Now wouldn't that be nice.

"That's the sound of guilt that is, Shapes. Positively deafening, it is." He scratched the side of his neck before addressing himself once more to Jones. "We'll leave you to think things over. When you're good and ready to tell us what really happened in that hotel room, then you just let the constable know. He'll know where to find us."

As the heavy metal door to the cell clanked shut behind them, Shapes asked, in a quiet voice, a question that had been on his mind since he'd set eyes on Jones once more. "What I don't get, is why did she stay around? Why didn't she just check out as soon as she'd shot Puncheon? That way she could have got rid of her loot before there was any chance of us pulling her in for questioning. She's only in that cell as suspect number one because of that lighter. It don't make sense to me."

"The trouble is, Shapes, you're thinking about it sensibly, with a level head, not when you're in a blind panic not knowing what the hell to do. I'd bet she reckoned it might look too suspicious if she cleared off like that, when she was booked in for the weekend. Thought it better to stay put and not arouse our suspicions. Shame for her and fortunate for us, she didn't think about getting rid of those stolen goods. Probably placed too much faith in her own ability to keep it all hidden."

"Suppose you're right, sir. Me, I would 'ave been out of there in a shot, so to speak. Take my chances if the police came knocking on my front door asking questions."

"Me too, Shapes. Me too."

The trouble was, as Dykeman led Shapes up the narrow stairs and on towards their office, he couldn't fend off a nagging doubt that his sergeant had a good point. The woman might not, after all, have behaved as you might expect if she'd shot Puncheon and was keen on not getting found out. The thought annoyed him. Things had become more complicated, not less, and that hardly helped matters.

SOMEONE HAD CHANGED the flowers that sat in a large blue vase in the reception area of the Marlborough Hotel. Yesterday's red roses had been replaced with a fresh, bright display of white lilies, the scent of which filled the large space so well it was almost overpowering, thought Dykeman. Personally, he would have gone for something with less scent, fine carnations, perhaps. He liked carnations. They were well-behaved plants. Never gave him any trouble in his garden.

That aside, the two policemen could hardly fail to notice the somewhat strained and irritable atmosphere in the hotel. It was there from the moment they set foot on the premises, a brooding undercurrent. Hardly surprising, thought Shapes, given the circumstances. It was often like that, people who were either scared witless or else highly excited on day one of a murder investigation had often turned into tired, irritable troublemakers come day two. All that most of them wanted to do now was clear off home. They'd had enough excitement.

Reginald Plowright, the hotel manager, seemed to have been waiting specifically for them to arrive. His eyes were dark and heavy and, noticed Dykeman, his suit wasn't quite as sharp as yesterday, nor his tie as perfectly knotted. He approached them in a tentative manner, one that suggested he was hoping they were going to announce their investigation was complete and the chief suspect had come clean. Hard luck, said Dykeman to himself.

"Good morning, Inspector. Sergeant."

"And what a lovely day it is, Mr Plowright. Just a bit of a shame I can't spend it in my garden."

"Yes, quite so, Inspector. Erm," Plowright fiddled with a cuff. "I was wondering if there had been any developments, significant ones that is, in your investigation."

"As it happens, there was a significant development about half an hour ago, wasn't there, Shapes?"

"Certainly was, sir. Very significant."

"Ah, well, that's excellent news. An arrest imminent, is it?"

"I wouldn't go so far as to say that, Mr Plowright. I would, though, say we've made some very good progress and, with a fair wind, who knows? We might just be in a position to finger someone's collar in time for Shapes here to have his Sunday roast at home."

If he was coming across as non-committal, Dykeman had no problem at all with that. Setting expectations he had no way of meeting for sure was a mug's game, one he'd played in the past; he wasn't making that mistake again. True, he knew he couldn't keep all the guests in the hotel indefinitely and it was only a matter of time before the more vocal ones starting making a fuss about being allowed to return home. That would present a new challenge, one he would happily dump on Shapes. At least he wouldn't get bored that way. The problem was, the changed atmosphere in the hotel suggested today was the day when they would start to hear the first rumblings of unhappiness. If he was really unlucky, some know-it-all would be on the phone to the newspapers or, worse still, his Chief Inspector. If that happened, he would have to deal with things personally. Yes, Sunday was looking more and more like the day when they needed to make some serious progress. The pressure was starting to ramp up.

Plowright grimaced. Shapes thought it made him look like one of his old uncles. Shapes didn't like the uncle in question.

"It's the guests, you see, Inspector," continued Plowright. "Some of them have other arrangements in place and they're starting to ask when they might be able to move on. There are also new bookings for tonight. I wouldn't want to cancel them if I thought there was any chance things would be, well, all sorted out today. I'm sure you can understand."

Dykeman did understand and wasn't entirely unsympathetic, but, frankly, it was just tough luck. If a few people had to be inconvenienced and the hotel missed out on a bit of money, so he and Shapes could get on with their job, then so be it. All the same, the inspector tried to sound concerned when he answered.

"I understand entirely, Mr Plowright. I appreciate you've got a business to run here and people have their plans. We don't want to cause any more inconvenience than we need to, but I'm afraid the investigation has to come first. I'm sure you appreciate that. If any of your guests turn particularly nasty, point them at Shapes here. He'll be only too happy to help."

Shapes twitched. There'd be words spoken later. What kind of crap job was that to land on him?

"Thank you, Inspector. That will be a help."

Dykeman didn't think Plowright sounded as though he meant what he'd said. Oh, well, he'd made an effort.

"Well, must be getting on. Won't get things done standing here talking all morning, will we. I don't suppose you could ask someone to bring me and Shapes a fresh pot of tea could you? Been ages since we had our last cuppa, eh Shapes?"

"Certainly has, sir." Well, twenty minutes at least, thought Shapes.

CAROL STITCH HAD BEEN standing behind the reception desk, trying hard to hear what Plowright and the two policemen were talking about. Sadly, she'd not been able to catch a word. It felt like a big lost opportunity to become the possessor of information none of the other members of staff would have. However, Mr Plowright had asked her to arrange for a pot of tea and a plate of biscuits to be taken through to the room the policemen were using and she'd decided to do the job herself; that way, she'd have the chance to ask a question or two.

As she rounded the final corner on her way back from the kitchen, she noticed a figure crouched on the ground in front of the door to the policemen's temporary office. It wasn't difficult to make out who it was: Joseph Pearling. She stopped and looked at him, wondering what he was doing. It was hard to blame him for being nosy when she was mad keen to find out more herself. Maybe he'd overheard something interesting.

Well, he'd certainly have to share it with her. She glanced around. Thank God, Mr Plowright wasn't to be seen. He'd go mad if he caught Joseph eavesdropping.

Stepping a little closer, she spoke in a quiet voice, hinting at conspiracy, "What are you doing down there, Joseph?"

Joseph Pearling had been crouched down by the closed door for only a few seconds. He felt embarrassed to be caught there. He looked up at the receptionist, a frown on his face.

"I'm not listening, you know." He realised, as he said the words, that the receptionist wasn't going to believe that. "Well, I wasn't. I dropped the toast."

Carol looked down at the small plate Joseph was holding. Two pieces of buttered toast were piled on top of it and she could just make out a scattering of crumbs on the carpet in front of her colleague.

"Don't suppose you could stop yourself then?" She smiled.

"No." He smiled back, confident she wasn't going to make a fuss or report him to the hotel manager. "Feel a bit stupid now, getting caught like this and I've only been here a few seconds. You could have waited a while."

She gestured to him to come away from the door, something he was more than happy to do, getting back to his feet with barely a sound, so the two of them could retreat to the relative safety of the reception desk.

"Well, what did you hear? You can't keep it all to yourself now, you know." Carol was excited and it showed in her voice.

"I didn't hear a thing. You found me too soon. Honestly, I'd only just picked up that toast. Although I'm not sure you can hear much through that door anyway, it's a solid old thing."

Carol didn't want to believe him, it was too disappointing, but before she could press him again Lucy Proud approached the desk.

"You want me to take that through to the nice policemen?" asked Joseph, pointing at the tea tray, a sparkle in his eyes.

"If you like. But don't think our conversation is done. I'll be looking for you later."

Pearling paused, uncertain how Lucy Proud might take that comment, then decided it wasn't worth an explanation and left her to Carol.

"WELL, HE WAS AN ODD one," remarked Dykeman, referring to Stanley Roundtree, as he reached for a rich tea biscuit. There were only two left and if he didn't grab one now, Shapes would have them both as soon as his head was turned.

"Bit of an old duffer," remarked Shapes, noticing there was now just the one biscuit left. "Reckon we can trust him? He might have made it all up or got confused about something else he'd seen."

"He might have lost a few of his marbles, Shapes, well, most of 'em maybe, but I think it's pretty clear the woman he saw with Puncheon was Lisa Kindling. She's not the kind of woman you're going to get mixed up with someone else."

"Yes, I suppose that's true enough."

The truth was, Shapes was already looking forward to having another opportunity to spend time in the presence of Lisa Kindling. It was the kind of perk he felt he should always make the most of and it was obvious they'd need to give her a proper grilling. No more pussy-footing around. She had some explaining to do.

"I think we need to have another word with Mrs Kindleman. She's not been altogether honest with us," asserted Dykeman.

"You can say that again. Major memory loss if you ask me. Makes you wonder why she happened to forget a little thing like that."

Stanley Roundtree had turned out to be in his seventies, hard of hearing and prone to losing his concentration halfway through a sentence. It had been hard work keeping him on track without risk of putting words into his mouth, but Dykeman was happy enough by the time Dartington had escorted the witness out of the room that the woman he'd seen going into James Puncheon's room was indeed Lisa Kindleman. They certainly hadn't encountered another woman at the hotel who came even close to matching the reference Roundtree made to Marilyn Monroe. What a stroke of luck Roundtree had seen the two of them going into his room.

"We'll have Dartington round her up once we've finished with Laura Sinkling. Seems we're in for a busy day."

LAURA SINKLING LOOKED tired, thought Dykeman, as she dropped herself on to the chair in front of him. Her eyes were dark, despite the make-up, and her hair hadn't been given quite the same level of attention as it had the day before, little stray bits trying to escape all over the place. The woman was clearly suffering with nerves. The question was, why? Just the usual worry people felt when they were involved in a murder case, especially when it concerned a friend or family member? Or was there more to it than that; something she didn't want them to know about? That was the whole point of this chat with her. They were going to do a bit more digging and that included finding out what it was she had been arguing about with Puncheon on the evening of their arrival and why she hadn't mentioned it to them before.

As Shapes went to shut the door, the handle slipped from his grasp and the door closed with a bang. Laura Sinkling nearly jumped out of her skin.

"It's just the door, Mrs Sinkling," said Dykeman, intrigued at the effect it had on her.

She held a hand up to her forehead and closed her eyes.

"It's the stress. I think things are rather catching up with me, Inspector." Her voice was thin, barely recognisable from the day before.

She pinched the skin between her eyes and took a couple of deep breaths. Things had seemed bad enough yesterday, she mused, but from the moment she'd awoken this morning she had felt awful. A nagging headache failed to clear up, despite a warm bath, a couple of aspirin, then a stroll round the garden after breakfast. Even at such an early stage in the day, she felt drained of energy. It was obvious, she concluded, that things had all been rather more stressful than she had initially anticipated and that was beginning to show in her health and general demeanour.

"Entirely understandable, Mrs Sinkling. These things always take a heavy toll on those involved, especially family and close friends. I am right, aren't I, to class you as a close friend of the deceased, despite your divorce?"

She nodded her head just enough so that Dykeman could see. "I don't suppose I would have chosen to remain on speaking terms with James, but after a while we found a way of getting along together. Surprising what you can do when you feel the need to."

Dykeman lingered for a moment on that last sentence, an interesting thing to say. Or was he overdoing it and seeing things for more than what they were?

"I suppose even good friends argue, don't they? It's only to be expected every once in a while."

She closed her eyes again, for a few seconds, wishing away the ache in her head. "I suppose so, Inspector."

"It's just that we're led to believe you and Puncheon were arguing in the garden on Friday evening."

There was a pause, only a very short one, but Dykeman made a mental note of it, all the same.

"Did we? Friday seems a long time ago now."

"Indeed you did. You were overheard by a member of staff. Said the two of you were really going at it."

Laura Sinkling's head tipped forward a little. She didn't reply.

"Did you know your former husband was in a relationship, Mrs Sinkling?"

Still she remained silent, her dark, heavy eyes vacant.

"I think you do," said Dykeman, with a little more force than he'd used up until then. "And I'd be willing to wager a few quid you know who he was seeing. I don't suppose this had anything to do with your argument, did it?"

"You're a clever man, Inspector. Far more observant than I perhaps expected." She raised her head and took a long, deep breath, before adding, "Yes, we were arguing about the relationship James was in. I really don't know who it was with, but he let it slip, as well as the fact the woman was married. Honestly, after all we'd been through together, I simply couldn't understand how he could do such a thing. It was so selfish and so bloody stupid. How did he imagine it was all going to end?"

Despite the disbelief they'd heard from other members of the party when the idea James Puncheon had been having an affair was put to them, Dykeman had, nonetheless, tended to believe it was true. There had been something in the way Frank Sinkling had shared the notion with him that suggested Laura's own husband was sure it was more than mere conjecture, even if he couldn't name the woman involved. There was a pleasant satisfaction for Dykeman now in finding that his hunch had been right. However, his sense of self-congratulation didn't linger for long. There was another question that needed answering.

"And why was it you didn't see fit to tell us this before?"

Laura Sinkling pursed her lips.

"The argument?"

"All of it. The argument and the illicit relationship."

"I'm very sorry, Inspector. I didn't think the argument was relevant. James and I, well, we... it was just an argument. I didn't murder him, so..."

She fell silent. If the world had already begun to feel as though it was pressing in on her now, all of a sudden, it started to feel as though it was in danger of squeezing the life out of her.

"You understand now, I hope, that either piece of information could make a considerable difference to our investigation?" prodded Dykeman.

She nodded.

"And you're sure you don't know who your ex-husband was seeing? Not even a suspicion."

"No. He wouldn't say who it was. He didn't even say how long it had been going on."

"Ah, that was my next question. I hope there's nothing else you've been withholding from us, Mrs Sinkling."

She shook her head. "No, there's nothing else."

"You should understand that it's a very serious matter to withhold information from a police officer investigating a crime. It's called obstruction of justice and it can result in a prison sentence."

He watched the woman's face with care for any sign whatsoever that might suggest she was still holding out on him, but if she was she was a pretty decent actress because he couldn't see anything of the sort. He glanced at Shapes, standing behind Laura Sinkling, notepad and pencil in his hands. Shapes merely shrugged his shoulders. Dykeman curled his bottom lip under the top one, feeling it rub against his front teeth, wondering if there was anything to be gained from continuing the conversation. There wasn't. He'd got what he came for.

"Let's hope you've not had any other memory lapses, shall we? That will be all for now, Mrs Sinkling. You're free to go."

Laura Sinkling didn't say another word. Indeed she didn't even give Dykeman a backward glance, but simply left the room in the same quiet, almost meek manner in which she had arrived.

Dykeman mulled over their exchange, not entirely certain he could trust her. It was true enough witnesses often left things out of their statements they didn't think were of any relevance to an investigation; an annoying habit that all police officers would prefer came to an abrupt end. But was that really the case with Laura Sinkling, or was there more to it? And if she did have some motive for keeping quiet, both about the argument and her ex's latest affair, what might that be? He couldn't help feeling that her assistance had been equal parts help and hindrance.

HAVING ESCAPED THE close and oppressive confines of the policemen's small room, Laura Sinkling sat alone in the hotel bar, feeling a little sick. She wondered if it wouldn't do her some good to actually be sick. Maybe that would act as some sort of purge, clear her body of the toxins that seemed to have built up inside her.

She had hoped no one had seen or heard her argument with James. She probably ought to have guessed that some nosy member of staff would have overheard them, though it seemed they can't have heard very much, otherwise surely the inspector would have said more than he did.

It was pretty clear the police didn't trust her now. The look on the inspector's face and the accusation in his voice told her that much. Well, there wasn't a great deal she could do about that now. In any case, if the inspector was to unearth the truth, that she knew full well who James had been seeing, then he wouldn't trust her any further than he could throw her. At least she'd not given away that little secret.

Chapter Eleven

By the time she walked into the room, Lisa Kindleman had kept the two policemen waiting for over ten minutes; something which irritated Dykeman considerably. The woman's show of petulance, or was it arrogance, wasn't going to do her any favours. And it didn't help matters that she chose not to bother with so much as an off-hand apology. It was as if she thought the rest of the world could dance to whatever tune she chose to put on.

It didn't leave Dykeman feeling any better disposed to her when he saw what she was wearing: a knee-length black pencil skirt that rode half-way up her thighs when she sat down and a red short-sleeved blouse that exposed a good deal of her cleavage. On another day he might have let his eyes linger a while on what she had to offer, but not this time; if she'd aimed to impress then she'd failed. He didn't like being taken advantage of and he'd make sure she understood that.

"I'd appreciate it, Mrs Kindleman, if you'd make your way here promptly in future. This is a murder investigation, not a social get together."

"You caught me unprepared for a public appearance, Inspector. I got here as soon as I could."

She appeared unperturbed. That also annoyed Dykeman. Even if it did eventually turn out she wasn't guilty of murder, he'd see to it that she had an uncomfortable time all the same.

"You always have to make a special effort before you go out in public, do you?" He tried to sound condescending, though wasn't sure he'd been all that successful, until he noticed Shapes lift his left eyebrow a good half-inch. Good, he must have hit the right note after all.

"I wouldn't want people to get the wrong impression."

"And what impression would that be?"

"That I can't be bothered, Inspector. I may have been blessed with some natural advantages, but I wouldn't look this good without a little effort."

The nerve of the woman. She didn't even look as though she'd got her tongue wedged in her cheek. Dykeman's nose twitched. Right then, he declared to himself, if that's how she wants to play things.

"Anyone in particular you like to impress with your... natural advantages?"

"I find it's always a good idea to make sure your husband doesn't have any reason to look elsewhere. There always seems to be so much temptation around, don't you think?"

She left her lips parted, but Dykeman ignored them.

"Your husband, eh? Is he the only man you like to impress? Or perhaps I should put that in the past tense, are you sure he was the only man you liked to impress?"

Bingo, you've looked away, trumpeted Dykeman to himself. Short of coming right out with name, rank and serial number, there was little more she could have done to make it clear there was another man in her life. But which man? Best not jump to any conclusions.

"So, I'm right. Care to name the man? No? How about James Puncheon, for example?"

"Inspector, how dare you."

"I'll damn well do as I please," snapped Dykeman. He got to his feet and began to circle his prey, confidence rising that he was close to a kill, so to speak. "You see, Mrs Kindleman, we have a witness who saw you and Mr Puncheon going into his room late on Friday evening. Very friendly, the two of you looked, if you get my meaning."

Any semblance of friendliness and ease left her face, replaced with a stone-like appearance that pleased the inspector no end. If he'd been playing darts, he would by now have scored a hundred-and-twenty with his first two arrows and been lining up another triple-top to give him a maximum one-eighty.

"James and I have been friends for a long time. Just friends." She spoke with determination, her hands coming together in her lap.

"Pull the other one, it's got bells on it." He continued to circle her, hoping it would make her feel even less comfortable than she already appeared to be. "According to our witness,

175

Puncheon nearly had your blouse off before the door was closed."

Well, that was a bit of an exaggeration, it was fair to say, but a little artistic licence rarely went amiss and he was confident this time he was very close to the mark. He could see that third and final dart winging its way towards the treble-twenty. Any moment now and the crowd would roar their approval.

Lisa Kindleman's head dropped forward. Silence from her, a roar from the crowd. One hundred and eighty, they bellowed.

"Well, Mrs Kindleman? Are you still going to tell me that you and Puncheon were nothing more than just good friends?"

She looked up. There was actually a tear in the corner of each eye. Genuine or for show, wondered Dykeman, a long way from being prepared to trust the woman.

"I didn't kill James, Inspector. Why would I do that, when we were having such a good time together?"

"I don't know. You tell me, because right now you're looking like our prime suspect. You certainly appear to be the last person to see Puncheon alive. Lovers' spat, was it? He wouldn't buy you a new diamond ring? Or was it worse than that? Did he want to end things? A woman like you wouldn't take too kindly to that, I should imagine. I bet you're not used to men dumping you. No, it's you who always gets to do the dumping. Am I right, Mrs Kindleman?" There was a brief pause before he barked, "Well?"

Lisa Kindleman flinched, caught off balance by the ferocity of Dykeman's attack, and almost shouted back her response. "No, to all your stupid accusations. We didn't argue and he wasn't about to end things. Why can't you stop wasting your time accusing me of killing James and find the person who really did? You're looking in the wrong place, you fool."

Dykeman looked at Shapes, who was scribbling frantically in his notepad. His sergeant grinned, a clear sign that he thought his boss was on the right track.

"How long had you and Puncheon being seeing each other?"

"Oh, I don't know. Five, six months, maybe."

She glanced up at the ceiling, as if looking for divine inspiration, thought Dykeman.

"You're not sure. Couldn't have been all that much fun then, if you can't remember when it started. And who initiated things?"

"Does it really matter?"

"Does if I say it does, and I do."

"I suppose I encouraged him, but it was James who suggested we go for a drive one Saturday afternoon. He took me to a hotel in Northampton. Thought there was little chance of us being seen there."

"That was the way of things, was it? Hotels in out of the way places or country lanes where it was just you and the birds?"

"If you speak to the staff at the Hanging Tree Hotel in Northampton, you'll find they know us there as Mr and Mrs Puncheon. We rarely went anywhere else."

"We will, don't worry about that." He was back in front of her now, leaning on the desk. "Do you know how to use a gun, Mrs Kindleman?"

"No, Inspector, I do not know how to use a gun. And I don't own one either. I told you, I didn't kill James. Why do you insist on thinking I did? What would I do that for?"

Her cheeks were flushed and her eye make-up smeared. But even that, Dykeman had to admit, if only reluctantly, did very little to dim the woman's beauty.

"Because, until and unless you can prove otherwise, you were the last person to see him alive and that means you could very well have shot him dead, Mrs Kindleman. What makes you think I should believe anything else?"

"The shots, surely someone would have heard the shots." She sounded hopeful, speaking quickly. "If I shot James then someone would have heard the shots while I was in the room. What about this witness who saw me and James going in to his room, surely he can tell you there weren't any gunshots while I was there. Well, can't they?"

"All in good time." She had a point, there had been no reports of gunshots after she had gone in to Puncheon's room. Trouble was, there had been no report of gunshots, full-stop, which was troubling and inconvenient in itself.

"So, what time did you leave Puncheon's room?"

"Ten o'clock. We were only there together for about twenty minutes. I didn't want to take the chance, but James was very persuasive and the wine did the rest."

"And did you both leave the room at ten?"

"No, James had already told the others he was going to have an early night. Claimed he was tired as a result of having had such a busy week. I went back to the bar. I think everyone else was there, apart from Sally and Bernard."

Dykeman realised with some regret that the woman had all but regained control of herself. It would have been helpful if he could have kept her off-balance for a while longer. People were more likely to make mistakes when they no longer had proper control of themselves. Oh well, you couldn't expect things to go all your own way.

"Did you see or hear anything of Puncheon after that?"

"No, nothing. As far as I was concerned, James really had chucked it in for the night. But doesn't that help. Knowing I was there with him until ten, I mean? Whoever killed him must have done so after that. Doesn't that help you narrow things down?"

Yes, she was definitely back in control of her emotions. This particular interview was about to come to an end. At least they now knew for sure who James Puncheon had been seeing. Whether or not that made a whole heap of difference, only time would tell.

He noticed she had pulled her skirt further down her legs. He took that as a sign that she had, at last, realised the seriousness of the situation.

"Perhaps. Did he say anything about meeting anyone else that evening, either before or after you went back to his room?"

"No. I think that was the whole point, Inspector, he wasn't expecting anyone else. We had the rest of the evening ourselves, as far as James was concerned."

Dykeman scratched an ear. The woman had opportunity, there was no doubt about that, but motive, that was much less certain. There didn't seem anything to be gained from carting her off down to the station, apart from giving Shapes an opportunity to slap a pair of handcuffs on her. Shame about that. He sat back down and brought his hands up on to his belly.

"Thank you, Mrs Kindleman. That will be all, for now."

As he watched Shapes show the woman out of the door, Dykeman couldn't help noticing that, despite her recent intimate relationship with the deceased, she hadn't exactly gone overboard in expressing her grief or frustration at the apparent lack of progress in effecting an arrest. In fact, she looked bloody happy to be leaving the room just as soon as she could. If a cold, self-centred heart was needed to pull the trigger and send a man to his death, she had it in spades. But maybe that was the problem; it was too obvious.

"You were on top form there, sir," remarked Shapes as the door closed once more on the outside world.

"Thank you, Shapes. I can't make my mind up about that woman. She's as cold and heartless as they come and she had the opportunity to murder Puncheon, but I can't help thinking if she did plan something of the sort then she'd do a lot better job of it. Wouldn't make the silly mistake of allowing someone to see them going into his room."

"Women like her, they're always trouble. Too full of themselves. She's the one out of all of 'em that's got the whatsits to top someone."

"I agree with your erudite observation, Shapes, but she'd need a motive first and right now all we've got is speculation that Puncheon might have decided to dump her."

"Bet she would have gone off like a rocket if he tried to do that. Anyway, if he dumped her that evening then she'd have needed to be a clairvoyant to have planned his murder, wouldn't she? I can't see her carrying a gun around with her all the time, just in case it comes in handy."

"That's true enough, though she could have left Puncheon's room in a huff, then returned, this time armed. Just because no one saw her return later on in the evening, it doesn't mean she didn't and we've only her word that he was still alive when she left him."

There was a moment of pause as both men wondered what they should make of things.

"I suppose there's a vacancy now," observed Shapes in a nonchalant manner.

"You what?" asked Dykeman, reluctant to interrupt his thought process.

"There's a vacancy. She'll be needing to find a new bit on the side now Puncheon has gone to meet his maker."

"Shapes." Dykeman's brow was deeply furrowed.

"Yes, sir." Then, after a brief hesitation as he searched for inspiration, Shapes added, "I'll go check how they're getting on searching for the murder weapon."

HIS SERGEANT HAVING excused himself from his presence, Dykeman decided to find some relatively quiet little spot away from the hotel. It was being away from the scene of the crime that was the important part. He'd recognised the signs of impending confusion in his over-worked brain. Without him asking it to do anything of the sort, his brain had begun working its way through all the new information they'd unearthed so far that morning, looking for patterns or omissions or any other sign that might point the way forward.

Dykeman had learned the hard way that whenever this happened it was beneficial to take a break, give his brain some breathing space to do what it was going to do whether he liked it or not.

Deliberately omitting to tell anyone where he was going, in order to minimise the chance of his being interrupted, Dykeman stepped out of the Marlborough Hotel and walked a hundred yards or so down the road to a bench in the shelter of two enormous chestnut trees. It wasn't exactly tranquil, what with it being adjacent to a busy road, but he was at least able to sit there alone, just him and his thoughts. It would do.

A fat, round pigeon landed at his feet, dropping out of one of the chestnut trees with all the grace of a one-legged overweight ballerina. It looked up at him, its face filled with expectation, then, realising it wasn't going to get any treats, began to wobble its way in an erratic pattern across the compacted soil beneath the trees, pecking every now and again at anything that might possibly resemble food. Would make a tasty pie, decided Dykeman, though he wasn't any too sure he stood much chance of catching it, even if he could be bothered to try.

A young woman, mid-twenties thought Dykeman, walked out of a side road some fifty yards further on. Her dark hair, cut so that it framed her pretty face, was topped with a small, round, straight-sided hat. She also seemed to be wearing a carpet, or, at least, that was what it looked like to him. It might have been cut into a dress, nipped in tight at the waist with a wide hemline just above the knee, but the eye-boggling pattern was definitely the sort of thing you saw in a carpet. She had two young children with her, neither of whom, guessing by the look on their faces, seemed happy with their lot. Sunday visits to grumpy relatives hadn't pleased him any too much either.

A bright red Triumph TR3, its soft-top folded down, rumbled along the road from the direction of the Banbury Cross, driven by a young man with a thick mop of blonde hair that whipped about in the wind. As the car reached the bottom of the hill that ran up past the hotel, there was a hearty roar from the engine as the driver pushed at the accelerator and the car raced up the incline. Dykeman couldn't help wondering if owning such a beast would have improved his chances with Sheila Delph. Best not linger on such thoughts, he decided, as the Triumph turned on to the Bloxham Road and disappeared out of sight.

Dykeman yawned, pulled a hanky out of a pocket and blew his nose, long and loud. On the stone wall behind him a pair of starlings squabbled over a tiny piece of bread. Life went on regardless of the murder he was trying to solve; a realisation that helped put things in perspective. Murder was murder, true enough, and a terrible thing for that. But it was just one, albeit unpleasant, thing to happen in a world where every second a hundred thousand other things occurred, many of them perfectly pleasant, happy even. It was a thought that helped to reduce the anxiety that had been building inside him since they'd spoken to Gwen Jones that morning.

It was, therefore, with some regret that Dykeman looked up towards the hotel to see the figure of PC Dartington legging it down the road towards him. He didn't need the intellect of a brain surgeon to know that something had happened. No doubt something bad. Hey ho, back to the grind. He stood up and started to walk towards his constable.

"Trouble at t'mill, is there, Dartington?"

"Sir, yes, sir." Dartington took a deep breath. "It's Mrs Kindleman. She's been attacked in her room."

Chapter Twelve

Lisa Kindleman seemed an entirely different woman to the one they'd interrogated only a half-hour earlier. For one thing, she was shaking, her efforts at holding a cigarette to her mouth almost comical to Shapes's eyes. Even a drunk would have made a better effort. Her eye make-up was smeared all over her face, her hair looked like she'd just rolled out of bed and her long, patterned dress had been ripped under the right arm.

Shapes found it hard to care much for the woman. It wasn't like she'd done a great deal to earn any real sympathy from them, so why should he be bothered. Sooner or later people tended to get their just desserts and, as far as he was concerned, that was the case here.

Harry Kindleman sat alongside his wife, an arm wrapped around her trembling shoulders, lines etched into his forehead and a warmth in his eyes that Shapes hadn't expected. He really cared. So what? They deserved each other, those two.

The room was something of a mess. Several items of clothing, both male and female, were strewn across the floor and every drawer in the single chest was open, the contents now in ruffled heaps. It reminded Shapes of his own bedroom come the end of an average week, when he'd not been much bothered about putting things away properly after a hard day's slog. He couldn't, however, imagine this was normal for the Kindlemans; people who, he got the impression, were more bothered about appearances than an ordinary bloke like him.

As Dykeman approached the Kindlemans' room, he saw Shapes standing in the doorway with another man. Dr Henry Pinch, a small, round man with thinning brown hair and an oversized moustache, had already arrived on the scene, having, by a stroke of luck, been on the premises attending to the needs of an elderly man who'd taken a tumble in the hotel's garden. Pinch had declared Lisa Kindleman to be fine, despite the obvious shock, and had given her a mild sedative to calm her nerves.

"Hello Henry. How's Mrs Kindleman doing?"

"Hello Leslie. Mrs Kindleman is in shock, as is only to be expected. There is some bruising to her left forearm, where she appears to have taken a blow, but apart from that I'd say she's in perfectly good health."

Dykeman knew Pinch well and, as he always did, he found the doctor's gentle, rhythmic way of speaking instantly comforting. It had occurred to him many times in the past that the man ought to have opened a practice as a psychologist, something to which he seemed perfectly suited.

"No reason we can't talk to her, then?"

"None at all, though I'd ask you take it easy. Nothing too taxing, you understand?"

"That's fair enough. With any luck, she'll have got a decent look at her attacker and we'll be in with a chance of apprehending him."

"I wouldn't hold out too much hope there."

"Eh?"

"She kept saying whoever it was came at her from behind. I got the impression she never set eyes on the man. But I'll leave all that up to you." Pinch closed his doctor's bag and gave it a firm pat. "She ought to sleep for an hour or two when you've finished with her. I imagine the sedative will make that easy enough. And you know where to find me if she needs any further treatment."

"That's the damn problem with this case; we keep getting nice, juicy clues dangled right in front of our noses, only for them to be yanked away at the last moment. Oh well, on we go. Thank you, Henry. Hopefully we won't need your services here again today."

The two men shook hands warmly before the doctor departed, at which point Dykeman turned to his sergeant.

"You spoken to her already, Shapes?"

"Only a few words, sir. She was hysterical. Kept saying she'd been attacked."

"No sign of whoever it was, I don't suppose?"

"Not yet. Her husband wasn't here. She was sleeping, so he'd gone down to the bar to read the newspaper. Bernard Dingle was there with him."

"Best get someone to speak to people in the neighbouring rooms. See if anyone heard or saw anything."

"Will do, sir."

Dykeman turned and looked again at Lisa Kindleman. It was interesting, he noted, that she'd changed her clothes since they'd spoken to her earlier. Seemed some people had more outfits than they knew what to do with. "She looks a right mess. Got a feeling we're not going to get much out of her for the time being."

"They were taking a chance, whoever did this, I mean. Jumping her here when the place is crawling with us lot. Makes you wonder whether they weren't desperate to get their hands on something in the room."

"I think you could be right there, Shapes. It was a big chance to take, though I'm guessing they probably weren't expecting there would be anyone in the room. If Mrs Kindleman was sleeping when they broke in, they might not have noticed her until it was too late."

"Makes you wonder what they were after and if it had anything to do with James Puncheon."

"It does indeed. Come on, let's see what we can find out, before the woman is too sleepy to answer our questions."

Their advance into the room was met by some firm resistance. "Do you have to do this now, Inspector?" snapped Harry Kindleman. "Can't you see the state my wife is in?"

"The sooner we speak to your wife, Mr Kindleman, the better our chances are of catching whoever attacked her. They've already got a bit of a lead on us and it's best not to give them any more of a head start, don't you think?"

"Well... I suppose so. But, seriously, take it easy, won't you. I've never seen Lisa like this before. She's normally as hard as nails and a damn sight tougher than I am." He turned to his wife and spoke in a soft, comforting voice. "Are you OK to answer a few questions, darling? I won't let them wear you out."

Lisa Kindleman's head lifted and dropped forward just enough for the others to notice. She took her husband's hand as it rested on her thigh and squeezed it tight. "It's for the best."

Dykeman seized on the opening at once. "Thank you very much, Mrs Kindleman. We'll let you get some rest as soon as we can. Now then, can you describe what happened."

"I was asleep, on the bed here. I don't suppose I'd been sleeping for very long. I think something must have disturbed me, but I'm not sure. Anyway, I woke up, still half-asleep, and had an odd feeling there was someone else in the room. Thinking it must be Harry, I called his name and then..." She took a deep breath and closed her eyes.

"It's alright dear, I won't leave you alone now. I'll stay here just as long as you need me." Harry Kindleman gave Dykeman a look filled with annoyance and frustration.

"That's when you were attacked, was it?" prompted the inspector.

"Yes," replied Lisa Kindleman, close to tears. "They were there, behind me. There by the curtains. I saw something move out of the corner of my eye and I started to turn. If I'd not got my arm up quickly, they would have hit me clean on the head. I struggled," she tugged at the rip in her dress with her free hand. "But I was thrown down on to the floor and whoever it was fled."

"Did you get a sight of their face, even a partial one?"

She shook her head. "Sorry, Inspector. It was dark and everything happened so quickly."

"Could you say if it was a man or a woman?"

"No. Sorry."

"What about a cologne or perfume? Or perhaps the noise of their shoes on the carpet? Take your time, give yourself a moment to recollect anything that stood out."

Lisa Kindleman remained quiet for a brief while, then shook her head again. "I'm so sorry, Inspector. I really am."

"That's fine, Mrs Kindleman. An attack like this can be very stressful and deeply upsetting." Dykeman had to admit that Lisa Kindleman both looked and sounded as though she was in a state of genuine distress and he couldn't stop himself from feeling a tad sympathetic, despite the annoyance and frustration she had caused them only very recently. It seemed that once again they had come close to making a potential breakthrough in the case, only for things to be snatched away from them at the last. The victim, for the time-being at least, couldn't provide them with any meaningful help at all as to who had assaulted her. Accepting things for what they were, Dykeman decided to let Lisa Kindleman get some rest and keep his fingers crossed that, once she was properly recovered, she might be able to recall something that was of use to them.

"I think we'll leave the questions there for now, Mrs Kindleman. You're understandably distressed and I don't want to go making things any worse. If should happen to remember anything else later then just ask for me or Shapes. We won't be far."

"I will. Thank you, Inspector."

Dykeman turned towards Harry Kindleman and said quietly, "Mr Kindleman, could I have a word before we leave?"

The three men made their way into the corridor, Harry Kindleman clearly reluctant to leave his wife's side, even for a short while.

"It would be very helpful, Mr Kindleman, if you could check on your belongings once your wife has settled down. Whoever it was attacked her was clearly here for a reason, most likely looking for something, and it would help us if you could identify whether anything appears to be missing."

"Of course. But, seriously, what would they want from us? I mean, it's not like we travel around with a trunk-load of gold bars. The best they'd get from us is Lisa's jewellery. Do you think that's what they were after?"

"It could be. Maybe an opportunistic thief looking to make the most of the confusion in the hotel at the moment. Frankly, Mr Kindleman, my mind is open to any possibility right now."

DYKEMAN AND SHAPES had retreated to their designated room, disappointed by the news that none of the other guests staying in the same part of the hotel as the Kindlemans had seen anything of an attacker. Only one couple, the elderly Firmins in the room next door, had heard Lisa Kindleman's initial scream and subsequent calls for help. Mr Firmin readily admitted it took him some time to get up and out of their room to see what the fuss was all about. By the time he arrived on the scene, the attacker was already gone.

Dykeman was slumped on the chair behind the desk. Shapes was inspecting a small landscape painting hanging on one of the walls. Two cups of tea were sitting on said desk, ignored and now only lukewarm.

"What the bloody hell is going on round here, Shapes?"

"Don't ask me, sir. I'm just your lackey. You're the brains in this partnership."

Dykeman gave his sergeant a withering look. "Well, at least we can be sure it can't have been that girlfriend of yours this time, because we've got her under lock and key down the station. Or I assume we still have. You haven't let her out, have you?"

Shapes ignored the jibe and continued his detailed study of the ropey painting.

"You alright, Shapes? You've been unusually quiet today, nothing like your normal self. And you hardly gave that Kindleman woman a second glance earlier on, which is definitely not like you."

Shapes shrugged his shoulders and remained tight-lipped.

"Come on, man, cough up. Something's on your mind. Is it that Welsh woman? Still getting to you, is she?" Dykeman hoped it was.

Shapes made a noise that Dykeman couldn't distinguish, then scratched his stubbly chin before half-turning towards Dykeman.

"Don't you ever get fed up of living on your own? No one there when get back from a hard day's graft, with dinner on the table and a smile on their face, and no one to warm your side of the mattress before you get into bed at night."

Dykeman looked at his sergeant, open-mouthed and, temporarily, too taken-aback to know what to say. He wondered what had brought on this rare comment on the state of their domestic arrangements or, more specifically, the absence of women in their lives. It wasn't the sort of thing they were in the habit of discussing.

"It is Jones, isn't it? Brought all this on, I mean."

"I've had enough living on me own. You reckon there's something wrong with us?"

"I like to keep my options open," said Dykeman, attempting to sound light-hearted, whereas he was, in fact, starting to feel rather uncomfortable. This was all a little too close to home, especially in light of recent developments with Sheila Delph. "And, no, there's nothing wrong with us. It's tricky finding a woman who'll put up with the life of a policeman."

Dykeman was about to say more when the door opened, then stopped ajar before someone knocked on it.

Shapes shook his head. Where did they get their constables from? "Come in Dartington."

"Thanks, Serge."

Constable Dartington wore a harassed look that spoke of further problems. Dykeman could hardly bring himself to ask the obvious question, but he did so, all the same. "What now?". There was audible exasperation in his voice.

"It's Mr Kindleman this time, sir. He's gone mad. Shouting and swearing at his wife, he is. Calling her all sorts of names. I reckon he knows she was having it off with Mr Puncheon and he's not happy about it. Can't say as I blame him, like. Wouldn't like it myself if Mrs Dartington took to seeing another man."

"In a bare knuckle street fight between you and the lovely Mrs Dartingon, I know who my money would be on, Dartington. And it wouldn't be you," cut in Shapes.

"Well, Serge, I reckon..."

"Never mind that, Dartington. I suppose we ought to see what's happened. In their room, are they?" asked Dykeman.

"Sir. PC Johnson is keeping them apart."

"I suppose he's the best man for the job. Come on, Shapes. No rest for the wicked, and all that."

Chapter Thirteen

Harry Kindleman was still simmering with rage when Dykeman and Shapes arrived back at the Kindlemans' room. His blue and red spotted tie was half-way down his chest and his hair was a mess. He had, thought Shapes, the look of a man who'd just got back home after a heavy session at his local pub. Sitting on the very edge of a chair a little way in from the door, he looked up at the two policemen, the rage not yet entirely gone from his wide and wild eyes. He didn't wait for Dykeman to start asking questions.

"I suppose you already know about this, don't you?" he snapped. It was definitely an accusation rather than a question. "Didn't have the decency to tell a man he's been made to look an idiot."

Dykeman glanced across the room at Lisa Kindleman. He'd thought he might find her submissive, filled with regret and keen for forgiveness. He should have known better. She sat on the edge of the bed, almost in exactly the same place as they'd found her a short while ago, her face now set like stone. If there were emotions bubbling around inside her, she was doing a grand job of hiding them. He turned back to her husband.

"Would you care to explain what's been going on here, Mr Kindleman."

"Come off it, you know what the bloody hell has been going on. That trollop was knocking off James Puncheon. Talk about stab a man in the back and after everything I've done for her."

"At least James knew how to show a woman some proper respect; something you'll never understand the meaning of." Lisa Kindleman delivered the words with cold, calculating precision.

Quite the contrast they made, thought Dykeman, one fire and brimstone, the other cold as the North Pole. If it was true that opposites attract, they made a good match. Quite why their marriage was in trouble was anyone's guess. Well, it wasn't, of course, because here were two people both of whom saw the world from only one point of view. Their own. They were bound to fall out sooner or later.

"Respect? How can you talk to me about respect after what you've done?"

Harry Kindleman was on his feet, jabbing a finger at his wife, who showed little sign of being intimidated.

"Mr Kindleman," demanded Dykeman. "Sit back down and get yourself under control, or I'll have to ask Johnson here to take you down to the station."

Kindleman looked at Dykeman, as if sizing him up, then did as he was told, careful to avoid further eye contact with his wife.

"Now then, who told you about the affair between your wife and James Puncheon?"

Dykeman was curious to know the answer to this question, since everyone else in their party had claimed to be entirely ignorant of who Puncheon had been seeing. At least one of them had been lying, but which one?

"No one."

"Eh? Your wife tell you, did she?"

Kindleman shook his head. "No. I overheard Laura Sinkling talking to Frank about it in the garden. She said she'd not told you the truth when you asked her about the rumours. Pretended she didn't know it was James. But she was worried she should have spoken up, in case it had anything to do with his murder. I didn't hang around to hear what Frank thought about that. I came straight back here."

"And does it have anything to do with James Puncheon's murder?"

Nice one, thought Shapes. Sometimes his boss could be an absolute genius.

Kindleman looked confused. It took him a moment to answer. "How can it? What's Lisa got to…" The words tailed off as it began to dawn on him what Dykeman had actually said. "Now listen here, Inspector, I never knew what those two were getting up to until ten minutes ago. Why would I have killed James two days ago, when I only found out now? It doesn't make sense."

"So you say, Mr Kindleman. But there is always the possibility that you knew full well what was going on before you arrived here. Would make a convenient alibi, claiming that you didn't know anything about it until after the event."

Lisa Kindleman's mouth had not formed a smile, but the look of amusement in her eyes was clear to see. Dykeman was sure everyone else in the room, her husband included, had noticed. For a brief moment he wondered, and not for the first time, if she wasn't the more likely of the two to shoot a man dead in cold blood.

"You're barking up the wrong bloody tree if you reckon I murdered him. I suppose I simply shot him dead on the off-chance something like this might crop up, did I? You'll be telling me next some gypsy woman told me it was in the tea leaves. Bloody ridiculous."

"Are you saying you wouldn't have confronted Puncheon if you'd found out about his affair with your wife before he was murdered?"

"Of course I would. I'd have broken his damn jaw, if I'd had the chance. But that's a long bloody way from murder. A man has a right to defend his reputation and his... marriage." Harry Kindleman looked daggers at his wife. She didn't respond. "Not that it seems to be worth much now."

"It's a common motive for murder, is revenge, especially when it's tied up with sex. You'd hardly be the first man to respond to such a discovery by murdering the other fella, Mr Kindleman. From where I'm standing, you have a very good motive for killing James Puncheon and we've only your word that you didn't know anything about his affair with your wife sooner than you claim. I'm sure you can appreciate that leaves you in a difficult position."

Harry Kindleman remained silent for a moment. He appeared to Dykeman to be mulling over his next words with care.

"I see your point, Inspector." Harry Kindleman's whole demeanour had changed in an instant. The anger in his words and the fire in his eyes had abated and he now spoke a good deal more calmly. He seemed to Dykeman and Shapes to have decided that co-operation was the best way forward. "Since I know I didn't shoot James, I'm more than happy to go back over my movements during the period leading up to his death, so I can prove my innocence."

"I'm sure we'll do just that, Mr Kindleman. But right now I think it would be a good idea if you and your wife put some space between the two of you. Give yourself some time to come to terms with recent developments, so you can have a grown up conversation about what happens next for the two of you. What we can't have is another incident like this, which makes our job of tracking down the killer even more difficult than it already is. Though, I suppose if you are our killer, that would be of benefit to you. Now then, I suggest you leave your wife here and find somewhere else to spend an hour or two."

Harry Kindleman looked again at his wife, wondering if he might see in her eyes some sign of regret. She simply ignored him, directing her gaze at Dykeman. It didn't really matter, decided the cuckolded husband, because their discussion, if you could call it that, was a long way from over. They'd be continuing it later, of that there was no doubt. Right now, as far as he was concerned, there was only going to be one outcome; one that involved his wife looking for a new home.

"Very good idea, Inspector. Think I'll have a coffee in the restaurant. Mull things over."

"Excellent. We're heading that way ourselves."

DYKEMAN WASN'T IN THE best of moods when they left Harry Kindleman safely ensconced in the hotel restaurant. It wasn't the attack on Lisa Kindleman or her husband's eruption at the news of his wife's affair that was annoying him, though both developments had left him somewhat perplexed. What was bothering him was having been lied to by one of the other guests. Words needed to be said and straight away. His brooding silence wasn't lost on Shapes, who thought it best to keep quiet as the two of them marched in double-quick time towards reception.

They hadn't done much more than exit the low-ceilinged hallway into the open expanse of the entrance hall when Dykeman made a noise like a grumpy cow before opening his mouth to speak.

"Mrs Sinkling."

There was an edge to the summons that had Laura Sinkling feeling immediately uncomfortable. Given the news concerning Lisa and Harry Kindleman, that seemed already to have reached every last person in the hotel, it seemed obvious why the inspector wanted to speak to her. There was little point now in denying the truth and she had nothing to gain from attempting to maintain her lie. It felt a little like it did on those occasions when, as a girl, she had to explain to her stern father why she'd been late returning home from school. At least Dykeman couldn't send her up to her room without supper.

She was standing in the middle of the entrance hall, flicking through one of the magazines that were placed there for the benefit of hotel guests. She turned towards the hastening policeman, effecting as natural and warm a smile as she could manage. "Inspector Dykeman. You look a little harassed."

"You could say that." He thought for a moment about finding somewhere more private, but dismissed the idea. A little display of authority wouldn't go amiss. "You lied to me, Mrs Sinkling. You told me that you didn't know who Lisa Kindleman was seeing, but you knew all along, didn't you? Would you mind telling me why you lied about something so important."

The man plainly wasn't happy, decided Laura Sinkling. Indeed, he sounded very annoyed, which she supposed wasn't altogether unreasonable. She hoped he wasn't about to throw her in a police cell and leave her there to fester for the night by way of retribution.

"You're right and I'm terribly sorry, Inspector." She placed the magazine on the table from whence it had come.

"So you damn well should be," snapped Dykeman.

Laura Sinkling gathered herself together. It was time to come clean.

"I couldn't believe it had anything to do with James's murder and I was so determined his selfishness wasn't going to lead to another marriage break-up after he'd already destroyed ours. I couldn't believe it when I found out." There was a momentary pause before she continued. "That's what we were

201

arguing about in the garden on Friday evening. I told him he should end it at once or I'd have to tell Harry. I was so angry with him."

"So, you don't think Harry Kindleman was aware his wife was having an affair with your former husband?"

"No, I don't think so. Not then, anyway. Harry is a... very confident man, not one much given to notions of self-doubt. I sometimes think Harry and Lisa are exceptionally well-suited. They're both so certain of themselves. Some might say they are a little self-centred."

"And the possibility didn't cross your mind that Harry Kindleman had found out about the affair and taken his revenge in the worst way possible?"

"Harry wouldn't do that, Inspector. He's not the sort. Anyway, he didn't know, not until this afternoon."

She felt herself blush. Perhaps she had made a mistake after all. But who ever seriously imagined one of their friends could be capable of murder? There again, she knew exactly what it felt like to find out that your spouse was sleeping with someone else. The humiliation. The pain. All those years together that seemed, in the end, to count for nothing. She had felt like she'd been used. She'd even felt dirty for a time, as if her husband's deeds had somehow soiled her. She shuddered at the memory. Maybe it wasn't so far-fetched to imagine Harry shooting James. Perhaps she was capable of such a thing herself, given the opportunity.

"Mrs Sinkling."

Laura Sinkling looked back up at Dykeman with a start. Her mind had wandered and he'd had to snap her out of things.

"I said," continued Dykeman. "What makes you think he wasn't the sort? You know what sort of person is capable of murder, do you?" Dykeman's words were heavy with sarcasm.

"I can't see Harry..." Her shoulders slumped and she let out a little sigh. "I'm sorry, Inspector. You're right. I don't have any idea what it takes to turn someone to murder and I should have spoken up. I hope it's not caused you too much trouble."

Dykeman was about to point out that it had indeed caused them considerable trouble, but before he could speak they were joined by Frank Sinkling, his face betraying the concern he felt inside.

"Laura," he said, taking his wife's arm. "Is there some sort of problem?"

"There is, Mr Sinkling." Dykeman didn't give the remorseful wife an opportunity to reply for herself.

"He knows," said Laura Sinkling to her husband.

"Ah. We disagreed over that, Inspector. I told Laura she really ought to let you know who James was seeing, but she was adamant she didn't want to risk breaking up another marriage. I think she could hardly believe he was getting up to his old tricks again and I can't say I blame her. I hear Harry knows all about it now. Don't suppose he's taken it too well?"

"You could say that. We've been with the Kindlemans just now. He blew a gasket. Did you have any reason to think he might already have known what his wife and Puncheon were getting up to?"

"If he did, he never said anything to me. Mind you, I'm not sure he would have. Think Harry would take it especially badly, finding out his wife was having an affair. Confident chap. Would put a particularly big dent in his self-assurance."

"And James Puncheon had never said anything about it? Not even hinted?"

"No, though I imagine that, as Laura's husband, I'd be one of the last people he'd say anything to."

"How did you find out about James's affair, Mrs Sinkling?"

"Woman's intuition, Inspector. Well, that and I noticed him fondling her bottom at a dinner party several months ago. She made no effort to put a stop to. In fact, she seemed to like it. After that, I watched the two of them very carefully and it became obvious there was something going on."

"Women's intuition, eh? Has a lot going for it, that does. Did you ever confront Mr Puncheon or Mrs Kindleman about your suspicions before this weekend?"

"I did. I got James alone, the week before last, and told him I knew what they were getting up to."

"How did he respond?"

"He was caught off guard. Started making up some stupid excuse about me misunderstanding and that he and Lisa were just being friendly. But I knew right away he was lying. Then he changed tune; told me it was none of my business now and that I should keep my nose out of things. I told him he was a fool and reminded him what had happened the last time he'd done something of the sort, but he didn't care."

"And Mrs Kindleman?"

"I did wonder about speaking to her, several times. But, well, she's not the most sympathetic of people. And she can be a little, well, intimidating at times. I couldn't really make up my mind what I might say to her. At least with James there was some history there; I had some sort of reason to butt in."

"Why not speak to Harry Kindleman?"

"As I said before, I was worried James's foolish behaviour would end up bringing an end to another marriage, so I decided not say anything to Harry. It's not as easy a situation as you might think, Inspector. Whatever you do, you're going to end up upsetting someone and, quite possibly, getting the blame for what follows."

"Mm." Dykeman found it hard to disagree with Laura's Sinkling's observations on the tricky situation she'd found herself in. It was all very well intending to do the right thing, but not everyone would end up seeing it that way.

"You know, I really can't see someone in our little party shooting James dead, Inspector," cut in Frank Sinkling. "Are you sure it can't be someone else?"

"We've not written off the possibility, Mr Sinkling, but when the evidence points us towards a particular individual it's hard to ignore. Motive and opportunity are what we look for, then it's a process of elimination that allows us to focus on the most likely suspect or suspects. Once we have the evidence we need, well, we can make our move. A solid, sound process makes all the difference."

What Dykeman didn't like to admit was the part that chance often played in resolving a case. He knew it to be true, but it didn't really do to share such thoughts with the public; they might get the wrong idea and downgrade the importance of talented, experienced coppers like himself and Shapes.

"I'm sure you're right, Inspector. After all, you chaps are the experts. If you don't know what you're doing there's not much hope for the rest of us."

Quite so, said Dykeman to himself, as he signalled his appreciation of her perception with a modest smile. He could practically hear the same thought flitting through his sergeant's head.

"May I go now, Inspector? Think I'd like to have a gin and tonic." Laura Sinkling's voice was soft, almost pleading.

"You can, Mrs Sinkling."

"Coming, Frank?"

"In just a minute, Laura. There's something I want to ask Inspector Dykeman first."

Laura Sinkling hesitated for a moment, then accepted her husband wanted to speak to the policemen on his own, so left him to it.

"What is it you want to ask us, Mr Sinkling?" prompted Dykeman.

"It's not so much a question, Inspector, as an observation."

"Oh?" Dykeman wondered if Sinkling was about to share some sage piece of advice with him. People often did that. Thought they were providing some penetrating insight he hadn't already considered. They were usually wrong.

"I know she doesn't like to let on about it, but Laura's divorce from James was more acrimonious than is common knowledge. He was very unpleasant to her at times, despite the fact he was the one responsible for the divorce. She came pretty close to a nervous breakdown by the end of it. I honestly don't know how she's put up with his presence since then. It says more about her strength of character than anything I could tell you.

"You think I'm wrong to be annoyed with her?"

"No, not at all. I made it clear to her, I thought she should have told you before who it was James was knocking off. No, it's just that... well, take it easy on her, will you? I'm worried this business might tip her over the edge. It's bad enough for the rest of us, but it's all much closer to home for her."

"I appreciate you being so honest with me, Mr Sinkling, but I'm sure you understand, Shapes and me, we can't go holding off simply on account of someone's nerves when we have questions to ask. What your wife did, holding back important information, could turn out to have serious implications for this case. However we're not looking to cause people undue stress, so I'll bear in mind what you've said."

"Thank you, Inspector. I appreciate that."

Dykeman watched Frank Sinkling as he strolled across the entrance hall in pursuit of his wife and wondered if they ought to pay more attention to him.

"We got anything interesting on him, Shapes?"

"Clean as a whistle, sir. Something up?"

"Don't know. Seems he might be the protective sort."

"You wondering if he's found something or someone that needs protecting?"

"I am."

FOR MANY OF THE HOTEL staff, the murder and subsequent developments had started to lose their sense of excitement, to be replaced by a growing feeling they were trapped in a real-life nightmare. The guests too appeared to be growing increasingly bad-tempered, while the hotel manager was clearly stressed and had started snapping at his staff, who were in turn struggling to cope with it all. One popular means staff were using to deal with things was to engage in as much speculation and gossip as possible.

Carol Stitch and her fellow receptionist, Maureen Close, were sitting at the reception desk, looking out on to a deserted entrance hall. The lack of anything else to fill their time resulted in the inevitable.

"I suppose you heard about Mr and Mrs Kindleman? What behaviour. You wouldn't believe it from such people."

Carol Stitch had been very happy at her colleague's recent arrival, since it gave her someone to talk to about the latest exciting turn of events. She'd been itching to talk to someone since Joseph had passed on the news, though he had himself been too busy to stay around to chat.

"I did. You wouldn't imagine it possible, would you, if you didn't hear it with your own ears." Maureen Close effected a tone that suggested she was appalled at the news Lisa Kindleman, as a married woman, had been hopping in and out of bed with James Puncheon. "D'you reckon he took her back to his room? Makes you wonder, doesn't it, what goes on in this place. There we are, quietly going about our work, while the guests are getting up to all sorts."

Stitch leaned in towards her friend and lowered her voice. "Well, I thought she looked the sort to..." But her speculation was cut short, as she whispered, "Here comes a guest."

An elderly man, supporting himself with a beautifully-turned chestnut walking stick, appeared at the end of the corridor that opened out into the entrance hall, away to the two women's left. He hesitated for a moment before setting off across the foyer at little more than a snail's pace.

"Hello, Mr Reams. That's a lovely tie you've got on." Stitch smiled as she spoke.

The old man didn't respond.

"He's a bit deaf," observed Stitch. "Poor old fella doesn't look like he's got long left before he pops his clogs."

The women then watched in silence as the old man made his way into the restaurant.

"Now then, where were we?" asked Stitch. "Oh, yes, that Mrs Kindleman. Well, I thought to myself as soon as I set eyes on her that she'd be the type to encourage trouble. They always do, that sort. Haven't you seen the way she flirts with Mr Plowright. Terrible, it is."

"The funny thing is, I did notice that man who got shot giving her a look the other day. You know, one of those looks that says there's something going on between the two of 'em. If only I'd known how things were going to turn out, I'd have said something to Mr Plowright. Might have stopped the randy sod from getting himself shot."

"You think it was her husband then, who shot him? Out for revenge."

"I do. He must have found out and, in a terrible rage, shot the man stone dead. There's so many guns around these days, after the war and all. Wouldn't be hard getting hold of one, not even here in Banbury."

"Hello ladies. Speculating on who murdered Mr Puncheon, are you?"

The two women were startled by the arrival of Joseph Pearling, who had arrived at the reception desk via the main stairs, which were slightly behind them and, therefore, out of sight.

"Oh, Joseph, you must stop sneaking up on people like that. Gave me a right fright," complained Close, holding a hand up to her chest.

"Takes lots of practice, does that," laughed Pearling, leaning over the side of the desk. "So, who did it, then?"

"Well, it's obvious, isn't it," replied Stitch, tapping Pearling on the end of the nose with a finger. "You did it. I bet you had your eyes on that Kindleman woman and couldn't bear it when you found out she was jumping into bed with Mr Puncheon. I've always thought you're the jealous sort." Her eyes sparkled with amusement.

"Damn it, I thought I'd done such a good job covering my tracks. Suppose it's the hangman's noose for me." Pearling took hold of Stitch's finger and kissed it on the tip. "Seriously, though, who is your money on?"

"The husband, I reckon." replied Close. She felt a little jealous of the attention Pearling was giving her friend. What was wrong with kissing her on the finger, or anywhere else for that matter. She'd wondered before why he was still single when he was such a good-looking young man. Surely, there was a queue of girls a mile long trying to get him to propose to them.

"So, it's jealousy and revenge for you? What about you, Maureen? You go for the husband, too?"

"Suppose it's the obvious one. Wouldn't any man get angry if he found his wife was having an affair?"

"But not every husband would toddle off and shoot the other man, would they now? Bit drastic. Give him a decent beating, by all means, but shoot him dead?"

"So, who did do it, clever clogs?" asked Close, wondering what her own husband would do if he caught her having a passionate, sordid affair.

"No idea." Pearling laughed.

"Get away with you," responded Stitch, poking him in the chest.

They might have carried on in a similar vein for a while yet, but were interrupted by the phone. As Stitch reached out a hand to answer it, Pearling gave them both a wave and walked off towards the restaurant.

"Why hasn't some young girl snapped him up yet? There something wrong with him?" asked Close, as soon as Stitch had finished on the phone.

"Oh, don't you know? He's seeing someone."

"Really? Who?"

"I don't know. I went into the garden the day before last for a smoke and he was standing with someone amongst the trees at the bottom of the lawn. I think he hoped no one could see them. But I could just make out there was a woman with him and they kissed. Proper kiss, like."

"On the lips?"

"It was. But I couldn't see her face or make out who it was. I was going to wait there until I could see, but I got called back inside."

"That's annoying. Well, now there's something for me to do; find out who this mystery woman is."

Close's eyes lit up as she spoke and the delight she felt was obvious in her voice.

"Let's try working it out together. It'll be fun."

"It will. We could always try locking him in a broom cupboard until he tells us who she is. My God, I'm so desperate to know already."

"Hello ladies."

For the second time, the two women were surprised by the arrival of someone at the narrow end of the reception desk. On this occasion it was Dykeman. He hadn't heard a word the women had said, but got the clear impression from their odd behaviour at seeing him that they had been gossiping and were, no doubt, worried he'd picked up on some of what they'd said.

Close stepped out from behind the reception desk and started to walk off towards the doorway that led through to the kitchen and store rooms.

"Well, I must be getting on. Lots to do."

"Hello, Inspector. Can I help you?" Stitch asked.

"Something I said?" asked Dykeman, nodding at the departing woman.

"Oh, absolutely." Stitch smiled. "Are you after a fresh pot of tea, Inspector? I think we should be able to rustle up some cake as well, if you'd like it."

"That sounds like a very tempting offer, thank you Carol. I'll take you up on that. Can you have it delivered to our office."

"Of course, Inspector."

"But I was looking for Mr Plowright. Don't happen to know where he is, do you?"

Stitch looked up at the clock on the wall behind the reception desk. "He's probably with the chef, making sure everything's fine for the restaurant this evening. He normally does that about this time. He speaks to the head waiter, too. Do you want to go through to the kitchen now, or shall I ask Mr Plowright to find you when he'd finished?"

"That's alright, Carol. I'll go to find him. Shouldn't keep him long."

But before he could take a step towards the kitchens, he was halted by another voice.

"Ah, Inspector, there you are? Been looking all round for you."

Dykeman turned round to find the smartly-dressed figure of Bernard Dingle standing behind him. The inspector wondered how the man managed to keep his clothes looking so flawless and sharp at all hours, when his own clothes had a habit of looking crumpled half an hour after he'd left the house. Dingle had, noticed Dykeman, a thick book in one hand. The title, what he could see of it, included the words Anglo-Saxon England. That was the man's specialist subject, if he remembered rightly.

"What can I do for you, Mr Dingle."

"Timing, old man. Appreciate it's a murder and all that you've got on your hands, but, as you know, I'm a director of Roche and Johnson, the furniture retailer, and I'm needed back at the office, pronto. Wondered if there was any sign of us being allowed to head off home."

"Not just yet, I'm afraid. But I shouldn't imagine we'll need to keep you all here too much longer. There's just one or two things..."

Dykeman tailed off and both he and Dingle turned their heads towards a minor commotion, as a uniformed figure struggled to avoid tripping over the large oriental rug that covered a large section of hall floor. The man appeared to be in a considerable hurry.

"Bunch," barked Dykeman. "What are you doing there, falling over your own feet?"

Constable Bunch, his face a little flushed, straightened up, pushed the rug back into place where'd rumpled it, then marched over to Dykeman. He didn't wait to be asked why he was there.

"It's a gun, sir. We've found a gun."

The constable's smile was broad and persistent. His news, he knew, was exactly what Dykeman had been waiting for. Truth was, they'd all been getting a bit desperate to find the murder weapon, if that's what it was. A murder investigation was never in a good place until you had the weapon.

"At last," boomed Dykeman. "Well done, Bunch. Where is it?"

Chapter Fourteen

The revolver, a Smith and Wesson, had been found, wrapped in cloth, shoved into a narrow gap between the window ledge and the brick wall outside one of the guest rooms. If he had been delighted at the news the likely murder weapon had been found, Dykeman was amused when told the occupants of the room in question. Given the very recent news about James Puncheon and Lisa Kindleman, things seemed to him to make for a nice, neat fit when informed the room was occupied by the Kindlemans.

Shapes had rubbed his hands together, his heart filled with glee, then immediately volunteered to frog march Harry Kindleman round to their temporary office, fully expecting they now had their killer in the bag. But, while he too felt more confident about things than at any time during their investigation, Dykeman thought it best to exercise a degree of caution. For one thing, they hadn't yet confirmed the gun was indeed the murder weapon and, for another, just because it had been found hidden outside the Kindlemans' room didn't automatically mean Harry Kindleman had used it to shoot Puncheon.

All the same, he agreed with Shapes, they should interview Harry Kindleman again, except this time they would do so down the road at the police station. Things were looking far more serious for the cuckolded husband, whose day had now gone from bad to worse.

While Shapes went off in search of Harry Kindleman, Dykeman made arrangements for the recovered gun to be sent off for analysis. With any luck, they'd get a match with the bullets removed from Puncheon. By the time he'd sorted that out, word had been passed to him to say that Shapes had a bad-tempered Harry Kindleman kicking his feet in Interview Room One. Dykeman didn't waste another minute, heading to the police station for what he fully expected would be a key interrogation.

Neither of the two interview rooms at the station had windows, meaning that, as usual, when he pushed open the door to Room One it stunk of body odour, cigarettes and stale coffee. A delightful mix. Put up with it a few minutes, he reminded himself, and he'd hardly notice the rank smell.

He found Shapes in casual pose on one of the chairs, legs stretched out, a mug of coffee in one hand, while he picked at his teeth with the other. Dykeman's arrival had no immediate impact on his sergeant's demeanour. On the opposite side of the single, rectangular table sat Harry Kindleman, a simmering, dark-faced volcano staring down into an ashtray half-filled with a hotch-potch of half-smoked cigarettes. On seeing who the new arrival was, Kindleman shot to his feet before Dykeman even had time to say hello, and exploded with rage.

"This is bloody ridiculous. How do you think it makes me look, dragging me down here? I've done nothing bloody wrong and now every man and his dog is going to think I shot that back-stabbing bastard. Why the hell couldn't you have spoken to me at the hotel?"

"Sit down, Mr Kindleman." Dykeman spoke calmly yet with a good deal of authority. "I said, sit down."

Kindleman fizzed with anger, but after a brief pause did as he was told, slamming a fist against the table-top. Dykeman pulled the one remaining vacant chair towards him and sat down.

"I take it you don't feel we have a good reason for bringing you here, Mr Kindleman?"

"Of course you bloody well don't. I never shot the man, I've told you that a dozen times already."

"But you've already agreed that you might well be thought of as someone with a motive to shoot James Puncheon and, since you've been staying at the same hotel, I think it is fair to say you've also had the opportunity to do just that."

"I still didn't do it." Kindleman spoke in a deep, strained voice, heavy with suppressed frustration.

"All that was missing was the means." Dykeman paused a moment, but Kindleman remained silent. "But it seems now we've also got that."

"What do you mean? James was shot. I don't own a gun."

"Are you sure about that, Mr Kindleman?"

"Of course I'm bloody well sure. I think I'd remember if I had a gun knocking about the place."

"So you deny the gun we found hidden outside your hotel room has anything to do with you?"

"What... Yes, of course, I do. I just told you, I don't own a gun."

"Just coincidence was it, eh?"

"Now look here, you're not going to pin this murder on me. I didn't know James was knocking off my wife until today, so why would I have wanted to kill him before then? It simply doesn't make sense and I'm damn certain any court will agree with that. Let me say it again, I did not kill James Puncheon."

As Kindleman wagged a finger in Dykeman's face, the policeman noticed the gold watch he was wearing. A Hamilton, if he wasn't mistaken. A nice piece; pricey too. Not the sort of thing the average man in the street could afford. He'd probably had a lucky break there; if Gwen Jones had seen it unattended, it was very likely she'd have walked off with it.

"You served in the Second World War, I assume?"

"Yes, despatch rider."

"See much action?"

"Enough. North Africa. Italy."

"So you'd know how to use a gun?"

"Of course. And I bet you do too. And what's-his-name sitting next to you and half the people in that damn hotel. If that's what it takes to make someone a suspect, you ought to have dozens of people locked up here."

Festival point, thought Shapes, impressed by Kindleman's line of argument. Almost every man over the age of forty would have served during WWII in some way or another and, as a result, knew how to use a gun. Mind you, that didn't let the man off the hook. As Dykeman had already pointed out, he ticked all the boxes: motive, opportunity and means.

"So, if you didn't hide the gun there, who did? Mrs Kindleman, perhaps?"

Kindleman sat back and eyed the inspector for a moment.

"I think you had better ask her that. We're not on the best of terms right now."

"Well, someone put it there, Mr Kindleman, and it seems mighty convenient it just happened to be tucked under the window frame outside your room."

"Then someone's trying to set me up. They've heard about Lisa and James and decided to make it look like I shot him."

Kindleman's rage had begun to abate. Some of the tension had left his body and his hazel eyes held steady as he met Dykeman's gaze. The inspector pondered the suggestion. It wasn't without its merits.

"That's something we'll look into, Mr Kindleman, as a matter of course. However, right now you are in a very difficult position and, under the circumstances, I am going to ask Shapes to take you down to the cells, where you can spend the night while we wait for the lab to carry out its analysis of the gun. I'm sure you can appreciate that it wouldn't be a sensible thing for us to let you roam free right now."

"Don't think I won't be taking this up with the authorities, Inspector. I don't appreciate being treated like a common criminal when I've done nothing wrong."

"Nothing? That's a bold claim, Mr Kindleman. Are you sure we wouldn't find something, however minor, if we went digging?"

Dykeman felt confident Harry Kindleman was the kind of man who had plenty of suspect, if not downright illicit, dealings he wouldn't want the police to unearth. He didn't appreciate Kindleman threatening him like that and it gave him a nice sense of satisfaction when the man responded.

"I want to speak to my lawyer," snarled Kindleman.

"Of course. Shapes will take you to a phone before tucking you into one of our cells. You'll be settled in just in time for tea." Dykeman turned towards Shapes. "Back to the office when you're all done, Shapes."

"Yes, sir."

"WHAT DO YOU RECKON then, Shapes?"

"Guilty. Who else has a motive as strong as his? He could have crept out of his room in the night, shot Puncheon and made it back to his room without anyone noticing, if he was careful. Wouldn't have been a hard thing to do in the small hours. And he probably had to hide the gun in a hurry, so stuffed it in that hole behind the window frame. We were lucky to find it."

"I agree he's the one with the best motive. In fact, I'm not sure anyone else has as solid a motive, as far as we can tell, with the possible exception of Gwen Jones."

Shapes sniffed. "Maybe."

Dykeman was tempted by the chance to have a laugh at Shapes's expense by winding him up again about Gwen Jones. Such an opportunity was not normally to be missed. But, on second thoughts, perhaps he'd leave it for now. They had important things to attend to.

"We can't write her off, Shapes. There's a potential motive there and the opportunity. Until we found that gun outside the Kindleman's room, it would have been a toss up for me as to whether Jones or Harry Kindleman was the most likely suspect."

"What about the ex? She could have done it. Revenge, sort of." Shapes couldn't help himself. He still couldn't quite let go of the thought of what might have been with Gwen Jones, despite what he'd told himself when they'd interviewed her the previous day. The soft spot he'd developed for her so quickly had yet to fully wear off. A woman showing an interest in him, whatever her real motives, was such a rare occurrence he couldn't stop himself from wanting things to turn out differently. It annoyed him, feeling that way. The woman had played him for a fool. What was he doing, having any sympathy for her? But he knew the answer. Though he hated to admit it, it was desperation, pure and simple.

"Laura Sinkling could," agreed Dykeman, leaning back in his chair, so he could lift his feet up on to his desk. His shoes, he noticed, needed a polish.

"I think her husband's comments about how bad her break-up with Puncheon was were very revealing. Does make you wonder how she could stand the sight of her ex. But I'm not sure I can see her going so far as to shoot him dead; not unless there's something we don't know about yet."

"She's a woman. They're capable of anything."

Dykeman couldn't help wondering if his sergeant's somewhat biased observation had anything to do with Gwen Jones. The poor fella had got his hopes up there, no doubt about that. She'd not had to do much; he was so desperate, was Shapes, that a simple smile would have him all weak at the knees.

Unfortunately, thinking about his sergeant's romantic difficulties reminded Dykeman about his own frustrations where women were concerned. Well, one woman in particular. But it didn't do to linger on what Sheila might be getting up to or, worse still, what her plans for the future might be. He thrust such thoughts to the back of his mind.

"Very observant of you, Shapes. She is indeed a woman. But a killer? Don't know about that. But let's keep her on the list for now. Who else can we add?"

Shapes picked at an ear as he worked his way through all the possible candidates. There were plenty of people involved, but it seemed almost impossible to put someone else in the frame, try as he might.

"I can't think of anyone else. Loads of 'em would probably have had an opportunity, but who else would have a motive?"

"Yep, that's my own thoughts. There's only two people here with a reason to shoot Puncheon dead. You never know, we might get lucky and find someone's fingerprints on that gun. Not everyone does a thorough job when they tidy up; whoever it is might have been a bit sloppy cleaning the gun before they hid it. We can but hope."

"I've been thinking about that," said Shapes.

"What? Fingerprints?"

"No, that gun. Convenient finding it outside the Kindlemans' room. The timing too, not long after the blow-up between the two of them when he found out about her and Puncheon?"

"Are you suggesting it's a set-up, Shapes?"

"Could be. If someone in the hotel was looking to bump off Puncheon, they'd have themselves a gilt-edged opportunity to point the finger of blame elsewhere. Harry Kindleman makes a bloody good suspect."

"But that would mean they must have known about Lisa Kindleman's affair with Puncheon beforehand. Thinks that possible?"

"Why not? Laura Sinkling had worked it out, so why couldn't someone else? Would be the perfect opportunity, all of them staying at the hotel for the weekend. We were bound to find out about Puncheon and Lisa Kindleman sooner or later. All the killer would need to do is sit back and wait, not giving themselves away in the meantime. Then, Bob's your uncle, Harry Kindleman takes the blame and the real killer toddles off home with us none the wiser."

"So, who would fit the bill, eh, Shapes? Who do you reckon is most likely?"

Shapes hadn't given that much thought. He was, in fact, basking in the glow of having been able to put together such a plausible case. It had come to him all of a sudden and he'd more or less pieced it all together as he spoke. That sort of thing didn't normally go down too well with his boss, especially when there was already a decent suspect or two in the frame.

"Don't know, though I don't trust that wife of his. She could have set him up."

"And why might she have done that?"

"Maybe they've got more money than we know about. Overseas property, that sort of thing. She could have decided she wants it all to herself."

Dykeman was impressed with his sergeant's line of thinking. Shapes wasn't always so imaginative; more of a plodder, most of the time. It had to be said, he did have a point. Harry Kindleman would indeed make the ideal scapegoat.

"True, they might have. So, she'd be hoping to bag the cash and start all over, minus her old man, having decided he was past his best?"

"That's it. Bang on."

"Well, let's keep that one on the back-burner for now. I want to see what comes back in the forensics report before deciding what to do next." Dykeman glanced at his watch. "I suggest, in the meantime, we take another look through the witness statements, to see whether anything new stands out in light of what we've learned today. Then we'll pack it in for the day. I've been told by the lab they'll do their best to get us their report first thing, so we'll have a bright and early start. With a bit of luck, the lab boys will come up trumps and we can put this case to bed without it dragging on beyond tomorrow."

"And without us having to lock up any more of the hotel guests," added Shapes.

"That too."

Chapter Fifteen

"So, what's happened here then Shapes?"

Dykeman was standing in the doorway of the hotel manager's office, which looked like it had been used as a playground by a horde of young children. Papers were strewn everywhere, drawers were open, their contents a mess, and a three-tier filing cabinet that stood against one wall had been forced open. More to the point, thought the inspector, was the open window in the middle of the wall opposite, above the manager's desk; a likely point of entry, especially if it hadn't been locked.

"Break-in, sir. Reported about twenty minutes ago."

Dykeman looked at the clock on the wall to his right. It was seven forty-eight. It had been fortunate he and Shapes had shown up at the station so early, looking to get their hands on the lab's report as soon as it came in. Shapes had taken the call from the desk sergeant shortly before Dykeman had arrived and decided not to wait around for his boss. Good call, thought Dykeman, never disappointed to see Shapes show some initiative.

"Do we know what's been taken?"

"The hotel manager's had a look through things and all he can see is gone is forty quid from the petty cash tin he keeps locked in his desk. Said he wouldn't normally have that much set aside, but wanted some extra cash on hand for the Hobby Horse weekend."

"Someone seems to have gone to a lot of trouble to get their hands on the hotel's petty cash. Came in through the window, did they?"

"Looks like it, though Plowright swears he always closes it before he finishes for the night. Very certain about that, he was."

"Signs of it having been forced open?"

"Nope. Reckon the manager must have forgotten to lock it after all." Shapes paused, then added, "I don't suppose you see this as a coincidence? Don't like coincidences, do you?"

"Coincidences? Nasty things, they are. Prone to tripping you up. No, coincidences are for the foolish and the lazy."

That pretty well summed up Dykeman's view of people who believed in coincidences; foolish and lazy. He had learned the hard way not to view things like that. If something else untoward happened at the scene of a crime, it more than likely had some sort of connection to the crime, even if it was a loose connection.

"Makes you wonder," continued Dykeman. "If that was all they were really after."

Shapes poked the toe of one shoe at the remains of a broken china pencil holder. It had been a big-bellied man with a huge smile, holding a pipe in one hand. Safe to say, it was beyond repair.

"They might have thought the safe was in here."

"Do they have a safe?"

"It's in a small room behind reception."

"Anything touched in there?"

"Not as far as we can tell. Plowright had a look in there as soon as he saw this mess. Anyway, there's someone on the desk most of the time, which means it would be tricky for any thief to get access without being spotted."

"Where's Plowright now?"

"Should be back any sec. Went off a few minutes ago to sort out a problem in the kitchen."

Dykeman looked again at the mess in front of him. Could this burglary really be connected to the murder of James Puncheon? What might someone want to take from the manager's office and why? If it was a case of simple thieving, did forty quid make it worth the risk? Maybe, if someone was desperate enough. On the other hand, if it was related to the murder then they'd most likely have been looking for something that might prove incriminating. He might be wrong, but he'd presume it was no coincidence and let the facts speak for themselves, as and when they were unearthed.

"Ah, Inspector Dykeman. You're here."

Reginald Plowright stood a yard behind the inspector, breathing a little more heavily than was usual, after his dash to the kitchens and back. His heart sank as he set eyes once more on the devastation in his office. He liked order, everything in its right place. It would take hours to sort things out.

Dykeman turned to face the hotel manager. He looked a little harassed, which was hardly surprising, given his office had been turned over. Mind you, he was as impeccably well dressed as ever, his orange tie an adventurous little number, thought Dykeman; not the sort of thing he'd ever wear himself; far too bright and cheery.

"Bit of a mess you've got here, Mr Plowright. Was it you that found it like this?"

"It was. First thing this morning. Seems to be one thing after another at the moment." The hotel manager let out a resigned sigh.

"Yes, the world's not being too kind to you recently. It looks like the window was left open, although Shapes tells me you're adamant you always lock it at the end of the day."

"I do, Inspector. I agree it doesn't look like it's been forced, but I never forget to lock it. Not ever. It's part of my routine and I'm a man of habit."

"You're certain you didn't forget last night? It's the sort of thing that's easy for any of us to do."

"I'm as sure as I can be. I've tried replaying the evening in my head, but I do that sort of thing on autopilot, so it's hard to remember things that clearly. What I can say, Inspector, is, if I did forget to lock the window, then it would be the first time I've done that since I became manager here."

Dykeman nodded his head in acknowledgement. From what they'd seen of the hotel manager, he did indeed appear to be a well-organised creature of habit.

"Shapes tells me that forty pounds has been taken from petty cash. Is that right?"

"It is. There's normally only half that amount in the box, but what with it being Hobby Horse weekend, I wanted to have more cash to hand."

"And nothing else seems to have been taken?"

"Well, it's hard to be certain, what with all the a mess. But I don't think there's anything else missing. One thing's for certain, they didn't run off with the staff shift book, thank

God. I left it on reception last night. I'd not get through a single day without that."

Plowright managed a smile, of sorts. He thought perhaps he ought to be grateful for small mercies.

"Shift book?" Dykeman glanced at Shapes. "Has anyone taken a look through that, Shapes?"

"Not sure, sir. Don't remember seeing any mention of it in the reports."

"Would you mind if Shapes had a look through that, Mr Plowright?"

"No problem at all, Inspector. You'll find it on the reception desk shelf, Sergeant."

"Shapes." Dykeman nodded towards the door.

"Sir."

Shapes departed without another word, stepping with care over the mess of objects that covered the carpeted floor.

"Am I likely to see my forty pounds back, Inspector? I suppose cash is easy to spend without drawing attention to yourself."

"Sadly, it is. We'll ask shopkeepers and landlords to keep an eye out for anyone spending unusually freely in the town centre shops and pubs. Something might turn up. Any disgruntled former employees you can think of that might have done this?"

"No. Only one person has left since I arrived and she only went because she was about to give birth. There's been a very settled staff here for some time, I'm pleased to say. I don't really want to be spending large parts of my time finding new employees, especially when good ones are so hard to come by."

"And you've not had any trouble with any of the existing staff?"

"Not this sort of thing, no."

Dykeman took another quick look around the room and back up at the window.

"Could be an opportunistic break-in. Happens a lot." He had no intention, for the time being, of mentioning his lack of belief in coincidences and his starting proposition that the break-in was somehow connected to James Puncheon's murder. It would only raise fresh concerns and almost certainly require him to spend valuable time trying to explain his hunch.

"Well, I'd better let you get on, Mr Plowright. There'll be some people here to dust for prints and take a few photographs shortly. Once they're finished, you'll be able to have your office back. Constable Dartington is outside and he'll keep guard until that's all sorted out."

As Dykeman left behind their latest crime scene and began to walk briskly along the street in the direction of the police station, his thoughts returned to the matter of a motive for the break-in. He'd bet his last sixpence that it had something to do with the murder, but what? That was the question. What could the killer possibly have been after that would justify the risk of breaking into the hotel manager's office?

As he reached the Banbury Cross, Dykeman's stomach began to rumble, his body apparently having exhausted the energy provided by his early morning toast. Since he wanted to find somewhere that would allow him a degree of peace and quiet, there seemed only one thing to do next.

IT WAS QUIET IN THE canteen at the station, the mad breakfast rush having finished and it not yet being time for the mid-morning tea break, so Dykeman sat alone at one of the corner tables, sipping at his tea now that he'd polished off a large bacon and egg roll.

The break-in at the hotel had him perplexed. For one thing, it was odd; odd that it had happened at all. What also seemed strange was the mess. Why make such a bloody great mess, especially if what you were after, the petty cash, was so easy to find and there was nothing else worth the trouble? And then there was that window. It hadn't been levered open from the outside and he had the feeling the hotel manager was as good as his word; he always locked it at the end of the day.

The sharp, ringing tones of a saucepan hitting the floor somewhere in the kitchen distracted him from his musings for a moment. He paused. Maybe that was the point. Was the burglary just an attempt at distraction? Were they indeed close to identifying the Puncheon's killer and whoever that killer was felt it necessary to try throwing them off the scent? It was plausible. He felt certain the motive for the burglary was either that or an attempt to retrieve some incriminating information. What it was very unlikely to be, he was confident, was a straightforward burglary for financial gain.

Hoping there might be news waiting for him by now, Dykeman picked up his cup of tea and made his way through the building, to the small office he shared with Shapes. His timing turned out to be excellent.

"Ah, Shapes, you're here already. Found anything interesting in that lot?"

Shapes was busy re-reading a small batch of statements when Dykeman walked in. He looked up, a bit of a twinkle in his eyes. "I have indeed."

Oh, no, thought Dykeman, recognising the look on his sergeant's face. Here we go, Shapes is about to play silly buggers and give me the run around. The man could sometimes be more trouble than he was worth.

"And what might that be, Shapes?"

"Don't fancy having a guess?"

"Do I get a clue?"

"Staff shift book."

"You mean, you've actually found something in there that's not right?"

"I have." Shapes wore what Dykeman could only view as a childish expression of triumph as he gave a little wobble of the head.

"Are we going to be here all day before you cough up?"

"There's a discrepancy. What two people told us in their statements doesn't tally with what's written in here," said Shapes, tapping a finger on the aforementioned book.

"Does it make any difference to our case?"

"It might do. I reckon..."

Shapes found his moment of minor triumph cut short by the phone on Dykeman's desk.

"Dykeman," snapped the inspector as he shoved the phone to his ear. As he listened, Dykeman's face lit up. "You're sure about that? No room for error there?" There was another moment of silence in the room as he listened again. "Excellent job. Well done. I think that's information we can put to good use right away."

As he dropped the receiver back into place, Dykeman looked across at Shapes. "Well, Shapes, that was the lab. They've done us proud."

"Not fingerprints?"

Dykeman's eyes danced with delight. "There were indeed."

"Harry Kindleman," asserted Shapes.

"Nope."

"No? Not Lisa Kindleman?"

"Not her either. No, they belong to a Welsh woman we've got locked up downstairs."

"Gwen Jones?"

"That's the one."

Shapes remained silent for a moment. The last vestiges of whatever was left of his attraction for the Gwen Jones slipped away. If he'd not already taken on board the full extent of his near miss with her and the possible ramifications, he certainly had now. Things could have turned out very tricky indeed.

"So, it was her after all. We shouldn't have trusted her in the first place. Bloody Taff."

Dykeman coughed. "We, Shapes? I seem to recall it was you who found her trustworthy."

"Yes, well. You know what I mean."

"I do. Now then, let's get downstairs and give her the good news. Something tells me it might come as a bit of a shock to her. Probably thought she'd cleaned all her prints off the gun before she hid it in that wall."

"MISS JONES," ANNOUNCED Dykeman in a confident tone as the two policemen stepped into the cell. "Been taking good care of you, have they?"

Gwen Jones had been laid out on the hard, narrow bed, wondering, for the umpteenth time, why she hadn't fled from the hotel before the police had picked her up.

The isolation and sense of being trapped, unable to do anything to effect an escape, had been eating away at her. Just as bad had been the lack of information about the progress the police were making with their investigations. She felt vulnerable, all too aware that her possession of that bloody lighter she'd stolen from James Puncheon put her, in the minds of the police, high on their list of murder suspects. She might have told herself that she regretted stealing the damn thing, given how events had unfolded, but the truth was she'd considered it a decent haul at the time. Things like that were always easy to sell on if, like she did, you knew the right people.

She had been wondering when she might next see Dykeman and Shapes. As she got to her feet, she glanced at Shapes. The poor man looked rather angry now. To be expected, she supposed.

"It's better than I would have expected," she replied. "Though they keep telling me there's no alcohol allowed, which is a bit of a shame."

The soft Welsh tones of her voice were more pronounced that previously and Dykeman found them very appealing. Wasn't going to save her from the hangman's noose though, he mused. She was wearing no make-up now and though her face looked very plain it still possessed a beauty many women would long for.

"Well, I don't imagine we'll be keeping you here much longer, eh, Shapes?"

The sour-faced sergeant grunted something neither of the others could make out.

"Has something happened?" ventured Jones, not sure whether the upbeat tone in Dykeman's voice was a good sign or not.

"It certainly has. We've found the murder weapon." Dykeman paused, for effect, a little disappointed there was no immediate reaction from Jones. "And that's not all. We've also found some fingerprints on the gun. Don't suppose you'd like to guess whose they are?"

Jones shrugged her shoulders. "I've no idea."

"You sure about that?"

"Don't see how I could know. I'd only be guessing. How about that nice hotel manager? Bit of a dark horse, I know, but isn't that how these things go?"

"Oh, no, definitely not him. It's someone much closer to home." Still not a twitch from the woman. That was a shame. Seemed it was time to make things crystal clear. "How about you, Miss Jones?"

Dykeman could have sworn some of the colour went out of Jones's cheeks, though it was hard to be certain in the dull light of the cell.

"That's not funny," she replied. "I suppose you'll be asking me for a confession next."

"It would help, that's true enough."

Dykeman waited, still a little disappointed at the lack of a panicked reaction from their suspect.

"Well, you won't be getting one, because I never murdered anybody."

"Oh, come now, your prints are all over that gun, clear as day. You did it, Miss Jones. You shot James Puncheon stone dead. It's like I've said all along, he caught you red-handed stealing his belongings and in a panic you shot him."

Dykeman was getting up to speed now, speaking faster and louder. He lived for these moments; where he had the guilty party bang to rights, squirming desperately for their life. She'd taken another human being's life, she knew it, and now she also knew she was going to pay the price. The panic that had appeared on her face told him everything he needed to know.

"No, no, no. You've got it all wrong. He never caught me and I didn't shoot him."

Gwen Jones was shaking her head vigorously, her hands squeezed into fists that she held up in front of her chest. Anxiety coursed through her words.

"Oh, come off it. Someone else stick those prints on the gun, did they?" Dykeman felt no need to hold back now and hurled his words at Jones.

"I didn't shoot him. I'm telling you the truth. I never shot that man and I never would have."

"So, who did, if it wasn't you? And why have we found your fingerprints on the gun?"

"I don't know who did it. For God's sake, I didn't shoot that man."

She was pleading now, but Dykeman had heard it all before. Remorse after the event was all well and good, but it was far too late to escape justice. Would have been better never to have pulled the trigger in the first place. He glanced at Shapes, who had remained silent the whole time. Ordinarily, he would have expected to find a look of satisfaction, enjoyment even, on his sergeant's face; reeling in a criminal was satisfying at any time, but when it was a killer it felt even better. But Shapes's ugly face was devoid of anything approaching a smile or look of contentment; instead, he wore a stern expression that was set so firmly it looked chiselled from granite. His eyes were fixed on Jones.

Now to bring things to a conclusion, decided Dykeman. Addressing himself once more to Gwen Jones, he slipped into his formal police voice, the one he reserved for occasions such as this. "Gwen Jones, I'm charging you with the murder of James Puncheon..."

As he spoke, Jones dropped on to the edge of the bed and buried her head in her hands. She began to sob. Dykeman continued reading his prisoner her rights, without a hint of a pause.

Chapter Sixteen

Always keen to pass on good news to the Chief Inspector as soon as possible, Dykeman wasted no time in heading upstairs to inform his boss the case was solved and Gwen Jones had been charged. The literal pat on the back he received, along with some enthusiastic compliments, had left him in an especially good mood. Too often his encounters with the Chief Inspector were far from happy ones, usually involving expressions of frustration with the rate of progress in solving a case, along with some useless advice on how to proceed faster. Moments of praise and congratulation were, therefore, all the more satisfying and to be cherished.

The good news having been delivered to one interested party, Dykeman wasted no time in returning to the Marlborough Hotel, where, after a minor misunderstanding as to the purpose of his latest visit, he managed to bring together most of the hotel guests to inform them of the recent developments. Most of those present were delighted, both at his success in catching the killer and their own freedom to now return home.

Reginald Plowright had been especially pleased to hear the news. The police insistence that all guests staying at the hotel at the time of the murder should remain on the premises had caused him to cancel numerous bookings, upsetting many people, some of whom were less than understanding of the circumstances. Now, at long last, there was the prospect of things returning to normal, given a little time to re-instate order and routine.

His mercy mission completed, Dykeman secured a cup of tea from the hotel manager and decided to take a short, well-earned break reading *The Daily Express* while ensconced in one of the comfy chairs in reception. All seemed well with the world and already he could detect a change in the atmosphere in the hotel as it began to return to something like its normal routine. One well-organised and, no doubt, keen couple were already in the process of checking out.

He had, however, not got past his second slurp of tea and the front page of the paper when the receptionist called across to him. Sergeant Shapes was on the phone. It was, she insisted, most urgent. She wasn't wrong about that. Gwen Jones wanted to talk and this time, she had insisted to Shapes, she would tell them everything she knew.

As Dykeman handed the phone back to the receptionist and turned towards the exit, he found himself experiencing an unsettling mixture of emotions. Some of them were not good ones. Doubt reared its head, as unwelcome as a slug in his veg patch. Either Gwen Jones had got creative in the time since he'd last seen her and felt she now had a believable alibi, or else... That was the option that bothered him most. Was she about to make him look an idiot? Others had done it, so why not her? He rubbed the side of his face and tried to push the unhappy thought to the back of his mind. Best to consider that she was about to make a last, futile attempt to wriggle out of her predicament.

"WHAT'S SHE SAID THEN Shapes?"

"Nothing worth the words."

Shapes had perked up a bit after they'd left Jones sobbing and shaking in the cell barely an hour earlier, but now he once again both looked and sounded like a man for whom life was not a happy experience. Dykeman considered telling him to wait while he spoke to Jones, but then he'd only have to go back over things afterwards. No, the man would just have to grin and bear it, so to speak.

"No clues then as to what she wants to tell us?"

"Nope. Just said she wanted to speak to you. Claims she's going to tell us everything she knows."

"Going to tell us a tall tale, you reckon?"

"Most likely."

Shapes sniffed and fiddled with the collar of his shirt.

"Right chatterbox you are sometimes, Shapes. I don't like going in there not knowing what her game is. Got a bad feeling about this."

Dykeman took a deep breath and squared up his shoulders, as much to boost his own confidence as in any attempt to come across as more intimidating to the waiting prisoner.

"Come on. Might as well get on with it."

The redness around Gwen Jones's eyes was an immediate reminder to the two policemen of the distressed state they had left her in. However, that aside, she seemed to both of them more certain of herself now. She met their gaze without hesitation and stood motionless by the bed, her whole demeanour that of someone with information they felt certain would dig them out of the deep, dark hole they were trapped in. Dykeman felt at once uneasy, unaware that he had started rapping the fingers of one hand on the side of his thigh. It was a sign of nervousness that others, Shapes included, were familiar with.

"Miss Jones, it seems you've been missing us." He hoped he'd been able to hide from his voice the unease he felt.

"Thank you, Inspector, for seeing me again." Jones sounded more nervous than the policemen had expected. "I couldn't bring myself to tell you the truth before. I couldn't..."

Jones seemed unable to find the words she needed. Dykeman stepped into the gap. "So, you admit you did lie to us. You did shoot James Puncheon?"

Jones looked alarmed, her eyes widening, shaking her head. "No, no. I didn't do that. You must believe me, I didn't shoot anyone. I wouldn't. I couldn't."

"So, who the hell did, if not you? I remind you, Miss Jones, it's your fingerprints on that gun."

"I did have the gun..."

"At last, some truth," snapped Dykeman.

"But it wasn't mine. I ... I borrowed it." She looked away, down at a corner of the bed, her voice faltering.

"You borrowed it? What do you mean, you borrowed it? Who from? And what for, if not to murder James Puncheon?"

Dykeman noticed Shapes begin to stir. He placed a hand on his sergeant's arm. Best to keep the focus where it was for now. No getting knocked off course.

"I was going to use it for a burglary." She looked back up, visibly struggling to get the words out. "There's an old couple living in a house on the Southam Road. The woman's supposed to have a lot of jewellery. Stuff from before the war."

"Bloody hell, is that the best you can do? Making up a story about another bit of thieving."

"I couldn't go through with it. I've never used a gun and couldn't bring myself to use one this time either."

"Alright, then. Let's pretend Shapes and I believe this little story. Who did you borrow the gun from?"

"I ... I can't say."

Whatever composure Jones had possessed when the policemen entered the room had now all but evaporated. She felt about ready to collapse.

"Now you listen to me," growled Dykeman, jabbing a finger in Jones's direction. "If you think for one minute we're going to believe this ridiculous story of yours and just brush over the little matter of who it was let you borrow their gun, then you're more of a fool than you already look. I want a name, right now, or we're leaving this cell and the next time you see us will be in a court room, where you'll be facing a charge of murder."

"But ... I love him."

At that, Jones began to sob, hiding her face in her hands.

Dykeman shook his head, but said nothing. Christ, whatever next? She'd uttered the only three words he genuinely didn't want to hear. 'I love him'. A straightforward case of greed or revenge was one thing, but when love came into it, well, practically anything was possible. Love had a very nasty habit of messing up the very best of cases.

For the second time, Shapes stirred, taking half a step forward. This time Dykeman made no attempt to restrain him from actively joining the fray.

"Seems to me, sir, we can't believe a word this woman says when it comes to matters of the heart. Best we leave her to it and let a jury decide whether she's to swing or not."

The bitterness in his voice was unmistakable to Dykeman, who wondered if it was at all possible for Jones to fail to notice it too.

"Well?" demanded Dykeman of the sobbing Jones. "Speak up now or that's it as far as we're concerned. Being in love makes no difference."

Her damp hands left Jones's face, but she was unable to look at Dykeman as she spoke, her eyes remaining fixed to the floor. "Alright, I'll tell you."

Chapter Seventeen

Standing at the end of the corridor, off which led the half-dozen cells in the basement of the station, Dykeman and Shapes took stock. Or, more accurately, Dykeman listened as Shapes spoke.

"She may be telling the truth," suggested the sergeant.

"What, you don't think she just made that lot up? A desperate attempt to shift the blame on to someone else? Something I don't know about here, Shapes?"

Dykeman gave his sergeant the eye, displeased at the prospect of having been kept in the dark about something of importance.

"Remember I told you that two of the witness statements didn't match what I found in the staff shifts book from the hotel?" Dykeman nodded. "Well, he was one of those."

"So? We'll need more than that if we're really to pin this murder on him. Not that I'm saying we should be looking to do anything of the sort."

"But there's something else."

Dykeman let out a sigh, closed his eyes and shook his head. He didn't care to think what was coming next.

"I phoned the central station in Bristol. Spoke to an Inspector Lightman. Turns out Jones's lover knew James Puncheon a long time ago and, by the sound of things, he'd feel he'd got plenty of reason to want Puncheon dead."

"What do you mean, knew him a long time ago? And why would he want Puncheon dead?"

Dykeman scratched at his head. He immediately regretted it because he scratched too hard and it hurt.

"His mum was widowed when his dad died in a road accident in 1934. Then along comes Puncheon. The widow was putty in his hands, so they reckon. Seems he persuaded her to invest everything she had in some useless business scheme he'd dreamed up. It went down the tubes and she lost the lot, house and all. It hit her so hard, a few months later she threw herself off the Clifton Suspension Bridge."

"So, he'd blame Puncheon for his mother's death?"

"Looks like it."

"But why wait until now to do something about it?"

"We don't know he hasn't tried before, do we? Might have given it a go and failed. Happened to do the job properly this time."

"Bloody Nora, Shapes, why didn't you tell me this before?"

"I tried to, then you went and decided it must have been Gwen Jones who did it on account of her fingerprints being on the gun. Seemed reasonable enough to me."

"But I might not have charged her if I'd known this." Dykeman fired a short, sharp blast of air between his lips, then rubbed the back of his head, not so hard as before. "I hope this didn't have anything to do with you and Jones, Shapes. Don't want to go thinking this was a nasty case of revenge."

Shapes's back stiffened. "I ain't pretending I wasn't attracted to the woman, for a bit, but there's no way I'm going to let her carry the can if it looks like being someone else who pulled the trigger. Like you said, those fingerprints had her done for."

"Good. We've got ourselves into a bit of a pickle as it is. What's the Chief Inspector going to say if I have to tell him we've charged the wrong person?"

"We? Seem to remember you taking all the credit for charging Jones."

Dykeman ignored his sergeant's riposte.

"Right then, there's no point in hanging around. We might as well get back to the hotel and confront our new suspect. You know, they could have been in on it together? If she really is in love, he'd have stood a good chance of persuading her to help him."

"Yeah, full of irony that is."

DYKEMAN AND SHAPES entered the hotel foyer at a brisk pace, both puffing a little from the rapid walk up the gentle hill from the station. Their enquiries as to the whereabouts of the hotel manager took them to the restaurant.

Reginald Plowright saw the two policemen appear in the entrance to the restaurant and it was clear from the look on their faces that something was wrong. Surely it didn't have anything to do with his hotel? The thought was too horrendous for words. He fiddled with his tie, praying that whatever it was, it had nothing to do with him and his guests.

Please, God, let it be someone else's problem. Surely that wasn't too much to ask?

The restaurant was devoid of guests, the breakfast sitting having just come to an end. While two waitresses tidied and re-set the other tables, Plowright was inspecting an up-turned table with the help of one of the male staff. It took Dykeman a moment to recognise Joseph Pearling; a man, like most of the other staff, he'd paid little attention to over the last few days. The two men ceased their work and turned towards the policemen marching in their direction.

"Inspector, a pleasure to see you again." Plowright sounded as he felt, uncertain. "Can I help you?"

Dykeman couldn't help glancing down at the table in front of him. One of the cross-braces appeared to be coming away, which had, no doubt, been causing the table top to wobble.

"It's actually Mr Pearling we've come to see."

Dykeman brought his gaze to bare on Pearling and held it there. As he did so, Shapes took up station a yard behind the waiter.

"Me, Inspector? Not sure what I can do for you, but happy to give it a go."

Pearling's mood was upbeat, his smile broad. Dykeman recalled his few encounters with Pearling over the course of the last few days and recollected he'd always seemed a happy individual. But now, looking into the man's eyes, perhaps he could see something more. Tension? Anxiety? Perhaps. But, there again, wouldn't all of the staff and guests have been riddled with such emotions over the course of the last few of days?

"It's Joseph Pearling, isn't it?"

"That's right."

"How long have you been working here, Joseph?"

"Started last November, didn't I, Mr Plowright?"

"Sounds about right, Joseph," replied the hotel manager, curious to find out what Dykeman wanted to talk to the waiter about.

"I suppose you'd worked in a few other hotels and maybe restaurants before that? I know it's common for people to move around such places."

"I did. I was at the Thistle in Stratford before I came here. Bit too big for my liking. I prefer a smaller establishment where you can get to know the other staff and the guests better."

"And if I didn't know better, I'd say there's a bit of West Country accent there."

Pearling seemed momentarily taken aback. "Not many people pick up on that these days, Inspector. Thought it had pretty much all gone."

"Where was it you grew up? I'm guessing it wasn't too far out west."

There was a slight pause before Pearling answered, as if he might be reluctant to own up.

"I grew up in Bristol. Only moved away a few years ago when I got the chance of a good job in Cheltenham."

"Tell me, Joseph, you weren't originally down to work the morning James Puncheon was killed, were you?"

Pearling glanced at Plowright before answering, with a little hesitation. "That's right. I needed to finish early for the day, so I could meet a lady friend in Adderbury. I wouldn't have been able to get there if I worked my planned shift."

"You didn't speak to me about that, Joseph," interrupted Plowright, the irritation he felt at hearing this news clear in his voice. "As well you know, there's a proper way to go about these things. We'll need to speak about that later."

The hotel manager's observation answered another question Dykeman had been planning to ask and reinforced his belief that all was not as it once seemed.

"I think that's not the only thing Joseph has kept from us, Mr Plowright. Perhaps you'd like to tell Mr Plowright yourself, Joseph."

"I don't know what you mean, Inspector."

Pearling effected the air of someone who hadn't a clue what the policeman was referring to.

"Really? Not even the slightest idea what it might be?"

Furrows appeared on Pearling's forehead and he shook his head a little.

"Erm, I don't know what to say. I can't think of anything Mr Plowright ought to know."

"Well, why don't I help you out. You'd met James Puncheon before, hadn't you? In fact, you knew him rather well, isn't that right?"

Pearling's eyes flickered and his body tensed, but Dykeman didn't wait for him to respond. He was on a roll now, increasingly confident of the outcome. He pressed home the attack, the words coming faster and more forcefully.

"In fact, from what we hear, you blame him for your mother's death, don't you? Claim the poor woman took her own life as a result of what Puncheon did to her. Isn't that right? Well?"

"That was a long time ago," stumbled Pearling, struggling to retain any kind of composure. "I'd forgotten all about it. In fact, it was only after Mr Puncheon had been shot that I remembered who he was."

"Come off it, Joseph," snapped Dykeman. "We've got your girlfriend locked up in a cell down the station and her fingerprints are all over the gun we found outside the Kindlemans' room. Going to leave her to take the blame were you? Watch her swing from a rope so you could save your own neck?"

"I don't know what you mean, Inspector."

Pearling's voice was unsteady now. He tried to take a step back, only to find the space already occupied by Shapes. The waiter's face began to twitch and his hands formed into fists.

"She's told us everything, has Gwen Jones. We know she got that gun from you. Very convenient that must have been, having someone to set up like that. She loves you, you know, though God knows why."

There was a pause as Pearling's head began to shake and his eyes widen. Now, thought Dykeman. Now was the moment. He hammered the accusation home.

"You killed him, didn't you Joseph. You saw your chance to finally get revenge for what he did to your mother and you shot Puncheon dead. Shot him in cold blood."

Pearling erupted like a volcano, rage exploding from his body as he brought his fists up in front of his chest and shoved his face, contorted almost beyond recognition, towards the startled inspector.

"He deserved it," shouted Pearling, his eyes bulging. "He should have swung for what he did to my mother. He destroyed her. Took everything we had. My God, I felt so good when I saw the look on his face. I laughed at him, you know. I laughed in his face before I pulled the trigger. Bye bye, I said. Off to hell you go."

Then, the anger and rage leaving him almost as suddenly as it had appeared, Pearling dropped down on to the nearest chair, and began to laugh so much that tears started to run down his cheeks. It seemed to Dykeman that the waiter really had lost control of his senses now; perhaps the release of all that pent-up anger and frustration, that had simmered away unseen for so many years, had been too much for the man to cope with.

Dykeman tilted his head towards Shapes, who slipped his cuffs of his belt and bent down to secure Pearling.

"Good God," gasped Plowright, his face filled with horror. "I've never seen anything like it. Do you think Pearling's had some sort of breakdown?"

"My bet is that's been bottled up inside him for so long that once the cork was removed he was always going to go off like a bottle of champagne that's been given a good shake." Dykeman stared at the pathetic figure of the collared waiter. "You never saw anything in his behaviour to suggest he had problems, I don't suppose?" he asked Plowright.

"No, nothing at all. I don't know what to say. It's a remarkable situation."

Plowright stood, rooted to the spot, staring in disbelief as Shapes helped Pearling to his feet.

"Well, we'll take him off your hands now. There's a nice, cold cell waiting for him down the road. Just need to work out whether he did it all on his own or if that besotted girlfriend of his helped out." Dykeman turn towards Shapes. "We all set, Shapes?"

"Think so, sir."

Shapes kept a firm grip on his prisoner as they began to move towards the door, all the time Pearling muttering that Puncheon deserved it. The waiter had gone so limp that Shapes feared if he was to let go he would fall flat on his face.

"Come on, then. Let's get him to that room we've been using, then I'll call for a car from reception. Don't want to make a spectacle by walking him down the road in this state."

Reginald Plowright remained motionless and open-mouthed as the two policemen and their captive disappeared into the entrance hall. To think that all this time he'd been working cheek by jowl with a killer left him feeling cold with fear. Who would he be able to trust in future, he wondered.

Chapter Eighteen

Three days had passed since Dykeman and Shapes clapped handcuffs on the emotionally unstable Joseph Pearling. The press had been informed in the usual manner and gossip about the killer was already common currency in the living rooms of Banbury. Reginald Plowright had called Dykeman the previous day, to tell him that, after an initial rush of last-minute cancellations, bookings had surged as people's morbid fascination at staying at the location of a murder overcame other emotions. It was a development that didn't surprise the experienced inspector one little bit; people were so very predictable.

"There you go, sir."

Shapes placed a pint of beer on the table in front of Dykeman, then sat down opposite him, keeping a tight grip on his own pint. The Kings Head had a good smattering of customers, though at six-thirty it was still a little early for most of the evening's drinkers to be in place. It was something that suited the two policemen; they had things to discuss.

"Cheers," replied Dykeman, picking up his pint.

"Cheers. Bloody nosey parkers at the bar started asking me questions about Pearling. As if I could answer them," grumbled Shapes, fidgeting in an effort to get himself into a comfortable position on the low stool.

"They recognised you, did they? Didn't know you were such a celebrity."

"I'm not, but you are," responded Shapes, eyeing his pint with true love and affection.

"Me?" Dykeman glanced over at the bar. In the gloom that filled the room, with its small windows and almost non-existent lighting, it was hard to make out the faces he suspected were looking in their direction. He turned back to Shapes, who was now busy savouring his beer. "Hope you told 'em what a genius I am, solving the case so quickly and all."

Shapes raised an eyebrow. "Do you think they would have believed me?"

"Maybe not."

What sounded to the two men like a tractor rumbled by on the road outside, before quiet descended again. They had picked the Kings Head because it was located in an out of the way spot on the eastern outskirts of the town. Even midweek most of the pubs in the centre would be busy; certainly too busy for them to expect to be left alone.

"Do you reckon he'll swing, then?" asked Shapes, in reference to Joseph Pearling. "He should bloody well do."

"I'm not so sure." Dykeman gave himself a moment to consider. "I suppose, if you put me on the spot, I'd say no. There has to be a good chance a jury will decide he's off his rocker. If I was his brief, I'd plead insanity and it oughtn't be too hard to put a decent case together, especially with his prior history."

"You mean that breakdown he had when he was supposed to be getting married?"

"I do."

"That was such a long time ago, I don't see why that should make a blind bit of difference. You murder someone, then you swing for it."

"Makes you think, though, about the role chance plays in our lives. If Puncheon and his friends hadn't happened to book a stay at the Marlborough when Pearling was working there, none of this would have happened. The two of them would still be going about their business none the wiser as to the whereabouts of the other."

"There's some people I wish I could avoid bumping into ever again."

"They probably say the same thing about you, Shapes."

Shapes ignored Dykeman's mocking comment. "I've lost count of the number of times a murder has been committed with someone's old service revolver. They should have collected all the damn things in at the end of the war, before people had time to hide them away."

"Wonder if Pearling kept it as a memento of his dad, or if he'd always thought it might come in handy one day?"

"Would be some serious forward planning if he thought he'd get chance to use it on Puncheon."

"Mm."

The two men remained silent for a while, each deep in their own thoughts. The deep, rich aroma of pipe smoke began to drift towards them from a thin, old man with scruffy white hair who was sitting on a stool at the bar. He was puffing energetically on a clay pipe he'd just lit. Behind the bar, the landlord, a short, balding man with large hands, stood and watched his customers. It was Dykeman who eventually broke the silence.

"Anyway, at least Gwen Jones won't be sent to the gallows, not with Pearling confirming she had nothing to do with Puncheon's murder."

"Reckon he's telling the truth about that?"

"Don't see why not. Think it was very clear he didn't really care for Jones half as much as he made out to her; maybe not at all."

"Serves her right."

"I should think she'll still do time for nicking those watches and that jewellery, especially as it's not her first offence."

"Good."

Dykeman eyed his sergeant. It was fair to say Shapes was a man who held any grudge close to his heart and that was certainly the case where Gwen Jones was concerned. She'd never be forgiven for attempting to mislead Shapes into hopes of romance.

"Laura Sinkling told me the Kindlemans left separately," continued the inspector. "Reckons they're not on speaking terms right now, though she suspects they'll end up back together. She thinks they're too well suited to go their separate ways and I'd say she's right about that."

"Bit of a looker like her wouldn't have any trouble finding herself a new fella."

"Maybe, maybe not."

"I'd buy her a fish and chip supper."

"Always the romantic, Shapes. Speaking of which, Mrs Sinkling also told me that unmarried friend of hers, Lucy Proud, has a new man in her life and, would you believe it, she met him at breakfast on her last morning at the hotel. Seems like at least one good thing has come out of all this mess."

"It's alright for her. What about the rest of us?"

Shapes muttered something else, that Dykeman couldn't hear, before downing half the contents of his pint glass.

Dykeman considered giving his sergeant a bit of a ribbing about his woeful record with women, something he'd done many times before, but then remembered he had something much better up his sleeve. Oh, yes, this was going to be good.

Effecting a casual air, as if what he was about to say was nothing much at all, Dykeman leaned back in his chair and caressed his pint glass.

"Oh, by the way Shapes, the Chief Inspector was saying to me yesterday that, seeing how you missed out on the chance to do your bit for the community at the Hobby Horse Festival, he's going to let you have a couple of days off at Christmas. It's so you can put on the old red coat and white beard and play Father Christmas for the kids at the Round Table's grotto inside Leach and Sons hardware shop."

Dykeman added a few bass-heavy ho, ho, hos for effect, then grinned at his sergeant.

"He can sod right off. I ain't wearing no Father Christmas outfit and there's no chance I'm letting all those horrible, snotty kids climb all over me."

Shapes wagged a finger at his boss and the expression that appeared on his face would have scared off even the most hardened of young children, keen to tell Santa what they wanted for Christmas.

"If you say so, Shapes."

"I do. The stupid old idiot can do it himself."

Dykeman began to laugh so much his shoulders jiggled up and down, while his eyes filled with tears. In one swoop, the Chief Inspector had given the whole station something special to look forward to at Christmas. It was as good an early present as you could ever hope to receive. Poor old Shapes, he'd never hear the last of it.

AN HOUR LATER, DYKEMAN stood alone outside the pub, watching Shapes walk to the end of the road and disappear around the corner, heading for the fish and chip shop on his way home. He'd continued grumbling about the Chief Inspector's plans for his Christmas right up to the moment they wandered outside and said their farewells.

A light rain had started to fall and the temperature had dropped a degree or two, thought Dykeman as his sergeant vanished. There was no sign of anyone else out and about, Dykeman's only company now a pair of noisy crows hopping from branch to branch on a nearby tree.

The inspector stood where we was, glad of the silence, and turned his thoughts to another matter altogether. Sheila Delph had called him not long after he got back to his office from lunch. She sounded nervous, which was odd, since he'd never known her to come across as anything short of relaxed and confident, It might have helped cushion the blow if he'd heeded that warning, but, sad to say, he didn't do anything of the sort. In fact, looking back, he could only describe himself as clueless, which was perhaps a little ironic, given his job.

She opened the conversation with a little gossip about another doctor at the hospital, before stumbling on to the real purpose of her call. She had decided, she went on, to accept her suitor's marriage proposal. The news went off in his ears like a bomb, blotting out most of what else she said, apart, that is, from something about moving to Canada after the wedding. Her intended had accepted an offer of work there.

Standing in the drizzle, he couldn't recall what he'd said in return and, anyway, doubted that it really mattered. Any happiness and sense of achievement he'd felt at solving his latest murder case had vanished.

Delph made it clear he would, of course, get an invitation to the wedding, as would Shapes. Very thoughtful of her. The inspector wasn't sure he'd find it in himself to accept such an invitation.

As he stood in the drizzle, that was turning into something more like proper rain, Dykeman felt a void had opened in his life; a big empty space where Delph was supposed to be. He didn't know what to do or where to go next. He had dithered when he should have made his own offer to Delph. She hadn't given him any indication she wanted to be anything more than friends, had she? Well, it was too late now.

He buttoned up his coat and pushed his hands deep into the pockets. The crows had stopped hopping and, instead, taken up residence in the branches of a big, spreading chestnut tree, whose large leaves provided some sort of shelter from the rain. Looking down at the ground, to keep the worst of the growing downpour from off his face, Dykeman began the walk home, where a silent, empty house waited for him.

THE HOBBY HORSE MURDER

The End

BEN WESTERHAM

A Note on the Banbury Hobby Horse Festival

There really is an annual Hobby Horse Festival in Banbury, Oxfordshire and it is a great deal of fun. I've been in town on several occasions (sometimes by design and sometimes by happy accident) to enjoy the music and the dancing and all the other things that make up the Festival.

However, I felt obliged to add a note here for fear I might be called out for a historical inaccuracy. The Festival has, in fact, only been running since 2000, when it was launched with the specific intention of bringing back to the town some sense of the many such events that used to be held across the country, once upon a time. It's done so well that, if you didn't know otherwise, you'd think it had been running for hundreds of years, which was exactly the original intention. So, while I have employed some artistic licence here, I think it is in keeping with both the spirit of the festival and the whole feel of these books.

These days, the Hobby Horse Festival runs alongside the Banbury Folk Festival each October. Of course, if you should happen to be in the vicinity of Banbury when the festival is on, then I'd encourage you to go along. That way, you can find out for yourself how enjoyable an occasion it is.

A Legacy of Death

If you've enjoyed reading *The Hobby Horse Murder* then why not take a look at the fourth story in the series *A Legacy of Death*.
https://benwesterham.com/books/book-details-a-legacy-of-death/

Free Book

IF YOU ENJOYED MEETING Dykeman and Shapes then why not find out how it all began as they investigate their very first murder case together. Download your free copy of *Murder at Stockton Farm*, sit back, relax and enjoy yourself as bruised egos and repeated misunderstandings ensure that solving the case isn't the only challenge the two policemen will need to overcome before the day is done.

https://benwesterham.com/bookoffer/

THE HOBBY HORSE MURDER

If you enjoyed this book then please consider leaving a review on the site where you bought it.
Many thanks,
Ben Westerham

From the David Good private investigator series

From 'Good Investigations'
"Mr Good," she purred like a hungry cat meeting a blind mouse, "and I do hope you will be." She slid beautifully, effortlessly in to the knackered old punter's chair, and I swear the thing wrapped itself lovingly around her sexy, lithe frame. Then she tempted me with those dark bewitching eyes, calling me closer, closer, closer

From 'Good Girl Gone Bad'
If you ask me, good girls can be the baddest there are, if the fancy takes them. Maybe it's because they save it all up for one big splurge, then go mad bad. I don't know, but what I do know is that anyone who tries telling you some little darling of theirs' wouldn't say boo to a goose is either stupid, misinformed or both. Any goody two shoes type should carry a health warning, 'Danger, Good Girl. May go bad at any moment'.

From 'Smart Way to Die'
Some people make you feel good about yourself whenever you meet them. They can't help it. It's like they've been sprinkled with fairy dust and whenever you get close to them some of it rubs off on you. He was one of those people; left me feeling

twice as chipper as I was before I'd met him and we'd only been chatting for 60 seconds.

BEN WESTERHAM

You can find out more about Ben Westerham here www.[1]benwesterham[2].com[3].

---

1. http://www.benwesterham.com/

2. http://www.benwesterham.com/

3. http://www.benwesterham.com/

www.ingramcontent.com/pod-product-compliance
Lightning Source LLC
Chambersburg PA
CBHW070857180626
46817CB00003B/800

* 9 7 8 1 9 1 1 0 8 5 8 1 2 *